ENTRANCED BY THE EARL

Perks of Being an Heiress, Book 2

By Jillian Eaton

DRAGONBLADE
PUBLISHING, INC.

ARE YOU SIGNED UP FOR DRAGONBLADE'S BLOG?

You'll get the latest news and information on exclusive giveaways, exclusive excerpts, coming releases, sales, free books, cover reveals and more.

Check out our complete list of authors, too!

No spam, no junk. That's a promise!

Sign Up Here

www.dragonbladepublishing.com

Dearest Reader;

Thank you for your support of a small press. At Dragonblade Publishing, we strive to bring you the highest quality Historical Romance from the some of the best authors in the business. Without your support, there is no 'us', so we sincerely hope you adore these stories and find some new favorite authors along the way.

Happy Reading!

CEO, Dragonblade Publishing

Additional Dragonblade books by Author Jillian Eaton

The Perks of Being an Heiress Series
Bewitched by the Bluestocking
Entranced by the Earl

CHAPTER ONE

London Residence of the Earl of Hawkridge
September 1870

"WHAT THE DEVIL are you doing in here?"

Evelyn Thorncroft, better known as Evie to her family and friends, did not flinch at the Earl of Hawkridge's harsh tone. Instead, she tilted her head, arched a dark brow, and said, "I could ask you the same thing."

"Me?" he said incredulously, slapping a hand on top of the carriage roof with such force that it startled the matching team of grays. With a snort, they began to prance nervously in place as the driver attempted to settle them. "This is *my* carriage."

"You are welcome to use it, if you'd like." Graciously sweeping her mauve skirts to the side, Evie patted the velvet upholstered seat beside her. "There is more than enough room for two."

Last night, when they'd met at the Countess of Beresford's ball, the earl's eyes had been a cool, soft gray. A gray that had turned black as a storm cloud when Evie had revealed her name to him.

This morning, his gaze was hard as steel, and his freshly shaven jaw all but radiated with tension. He was absolutely *furious* to see her. But then, she'd suspected he would be. She'd even prepared herself for it, which was why she hadn't jumped when he had wrenched the door open and glared at her with all the ferocity of a snarling bear.

All things considered, his anger was a compliment. After their waltz had abruptly ended with the earl stalking away, Evie had taken it upon herself to ask a few discreet questions about Weston, the Earl of Hawkridge.

She'd learned that he was outrageously wealthy. She'd learned that he was an adept equestrian. And she'd also learned that he was as notorious for his self-control as he was for his lack of emotion.

Cold as a glacier, one woman had said.

But handsome as sin, another had sighed.

Evie agreed with both opinions, although there was nothing the least bit *cold* about the fire burning in the earl's eyes as he stared at her. She liked that her unexpected appearance had sparked such a volatile reaction. It revealed a crack, however slight, in all that armor.

And she was the one yielding the chisel.

"Get out," Weston growled, jabbing a finger at the ground. *"Now."*

"Are you inviting me inside for tea?" she asked brightly. "How splendid."

A vein bulged in the middle of his temple. "I am not inviting you anywhere, Miss Thorncroft, except out of my sight. I do not know how you came to be in this carriage, and I do not care. But you *will* depart it immediately."

"Do people do what you tell them?" she asked curiously.

"Unequivocally."

Her lips curved. "Well, I pride myself on being the exception. If you're not going to share the carriage with me, Lord Hawkridge, would you mind closing the door? There is a slight chill in the air, and I wouldn't want to catch a sniffle."

"Did your sister put you up to this?" he demanded.

Evie clucked her tongue. "Joanna is as much my sister as she is yours."

Courtesy of the private detective that Joanna and Evie had hired to help them track down their mother's stolen ring (their reason for coming to London in the first place), they'd discovered that Weston was Joanna's half-brother. And that *he* was the one who had taken the ring. Or had it taken. The exact details were still a tad murky and it was *all* a tad confusing.

In short, Joanna was the result of a scandalous secret affair between Anne Thorncroft, Evie's mother, and the Marquess of Dorchester, Weston's father. The affair had been *so* secret that even Joanna hadn't known who her real father was until the sisters followed the trail of the stolen ring all the way to London and everything had started to come to light.

Including the fact that Weston was their thief.

And he had no intention of returning what he'd taken.

"You and your sister can sod off all the way back to Boston because you're not getting your greedy hands on my family's ring ever again," she believed had been his exact words when she'd asked if she could have the ring.

If his current thunderous expression was any indication, it didn't seem as though a good night's sleep had changed his mind any.

Pity, really.

For *him*, that was.

If Weston had been more agreeable, they could have handled things the easy way. The *polite* way. If there was anything Evie had learned during her time in England, it was that the British were exceedingly polite.

But she was an American.

An American who wasn't going to be leaving England without that ring on her finger...one way or another.

"My father's illegitimate offspring means nothing to me," Weston said coolly. "And you mean less than that, Miss Thorncroft."

Evie winced. "This is going to be very awkward then, I'm afraid."

The corners of his mouth tightened. "What is?"

"Why, it's just that we're going to be sharing a roof for the next four weeks. I'd hoped we might be able to start off on better footing, but..." she trailed off with a delicate shrug. "I suppose that we will have plenty of time to strike up an amicable relationship over the coming days."

"What are you talking about?" he scowled.

"She hasn't told you?" Evie said in feigned dismay. "Oh, dear."

His eyes narrowed with suspicion. "Who?"

"Lady Brynne. She's invited me to Hawkridge Manor. For the house party," she clarified when Weston remained silent.

At the news, a muscle leapt high in his cheek. His hands curled into fists. For an instant, Evie thought he was actually going to lose his temper. But it seemed his callous reputation was well-earned, because Weston didn't yell. He didn't even speak at all. Raking her with a final scornful glance, the type of look generally reserved for a piece of trash after it was scraped off the bottom of a shoe, the earl turned on his heel and strode away.

Goodness, Evie thought, her blue eyes sparkling with anticipation. This *is* going to be fun.

"BRYNNE!" WESTON'S BELLOW echoed through the large foyer, reaching all the way through his seven-bedroom brick manor to the rear gardens and sending the servants scurrying out of his way as he marched down the main hallway in search of his quarry.

Normally, he detested raising his voice, having been taught that if a man could not get what he wanted with a civil tone, then he didn't deserve to have it. But if there was ever a time to shout, surely it was upon learning that his twin sister had invited his sworn enemy to spend a bloody *month* with them in the countryside.

He hadn't been able to abide the sight of Evelyn Thorncroft for thirty seconds after he'd learned who she really was! What made Brynne think he could possibly be in the same company as that money-grubbing hoyden for thirty days?

After looking in the music room, the library, and the parlor to no avail, he stepped out onto the rear terrace and stopped short when he saw his sister painting in the shade of an oak tree, her fair brow furrowed in concentration as her brush swept across the canvas in swift, agitated strokes.

"Do you mind?" she said without bothering to lift her head. "You're blocking my natural light."

It was fitting, he supposed, that the last time they'd discussed Joanna and Evelyn Thorncroft they were in this very spot. Brynne had been painting then, as well. But then she was *always* painting, her quiet nature much more suited to the arts than socializing over a game of whist.

If he recalled correctly, she'd asked him what he planned to do if Joanna requested the ring back. The ring that family tradition dictated belonged to *his* future bride, not in the hands of one of his father's by-blows. And he'd replied that he would give it to their dear half-sister...over his cold, dead body.

Weston stood by that proclamation. He'd rather see the damned ring destroyed than return it to the daughter of his father's mistress. A mistress that Jason Weston had taken before his wife, the Marchioness of Dorchester, was barely in her grave.

She'd died giving birth to Weston and Brynne.

A tragic demise made worse by her husband's betrayal, or so that was how Weston viewed it. Which was why he wanted nothing to do with Joanna *or* Evelyn.

Especially Evelyn.

Evelyn Thorncroft, with her guileless blue eyes and perfect porcelain skin and pink, voluptuous mouth, was the last person on earth he would *ever* want at Hawkridge Manor. Let alone for the annual Weston house party!

The exclusive event, held every year right before the beginning of the London Season, was another tradition. Started by Weston's grandfather, the Duke of Caldwell, as a means to celebrate his recent engagement, it had been carried on by Weston's father before it finally passed to Weston himself.

It was an obligation he took seriously, both as an earl and an heir. His grandfather, while alive at the advanced age of seven and eighty, was in no condition to play host to two dozen guests, and his father, quite frankly, couldn't be bothered.

As soon as Weston came of age, the marquess had tossed the party into his son's lap with all the carelessness of a horse swatting at a fly before he took off on a six-month holiday to his hunting lodge in Scotland.

He was there now, or so Weston assumed, having not seen hide nor hair of him since the Thorncrofts came to town. Good riddance, as far as he was concerned. Weston and his father had never been particularly close, and after Weston found a letter that had led to his discovery of the secret affair between the Marquess of Dorchester and Anne Thorncroft, an affair that had resulted in a *child* his father had never bothered to mention, the distance between them had grown to an immeasurable length.

When confronted by his son, Jason claimed that Anne Thorncroft was the "love of his life". As if Weston men were actually capable of falling in love.

For five generations, they'd married for duty and little else, resulting in marriages that were as passionless as they were practical. Weston had been set on continuing in the path forged by his predecessors with Lady Martha Smethwick, a bland woman with impeccable manners whose family was known for producing sons.

But when he'd gone to his father to ask for the family ring, a priceless heart-shaped ruby framed on either side with diamonds, he had been shocked (and subsequently enraged) to learn that Jason had *given the ring away*.

To his American mistress!

"If you want it, then go find it," his father had said, and so that was exactly what Weston had done.

It had cost him a small fortune, but he'd gotten what he wanted in the end.

He always did.

And what he wanted right *now* was an explanation for why Evelyn Thorncroft, of all people, was sitting in his carriage outside of his house.

"Do you have something you'd like to tell me?" he asked his sister after stepping out of her beloved "natural light".

"You know, there was something..." Tapping the edge of her brush against her chin, Brynne's nose wrinkled thoughtfully. "That's it. Now I remember. The green fabric I wanted to reupholster the dining room chairs in doesn't complement the wall in the way that I'd hoped, and I will need to choose another. Do you prefer eggplant, or more of a plum shade? I like the eggplant, personally, but I'm afraid it may be a tad too–"

"I don't care about chairs," he interrupted between clenched teeth. "Why the hell is Evelyn Thorncroft under the impression that she's been invited to Hawkridge Manor?"

"Oh!" Brynne smiled brightly. "That's because she has. Once the chairs are reupholstered, I really think we should commission a new sideboard. There's a lovely furniture maker in Berkley Square that everyone has been raving about, and–"

"No," he snapped.

His sister's smile faded. "No, you don't want a new sideboard, or no, you don't like the furniture maker? Maybe if you saw a few of his pieces you'd change your mind. We could go this morning, if you'd like, before we depart for the country."

Tilting his head up to the clear blue autumn sky, Weston prayed for patience. While sisters had their merits, and Brynne was better than most, it went without saying that siblings were a burden. Was it any wonder that he didn't want another?

"I did it," said Brynne after a long, heavy pause. "I invited her."

"I figured as much." Dropping his chin, he met his twin's hazel eyes. "The question is what you hoped to accomplish with such a ridiculous stunt."

"It's not ridiculous," Brynne said defensively. "Evie is our family, and–"

"She is *not* our family." For some reason, Weston felt a primal urge to make that distinction. Maybe it was because–for a very, *very* brief moment–he'd fancied himself attracted to the raven-haired beauty who had stunned him with her beauty and charmed him with her wit. He hadn't known who she was, of course. If he had, he never would have asked her to dance. Never would have leaned in to detect the scent of her perfume, an exotic blend of jasmine and citrus. Never would have admired the play of the candlelight across the top of her breasts. Never would have gazed at her plump pout and imagined what it tasted like. What *she* tasted like.

But that was all before.

Before he knew her name and what she was after.

Now he wanted nothing to do with her. This woman who was his half-sister's sister.

Unfortunately, it appeared Brynne had other ideas.

"Evie may not be our family by blood, but she *is* connected to us," his twin countered. "I should like to get to know her. We met last evening at the ball, and I found her to be exceedingly fresh and facetious."

Weston glowered. "I think we have a different definition of the word facetious."

"To be completely forthright," Brynne went on, ignoring him, "I extended the same invitation to Joanna, but it seems she will soon be returning to Boston."

"Good riddance," he said bitterly. Then his eyes narrowed. "Why isn't Evelyn accompanying her?"

"Because she is attending our house party," Brynne explained with the patient tone of a parent speaking to a child who was having great difficulty grasping a simple arithmetic. "I've already sent our driver to collect her."

"Oh, I'm aware. She's here."

"She *is?*" Brynne gasped. "Why didn't you say anything?"

Crossing his arms, Weston watched in tightlipped silence as his sister leapt to her feet, nearly toppling her easel in the process. She whirled in a circle, then spun back, before glancing down at her own hand still clutching her paintbrush.

"There it is," she said in relief before she swished the bristles clean in a cup of water and carefully returned the brush to its rightful box. Then she untied her painting frock, straightened her hat, and all but skipped up the stone steps to the terrace where Weston was standing. "I suppose we won't have time to visit the furniture maker after all."

Weston smiled pleasantly at his sister.

She smiled back at him.

His mouth flattened. "You're going to march yourself out there and explain that you made a mistake. Tell her we don't have the room to accommodate a last-minute guest."

"But we *do* have the room. Hawkridge is enormous."

"Then tell her we don't have the means to get her there."

"She is sitting in our carriage as we speak."

He threw his arms up. "Then tell her the bloody sky is falling! I don't care. Evelyn Thorncroft is *not* attending this house party. And that's final."

Now it was Brynne's eyes that narrowed. Although renowned the *ton* over for her ladylike demeanor and quiet grace, his sister possessed the same spine of steel that he did, and when she put her foot down on something she rarely removed it. "Don't you dare take that tone with *me*, Weston Weston."

He grimaced. "You know I hate it when you call me that."

Why his parents had seen fit to give him the same moniker twice, he hadn't the faintest idea. It was an embarrassment he'd overcome by referring to himself as Hawkridge to his peers, and the more familiar Weston to his personal friends and family. Only Brynne dared bring up the unusual name, and every time that she did, he couldn't help but wince.

"And *I* hate it when you treat me as if I were your subordinate!" she retorted. "Just because I happened to be born the female twin and you the male does not make me less than you."

"According to British law it does," he pointed out.

"You're just trying to make me angry enough to forgo the party entirely, so that you can tell Evie she has been disinvited."

"Yes," he admitted unabashedly. "Is it working?"

"You're a cad, Weston."

He shrugged off the insult. "I'm much worse than that, sweetling."

"Oh, I am aware. But as a lady, it's the only word I can use."

Shifting his weight, he skimmed his nails, filed to blunt edges, along his jaw. "Why is this of such importance to you, Brynne? You didn't even know we *had* another sibling until a few weeks ago. We've gotten along fine until this point. Why complicate matters unnecessarily?"

"I'd hardly call being raised by an army of governesses and sent away to Cheltenham Ladies' College for a year of my life as *fine*," Brynne retorted, referring to England's most acclaimed boarding school for young women of distinguished families.

Weston's experience had been similar, except he'd attended Eton for four years instead of one. From fourteen to seventeen he'd only seen his father and sister over Christmas, and even then, the marquess had rarely made an appearance, abandoning his two children to celebrate the holiday in the company of servants.

He and Brynne couldn't complain, and they never had. Not when they'd been blessed with a roof over their heads and food in their bellies and more money than either of them could spend in a lifetime. Money that Weston had increased tenfold with a variety of entrepreneurial investments that expanded far beyond the passive income brought in by tenant farmers.

But while he and Brynne had never wanted for anything of a materialistic nature, there were other ways to starve a child, and they'd both longed for love. For affection. For even the simplest gesture that would indicate their father considered them as more than just another obligation to be met.

As Weston grew older, his paternal expectations had grown lower until they'd all but disappeared. But Brynne, he suspected, had held out hope that their sire might suddenly turn into the father-figure they'd yearned for all those years spent alone in a vast, empty house.

His hope had been that things would change when he went off to boarding school. While Brynne had dragged her heels, afraid to leave him, Weston had secretly counted down the days until he could start a new life far from the loneliness of his old one.

Instead, he'd learned two valuable lessons he'd carried with him into adulthood.

That he could be surrounded by people and still feel terribly alone.

And the only person he could depend on was himself.

"Given our upbringing, I understand why you might have an...*attachment* towards the Thorncrofts," he allowed begrudgingly. "But they are not our family, Brynne. They're nothing like us."

Her lips twisted in a humorless smile. "At this point, I surely think that is to their credit. Why would anyone in their right mind *want* to be like us, West? Yes, we've titles and wealth and prestige. But what have we really accomplished with our lives? I spend all my days painting because I haven't a single friend I'd genuinely like to spend time with. Father would prefer to sit in a hunting lodge than have tea with his children. And you're about to propose to a woman you don't even like."

"I like Lady Martha."

"What is her favorite color?"

"Why is that of any importance?"

Brynne rolled her eyes. "That is exactly as I assumed. You've only selected her because she will make a suitable countess. And once she's given you an heir, the two of you can ignore each other for the next thirty years."

"And?" he said, not seeing the problem.

"Shouldn't we want *more* for ourselves?"

His sister's words struck a chord deep down inside of Weston. A chord he'd gone out of his way not to touch. Did he want more than a loveless marriage to a lady who invoked nothing more than vague stirring of apathy?

Of course.

He was a cad, not a fool.

And it was because he *wasn't* a fool that he understood the merits of shackling himself to someone like Martha Smethwick. Someone who would never question him. Never challenge him. Never provoke him. She was going to be the perfect wife because she *wouldn't* require more of him than he was willing to give.

Frustrated, he raked a hand through his hair. The thick dark strands fell in a disheveled wave across his temple. What the hell did Brynne expect of him? That he marry a woman like Evelyn Thorncroft?

Now *there* was a bloody brilliant idea, he thought sourly. Why spend the rest of his life in relative peace and quiet when he could spend it arguing with a stubborn black-haired beauty who derived pleasure from making his blood boil?

Good God, he'd rather die a monk than marry *that* shrew.

"We are far more fortunate than most, Brynne." He gave his sister a stern look. "We'd do well to appreciate what we have." *And never bring up this conversation again,* he added silently.

"I *do* appreciate what we have." Her chin jutted. "You know that I do. But I also want–I *need*–a friend, West. Someone with whom to go shopping on Bond Street with, and gossip at a ball with, and share girlish secrets that I cannot divulge to my brother."

"And Miss Thorncroft is that friend," he said skeptically. "You've an entire city of eligible companions to choose from, and *that* is who you pick."

Brynne's paint-smeared hands went to her hips. "It isn't the same as a man selecting his wife. I actually want to *enjoy* myself when I am in their company."

As he gazed at his sister, Weston was reminded of his one vulnerability. Namely, the fact that he'd never been able to deny his twin anything.

When she was fourteen and distraught over the loss of their beloved family hound, he'd immediately gone out to the nearest farm and bought her two basset puppies, Ellie and Emma, who were now fully grown and no doubt eagerly awaiting her arrival at Hawkridge Manor where they patrolled the grounds in between eating and naps.

When she broke her ankle at sixteen and was made to remain indoors for the entire summer, he'd stayed with her every day to keep her company.

And when she turned eighteen and desperately wished for a white horse with black spots for her birthday, he'd scoured the entire country before importing an appaloosa mare from a private breeding farm in New York.

"I don't want to see Evelyn," he said, setting his jaw, "for the duration of the house party."

Brynne gasped in delight. "You won't! Except for when we all dine together, but I'll make sure that you're at opposite ends of the table. Oh, thank you, West!" Flinging her arms around his neck, she hugged him tight. "You're the best brother I have."

Weston gave his sister an awkward pat on the top of her head before he stepped back. Having been denied physical contact as a child (his governesses had been under strict orders to never embrace him, or even so much as wrap their arm around his shoulders, even if he were crying–*especially* if he were crying), he did not like to be touched as an adult.

Accepting comfort was a sign of weakness.

And the Earl of Hawkridge did not permit himself to be weak.

"I am the *only* brother you have."

"That's right. Which is why I hope you'll grant me one more *very* small favor," she said, squeezing her pointer finger and thumb together. "Miniscule, really."

Weston wasn't fooled for an instant. "What is it, Brynne?"

"You'll need to travel with Evie to Hawkridge."

"The devil I do," he snorted. "It's out of the question."

"But you know that with my travel sickness I'm far better suited to make the trip in the brougham. And with all of my art supplies, another person simply wouldn't fit. At this stage, it would take another hour, at the very least, to prepare the second town coach. Then you wouldn't arrive at the estate until well after sunset. It only makes sense that you and Miss Thorncroft share the conveyance that is ready to depart immediately."

"No," he said flatly.

"West…"

"*No.* Absolutely, unequivocally, *no.*"

CHAPTER TWO

"M INT?" EVIE ASKED, prying the top off a circular metal tin and holding it out to the Earl of Hawkridge. "I find on long journeys there's nothing worse than stale breath."

"Oh," Weston replied icily from the far corner of the carriage where he sat wrapped in shadows and silent disdain, "I can think of at least one thing worse."

"Suit yourself." Slipping a hard peppermint between her lips, Evie used her tongue to press it to the roof of her mouth as her gaze went to the window. They'd exchanged the busy streets of London for the rolling countryside of southern England. Here the houses were few and far between, with more sheep dotting the sprawling green fields than people.

The passing scenery reminded her of home. But unlike Joanna, who was boarding a ship at this very moment to return to the sleepy village of Somerville, and their sister, Claire, who'd been unable to leave it, Evie knew that she was exactly where she wanted to be. In a fancy carriage, sitting across from a handsome earl, on her way to an exclusive house party.

Of the three sisters, Joanna was the boldest. Claire, with her quiet scientific mind, was undoubtedly the brightest. But Evie, more than anything else, had always desired to be the *best*. And for her, that meant having the unparalleled admiration of her peers.

She'd started her quest for prestige at a young age when she'd made herself into the most popular girl at Chesterbrook Academy for Young Ladies. Some thought that popularity was accidental, a whim of fate, such as it were, but Evie knew that it was much more than that. It was hard work, and cunning, and knowing just the right thing to say to just the right person.

There were those (including Joanna) who considered her aspirations to be superficial. Silly, even. But having her peers gaze at her with envy as she sauntered down the street wasn't *silly* to Evie. Having the best, most beautiful gowns wasn't silly. Living in the biggest house in the entire village wasn't silly. Marrying Evan Bridgeton, the eldest son of a senator, wasn't silly.

It was smart, and practical. It was using the natural traits afforded her as a woman to thrive in a world controlled by men. And if *occasionally* she became a bit too consumed with how she looked or how others perceived her, well, that was all part of it.

For all intents and purposes, Evie was on the verge of living a perfect life. She was going to marry the best bachelor in all of Somerville (even if he didn't know it yet). They were going to have the best children. Host the best parties. Travel to the best places. It was all but etched in stone, really.

Until the War of the Great Rebellion happened and Evie lost…everything.

Including her father.

A skilled physician, Jacob Thorncroft had felt it was his civic duty to help the Union in whatever capacity they needed him. Leaving his three daughters in the care of his mother, he had marched off to war…and ten months later his remains were returned to them in a pine box.

To this day, Evie had never known pain like that. The bewildering, baffling hurt of realizing the last time she had held her father's hand, kissed his cheek, and told him that she loved him had been just that...the last time.

In her head, she'd understood the risk of war. What it could give, and what it might take. But in her heart...in her heart, she'd never really believed that it was *her* father who might be killed. *Her* father who might never come home. *Her* father who she would never see again.

It still ached, to think of him. Like a bone that had broken and never set right. Enough time had passed that the ache was no longer sharp enough to steal her breath, but all it took was a color, or a smell, or the sound of a deep laugh and she was found herself recalling all of the memories they had made together.

And mourning all the memories they never would.

Without their father's financial support, it wasn't long before the sisters were forced to sell their grand house in the middle of town. With tears in her eyes, Evie had watched from the window of her empty bedroom as all of their worldly possessions were loaded into carts and carried away to be sold at auction.

The servants were let go next, and then the carriages were sold, followed quickly by the horses. In the blink of an eye, the Thorncrofts went from being one of the wealthiest and most highly regarded families in Somerville to living in a drafty cottage outside the village with hardly enough room to accommodate the mice living in the attic, let alone three young women and their grandmother.

It was a tremendous fall.

A fall that Evie took personally.

And she'd promised herself, she'd *vowed*, that the day would come when she returned to the top of that ladder. She would claw her way there if necessary, but she'd be damned if she stayed on a rung where people looked at her with pity in their eyes.

"Would you stop that?" Weston said irritably, drawing Evie out of the past and back into the present.

Blinking, she glanced away from the window to where her carriage companion was slouched in the opposite diagonal corner, his long legs sprawled out in front of him and his arms crossed.

He'd closed the curtain to *his* window before he even sat down, leading her to assume that he intended to sleep for the duration of their journey. After attempting to engage him in a mild conversation about the weather which he replied to in a series of grunts and glares, she'd decided to let Weston sulk while she enjoyed the luxury of traveling across England in the most magnificent coach she'd ever seen, let alone had the pleasure of riding in.

Marked with the Earl of Hawkridge's insignia in gold on the outside, it was upholstered with rich emerald green velvet within. Wood trim gleamed in the subdued light, and silk tassels hung from the canopied ceiling. The seats were large and roomy, and the carriage's suspension was well sprung for she'd felt nary a jolt on their trip thus far. If not for Weston's unpleasant demeanor, the trip would have been downright heavenly.

"Stop what?" she asked, bemused by the request.

Scowling, he leaned forward ever-so-slightly. "Making that noise."

"*What* noise?"

His scowl deepening, he gestured at her mouth. "That noise. That–that sucking noise."

"*Sucking* noise? I don't...I...oh, you mean *this*." She stuck out of her tongue, revealing what remained of the peppermint, before tucking it into the side of her cheek. "I wasn't aware I was being unduly loud. I *did* offer you one, you know."

"I don't want a mint," he said in a strangled voice. "I want you to not do that again."

"Not do *what* again?"

"That *thing* you just did with your tongue."

"I was showing you the peppermint."

His ebony brows pulled inward to form a line of disapproval. "As an uncivilized American, you most likely aren't aware of this, but

British ladies do not go around sticking their *tongues* out of their mouths. If you are to be a guest at my estate, I expect a *modicum* of common decency and good manners."

"If you don't like it, then look the other direction," she suggested before she resumed staring out the window...and slid the peppermint to the roof of her mouth with a loud *pop* of suction.

"That does it," Weston snarled. "Give it to me."

She flicked a disdainful glance at the arm he was holding out to her, his palm raised flat. He'd worn gloves when he'd entered the coach but had removed them sometime after they'd set off, exposing his hand to her gaze.

In her (admittedly limited) experience, Evie found that men of leisure often had the soft, lily-white hands of a lady. Unsurprising, given the most vigorous physical activity required of them on any given day was pouring themselves a glass of scotch. And even then, they had a footman at their beck and call if the task proved to be too arduous an undertaking.

But with some interest, she saw that Weston's hand was neither soft nor the same shade as a fish's underbelly. Instead, his fingertips were marred with rough calluses and his skin was a warm brushed gold, indicating that he often saw fit to discard his gloves.

A wicked part of her wondered at the rest of his body that she *couldn't* see. Were his gloves the only article of clothing he went without? Or was he in the habit of roaming his private estate sans a waistcoat and cravat with his shirt partially unbuttoned?

It was an intriguing image, to be sure.

One she might have allowed herself to imagine a bit further if he wasn't currently looking at her as if he wanted to yank open the door and toss her out.

"What is it you want *now*?" she asked with a sigh.

"I want you to give me that cursed tin," he gritted.

"What tin?"

"The tin with the mints!"

"Why?"

It was evident by the way his eyes flashed that he wasn't accustomed to having his orders questioned. "Because I'm going to throw it out the window."

That was better, she supposed, than throwing *her* out the window. But still not preferable, as it was her last batch of peppermints and she hadn't the money to purchase another. Truth be told, she hadn't *any* money. None of the Thorncrofts did, and that was why their mother's ring was of such importance. Why they'd made the painful decision to sell it. Why they'd gone to Boston to have it appraised. And the ring was why she was here right now, sitting across from an earl who, by all outward appearances, despised the very sight of her.

Of course, if he hadn't paid off every jeweler in Boston and its surrounding areas to alert his detectives when the ring surfaced and then have them *steal* it, she and Joanna wouldn't have had to come to London in the first place.

It was Weston's fault, really.

Everything.

Although Evie thought it best to keep that particular fact to herself at the moment lest he *did* open the door and toss her out.

"I shall gladly discard the peppermint," she said, "*if* you stop glaring at me and agree to indulge in pleasant conversation. What is your opinion of the weather today? I am glad to see that it has finally stopped raining."

His jaw tightened. "This is not a *negotiation*, Miss Thorncroft. And I don't give a damn about the weather."

No, the only thing he cared about was hating *her*. Even though she'd done nothing except befriend his sister, invite herself to his house party, and abscond with his carriage. Hardly anything of notable consequence.

Then there was the small matter of her mother having a secret affair with his father, but that wasn't *her* fault, was it? She hadn't even been born. Unfortunately, if Weston's persistent glower was any indication, he didn't see it that way. And he clearly had no intention in indulging her request for amicable discourse.

Pity, as the weather *was* lovely.

Outside the carriage, at least.

Turning her head to the side, Evie discreetly swallowed her mint and cast her gaze to the passing scenery. She'd have plenty of time to antagonize Weston over the coming days. No need to poke the bear unnecessarily. Especially if her goal was to win the bear's favor.

It really was the height of irony. There wasn't a man alive in Somerville she could not have wrapped around her little finger if she but expelled the tiniest amount of effort. Including Evan Bridgeton, whose father was now considering a bid for the presidency after Grant ran for his second term.

What a wonderful match *that* would have been! Evan's political ambitions paired with her social ones. They could have taken Washington society by storm. Only her grandmother's absurd rule that Joanna had to be the first of the three sisters to marry had prevented Evie from becoming the daughter-in-law of a senator. Well, that and the fact she'd never *technically* received a proposal.

Joanna still did not have a husband. But as their grandmother wasn't in England, and as she hadn't specifically stated whether her rule extended beyond international waters, Evie did not feel obligated to adhere to it. Desperate times called for desperate measures, and she *was* going to marry the Earl of Hawkridge.

He just didn't know it yet.

CHAPTER THREE

E VIE HADN'T EVEN realized she'd fallen asleep until a hard jolt startled her awake.

"What...?" Blinking the sleep from her eyes, she sat up and swiped a hand across her chin. Goodness. Had she been *drooling?* Perish the thought. "What's happened?"

"We've cracked an axle," Weston replied tersely.

She sat up a little straighter. "That doesn't sound good."

"It isn't." He began to pull on his gloves as the carriage limped to the side of the road and rolled to an unceremonious halt. "Especially since we're three miles from the nearest inn."

"Three *miles?* I–where are you going?" she demanded when he pushed open the door.

"To help the driver." In a single lithe motion, Weston leapt from the carriage and landed in several inches of mud, its thick consistency most likely responsible for their cracked axle.

"Wait!" she called, scrambling across her seat. "You cannot just leave me here."

After flicking a spot of wet dirt off his coat, he gave her a cool smile. "Oh, but I can."

With that, he slammed the door in her face, leaving her to glare out the window at him as he made his way around the front of the cumbersome town coach to where the horses were nervously prancing in place.

On a huff of breath, Evie flopped back and crossed her arms. She knew Weston didn't like her, but did he have to treat her as he would a child?

When they were dancing together at the Countess of Beresford's ball he hadn't treated her like a child. Before she told him her name, their banter had been flirtatiously playful. And the heat in his gaze had burned hot enough to scorch the entire room.

Part of her wished they could return to that moment in time when neither one of them had known who the other was. When there was nothing between them but raw, unapologetic attraction and the seductive whisper of lust. Oh, what might have been if they'd remained anonymous! Another dance, perhaps even a venture out into the moonlit gardens where the air was heavy with the scent of gardenias and temptation.

But instead of flowers and moonlight, she had a crippled carriage and mud.

Hardly the ingredients for a blossoming romance.

Biting down hard on the inside of her cheek, Evie eyed the door. She considered joining West outside, but the only traveling habit she had, a plain, long-sleeved beige jacket with matching skirt and modest bustle, was the one that she was wearing, and she didn't want to dirty it. But neither did she want to remain inside a carriage that was growing warmer by the second. Maybe if she opened a window, the wait would become more bearable and she could hear what the earl and the driver were discussing. As it stood, their muffled voices provided no insight into how long they might find themselves stuck in the ditch.

She'd just begun to fidget with the latch holding the glass pane shut when the door was abruptly yanked outward and Weston poked his head in.

"Gather your things," he said grimly. "We're going to walk."

"*Walk?*" she repeated, incredulous. "But you said the nearest town was three miles away!"

Something indecipherable flickered in the depths of his cold gray gaze. "By all means, stay here with the driver and the horses. Another carriage should be round before nightfall to collect you."

He started to close the door. Would have closed it, if Evie hadn't thrust her foot out.

"I am not going to sit here for hours in hopes that help *might* arrive before it gets dark." She extended her arm, wrist gracefully bent and fingers pointed. "If you'd be so kind as to assist me, I'll–*ahhh!*"

With all the care of a butcher tossing a slab of beef onto his shoulder, Weston grabbed her hand and pulled. Caught unprepared and off balance, she shrieked as she fell straight towards the watery muck, her arms flapping wildly in the air.

At the last possible second, the earl grasped her by the waist and set her on her feet, his thumbs digging into the jut of her hipbones as he scowled down at her.

"You're impossible," he growled, as if it were somehow *her* fault she'd nearly ended up with a mouthful of mud!

"*Me?*" Glaring up at him beneath the brim of her bonnet, a narrow concoction of silk and ribbon that sat low over her brow and was held in place by a bow that ran beneath her chignon, she struggled to rein in her temper.

Unlike Joanna, who always spoke her mind, Evie had learned at an early age that it was often advantageous to keep her opinion to herself. Particularly if that opinion reflected negatively on the only person in a three-mile radius who knew where they were going.

Up ahead, the main thoroughfare branched into three separate roads, and she had a feeling that if she picked the wrong one that she could be committing herself to wandering the countryside for the next several hours.

"Is there something you'd like to say, Miss Thorncroft?" Weston asked, blatantly searching for a reason–*any* reason–to leave her behind.

Unfortunately for the earl, she had no intention of giving him any excuse to leave her sitting in the carriage. Until they reached their final destination, she would strive to be on her very best behavior. However, if the opportunity presented itself to shove her traveling companion into a watery ditch and giggle mercilessly as he climbed out of it…well, she *was* only human.

And an occasionally vindictive one, at that.

Despite her delicate build, love of fashion, and general abhorrence of anything icky (including, but not limited to, mud), Evie's sugary smile disguised a woman who was ruthless in her pursuit of what she wanted. She may have been small and weak in stature, but her determination was as strong as iron, and she wasn't going to stop until she had the three things she desired most: a wealthy husband, her mother's ring, and the respect of her peers.

She rather thought it was to her credit that she'd found a way to get all three at once…and become a countess in the process. Although if she'd had the choice, she would have vastly preferred one of her malleable Somerville admirers to the ill-tempered Earl of Hawkridge.

They'd not shared each other's company for any considerable length of time, but she intuitively sensed that he was not a simple-minded dandy whose eyes would cross and tongue would wag at the sight of a discreetly flashed ankle. Courting him–and convincing him to propose–was going to be a great challenge. Perhaps the greatest of her lifetime, excluding the gloomy months following her father's death.

But Evie was not daunted by the uphill battle that awaited her.

Instead, she found herself invigorated by it.

Not to say that she wouldn't *prefer* Weston drop to his knees and declare his undying love. It would certainly make her ascension to British nobility an easier ride than the bumpy, axle-breaking journey she currently found herself on. But she'd never shied away from a little adversity before, and she wasn't about to start now. Thorncroft women were made of stern stock, and they'd overcome far more difficult obstacles than arrogant, scowling earls.

Speaking of which...

"Why, I was just going to compliment you on your amazingly quick reflexes, my lord." Batting her lashes, she gave a simpering smile that had been practiced and perfected in the cracked mirror hanging on her bedroom wall. "You are surely a gallant knight sent from above, and I could not have asked for a better champion to keep me safe on the arduous trek that awaits us."

Her gallant knight loomed above her, suspicion clouding his gaze and a muscle pulsing in his jaw. "I do not know what game you are playing, Miss Thorncroft, but I can assure you that I want no part of it."

"I'll be the first to admit I enjoy a good round of solitaire now and again," she said. "But as I haven't any cards with me at the moment, I am afraid I don't know to what game you are referring, Lord Hawkridge."

Delivering a flat, humorless laugh, Weston released his grip on her and stepped away.

"If you don't keep up," he said curtly, "you can stay behind."

And with that uplifting note of encouragement, he headed off down the road, leading Evie to impulsively stick her tongue out at his back before she picked up her skirts and hurried after him.

WESTON WALKED FOR the better part of a mile before he allowed himself to steal a sideways glance at Evie. To his surprise–and reluctant admiration–she'd managed to keep pace with his longer stride, but she looked far from happy about it.

Suppressing an unexpected grin at her disheveled appearance, he held up his arm and motioned for her to follow him into the shade of an oak whose thick branches provided a welcome relief from the unrelenting sun.

"We can stop here for a minute to catch our breath," he said brusquely. "Then we'll continue on."

"How much *further?*" Evie groaned, swatting at a tendril of hair that had come loose from her chignon and was tickling the side of her neck where a layer of perspiration caused her ivory skin to gleam in the dappled light.

Inside the carriage, she'd been the epitome of ladylike perfection. Every ebony tendril had been artfully arranged, her habit had carried nary a wrinkle, and her tiny bonnet had been tidily pinned to the middle of her head.

But now, after twenty minutes of walking in the unseasonably warm autumn heat, her skirts had wilted, her hat was dangling low over her left brow, and her color was high; her cheeks as rosy as two ripe apples.

Two ripe apples that Weston suddenly and inexplicably wanted to bite into.

Would she taste sweet or tart? A combination, if he had to guess. Like a chameleon, Evelyn Thorncroft had the unique ability to change her demeanor at will. But he found that of all the Evie's he had encountered thus far (the coquettish Evie at the ball, the smirking Evie outside his townhouse, the suspiciously agreeable Evie in his carriage), he preferred this version of her the best.

This rumpled, hot, sticky version that had peeled away her carefully constructed polished veneer to reveal a glimpse at the raw, authentic woman beneath. The woman, he suspected, not many people ever had the chance to see.

"We've only gone a mile," he said, and found himself struggling not to chuckle when Evie's plump lips parted in dismay. As someone not given to great bursts of humor, it was an uncharacteristic reaction. One that caught him off guard, and caused him to frown.

Evelyn Thorncroft was his *enemy*. An opportunistic, scheming shrew who had taken advantage of his sister's cordial nature and all but forced herself upon him for the next four weeks. *If* she lasted that long. Weston hadn't told Brynne, but he had every intention of making Evie's stay at Hawkridge Manor so miserable that she was begging to leave within a fortnight, if not sooner.

The American was a problem he didn't want. Especially now that she was invoking unwanted...*feelings* inside of him. And when Weston found himself faced with a problem, there was only one thing to do.

Eradicate it.

"A *mile?*" she exclaimed, gazing at him disbelief. "It feels as if we've walked for ages!"

"We have at least another two to go." Not the list bit sympathetic to her discomfort (he *had* offered to let her stay in the carriage), Weston removed a silver plated flask from the inside pocket of his coat and took a swig. "Maybe three."

"Three more miles?" At that, Evie's legs crumpled beneath her and she sank to the ground in a plume of tan skirts, tangled hair, and despair. "Can't we wait here for another carriage to come along?"

"We could," he acknowledged. "But if one did not, we'd soon find ourselves stranded out in the elements after sunset."

"What about Lady Brynne?" Evie said hopefully. "Surely she'll be along."

"My sister suffers from traveling sickness, and takes a less direct route where the roads are wider and more smoothly grated."

"Well why didn't we go *that* way?"

He smiled thinly. "Because I desired to divest myself of your company as quickly as possible. If you're done resting, we need to continue on."

"Help me up," she said, extending her arm.

Of its own accord, Weston's gaze dropped to her hand. Without his noticing, she'd removed her gloves while they were walking. Her fingers were long and elegant, her nails filed to a rounded edge. She may not have borne the title of a lady, but she had the soft, lily-white hands of one. Or so he thought before she turned her wrist with an impatience flick and he saw the rough calluses on her palm.

As he couldn't fathom Evie doing any sort of manual labor, he wondered what had put them there. By all impressions, she was a pampered Boston socialite without a care in the world. But those blisters belonged to someone who had endured hardship. Someone who had used their hands in such a repetitive manner that their skin had literally died and then hardened.

They didn't hurt, calluses.

From years of riding, Weston's hands were riddled with them.

But then, he wasn't a woman.

And maybe...maybe Evie wasn't the woman he'd assumed she was. Namely, a spoiled brat who'd had her shiny toy taken away and, on a frivolous whim, had sailed across the ocean to get it back. Out of boredom, and spite, and a general lack of respect for the fact that the ring she'd asked him to return belonged to *his* mother, not hers.

But what if she wasn't here because she wanted to be?

What if she was here because she *needed* to be?

What if the ring wasn't a merely a token, but a means for survival? After all, the only reason his investigators had found it in the first place (aside from sheer luck) was because Evie and her sisters had brought it to a jeweler in an attempt to have it appraised. Which they wouldn't have done unless they had plans to sell it. But why part with the ring *now* after having it in their possession all these years?

It didn't make any sense.

Unless the Thorncrofts found themselves in dire straits...and desperate for money.

His brow furrowing, he made himself look at Evie. *Really* look. Something he hadn't done since he had first seen her across a crowded ballroom where her breathtaking beauty had called to him like a siren singing out to a sailor. Right before she caused the poor bloke to dash his ship upon the rocky shoreline.

For the first time, he noticed that her traveling habit was nearly worn threadbare in several places and the buckles on her shoes were tarnished and old. She wore no jewelry, not even a modest pair of pearl earrings or an agate brooch, and the feathers on her hat had clearly been replaced more than once, the remnants of past thread not matching the new.

"Is there something on my face?" she asked, self-consciously swiping her thumb along her bottom lip.

"No," he said gruffly.

"You're staring."

So he was. Averting his gaze, Weston held out his arm and waited until he felt the slight weight of her fingers pressing into his hand before he briskly hauled her to her feet. He knew he was being a tad rough with her. Rough *on* her. But the alternative–kindness, compassion, understanding–was not an option for the cold-hearted earl. Poor or not (and closer inspection had revealed that Evie was the very definition of genteel poverty), she was a thorn in his side that he couldn't wait to be rid of.

And now he had his solution.

Weston was a shrewd businessman, not a kind philanthropist, but he had donated a lofty percentage of his inherited wealth over the past decade to a variety of charitable organizations running the gamut from orphanages to hospitals. Evie was no charity, but if throwing money at her removed the vexing chit from his sight, what did it matter to him?

No to mention that his father, the Marquess of Dorchester, was likely to settle a large amount on his bastard, Joanna Thorncroft, whenever news reached of him of her arrival in London and the subsequent stir that had been created after the *ton* learned that the marquess' American mistress had given him a daughter.

Brynne may have wanted to become acquainted with their half-sister, but Weston had no such illusions regarding loving family reunions. For the love of God, they couldn't even function properly as a family of three. Why the devil would they want to bring *Americans* into the mix?

By all accounts, Joanna was on her way back across the Atlantic.

Good riddance, as far as he was concerned.

But that still left Evie to contend with. The most dangerous of the Thorncrofts, to his mind, solely because she *wasn't* his half-sister. There was no blood shared between them. Meaning there was nothing to keep him from sinking his fingers into all those messy obsidian curls, pressing her against the oak tree…and ravishing her senseless.

Weston had never realized how closely lust and loathing were intertwined before he'd found himself tempted by a dark-haired hellion with the clear, crystal blue eyes of an angel.

"You're staring again," the hellion angel said crossly. "Has your mind been addled by the sun? It would explain a lot. Including why you'd lead us to be stranded twenty miles from the nearest village when there was another perfectly good road at our disposal."

"We're three miles," he corrected. "And it's hardly my fault the axle broke. I've gone this way a hundred times before and never had any issue. If there is blame to be given out, I assign it to you."

Evie frowned. "What did *I* do?"

Everything, he thought crossly.

And nothing.

Weston was a hard man. A heart of stone, his last mistress had said after he'd ended their eighteen-month affair with all the pomp and circumstance of dashing a cheque off to his tailor. But he was also a fair one. He acknowledged that in *her* mind, Evie believed the ring she sought rightfully belonged to her and her sisters. He couldn't fault her for wanting it back. Not if his suspicions were true, and its return was necessary to their very survival.

Neither could he fault her for his own desires. Aside from a flirtatious exchange at the ball before either had realized just who the other was, she had not done anything to fan the flames of his ardor.

Why, then, had he pictured her naked more times in the past two hours than he ever had Lady Martha, whom he'd known for two years?

His unparalleled attraction to Evie was as infuriating as it was baffling.

And he needed it to end before he did something he'd soundly regret…like making good on his fantasy to kiss her.

Which was why, as soon as they finally got to Hawkridge Manor, he was going to pull her aside and offer her a ghastly amount of money to hop on the next sailing vessel bound for Boston and never return.

He'd do it now, of course.

There wasn't a single reason not to.

Except…except he didn't want to upset Brynne.

Yes, that was it, Weston told himself.

For some reason, his sister wished to forge a friendship with Evie, and who was he to deny her such a small, insignificant request?

Especially this near to her birthday.

In seven months.

"Just drink this," he growled, thrusting his flask at Evie. "The last thing I need is you fainting from dehydration."

Warily accepting the flask, she raised it to her nose and gave a delicate sniff. Her gaze flew to his. "Is this *brandy*?"

"What else would it be?" he said impatiently.

"It's eleven in the morning!"

"And?"

"Fine." Tilting her head back, she took a sip from the flask, gave a cough, and then (to Weston's amusement and slight alarm) indulged in a deep swig that would have done a sailor proud.

"All right." He snatched the flask away from her. "That's enough."

Eyes watering, Evie gave another cough. "I've had wine before, but never brandy. It's rather strong, isn't it? Like drinking fire and smoke, all wrapped into one." She smiled at him. "The aftertaste is quite pleasant."

32

"Bloody hell," he muttered, shaking his head even as the corners of his lips twitched reluctantly. Evie was no bigger than a teacup. When he'd lifted her out of the carriage, his hands had easily spanned her waist. A sip or two of his best cognac, which he had directly imported from Charente, France, and he wouldn't be surprised to see her toddling on her feet.

But when they set off back on the road, her gait was remarkably steady, her bustle lightly flouncing as her hips swayed rhythmically from side to side.

Not that he was looking at her hips.

Or any other part of her anatomy, for that matter.

Definitely not the rounded curve of her breasts. Or the slender line of her neck. Or the tips of her earlobes peeking out from beneath her heavy curtain of hair.

Who knew *ears* could be so damned attractive?

Scowling, Weston deliberately lengthened his stride as he banished any and all lascivious thoughts regarding one Miss Evelyn Thorncroft to the back of his mind where, God willing, he'd be able to keep them until she was gone.

A week, he vowed to himself as they trudged past a field spotted with white, fluffy sheep who lifted their heads in collective curiosity, unaccustomed to seeing humans strolling down the carriage path out in the middle of nowhere.

He would allow Brynne a week with Evie, to gossip and play whist and do whatever it was that women did when they were together. Compare recipes, work on their embroidery, conjure Lucifer...who knew, really?

Seven days, and then he'd do what Weston men did best when they were faced with something they had no interest in dealing with. Mistresses, wives, children. The answer was always the same.

Toss money at the problem and hope it disappeared.

CHAPTER FOUR

E VIE'S HEAD FELT pleasantly fuzzy, like it had when she and her sisters were children and they'd linked arms and spun in a circle until one (or all) fell down.

When they hadn't a care in the world.

When everything was new and innocent.

When they weren't struggling to keep pace with curmudgeonly earls.

"Would you wait up? You're going much too fast," she complained to Weston's broad shoulders as he marched along ahead her with all the steely determination of a solider heading off to battle.

Without giving any verbal indication that he'd heard her, Weston nevertheless shortened his stride, allowing her to catch up so they could walk abreast of each other instead of her trailing behind like a scolded child.

She slanted him a glance out of the corner of her eye, and couldn't help but giggle at what she saw.

"If you find something remotely frivolous about this situation, Miss Thorncroft," he said darkly, "by all means, please enlighten me."

"It's–it's your *face*," she gasped before she doubled over with a peal of laughter, wrapping her arms around her belly as her entire body shook with mirth.

Weston stopped short. "Pray tell, what about my face is so humorous?"

Between chortles, Evie managed to say, "It is very *very* serious."

A long pause, and then...

"Miss Thorncroft, you're foxed."

"Where's the fox?" Popping upright, she slanted a hand across her brow and peered off across the field. "I've only seen sheep."

"My point exactly." Weston removed his hat, ran his fingers through his hair, and regarded her with a lifted brow. "What am I supposed to do with you, Miss Thorncroft?"

"I'm rather thirsty," she said with a hopeful glance at the pocket that held his flask.

Although his mouth remained stern, his gaze held a faint, unmistakable glint of amusement. "I should think not, Miss Thorncroft. I believe you'd had more than enough cognac."

"I thought you said it was brandy."

"Cognac is a type of brandy. Like a thoroughbred is a type of horse," he explained when her temple creased in confusion.

"Oh. I understand." She didn't really, as she knew as much about horses as she did different types of liquor, but nodding along seemed as if it were the most prudent thing to do. "I did not mean to insult your appearance, you know. No offense was intended."

"No offense was taken."

"Good. Because you're really very handsome."

"Thank you, Miss Thorn–"

"Almost as handsome as Evan Bridgeton," she went on.

Weston's eyes narrowed. "Who the devil is Evan Bridgeton?"

"The man I was going to marry. Oh, look! That sheep has a lamb."

"You were *engaged?*"

"No, I...why Lord Hawkridge," she cooed, lashes fluttering. "Are you envious of Mr. Bridgeton?"

Evie's head may have been fuzzy, but she wasn't so inebriated that she didn't recognize a flash of jealousy when she saw it. And Weston, with his taut jaw and drawn fists, was most *definitely* jealous.

How…interesting.

"You needn't be, you know. Envious, that is," she said when his only reply was a low, rumbling growl. "It's true, Mr. Bridgeton was renowned throughout our village for his striking blond hair, piercing green eyes, and chiseled countenance, but it is not as if he was a Greek god or anything. However, come to think of it, I *did* hear him compared to Adonis on occasion. And yes, he *was* the son of a senator, which, in America, might as well have made him a marquess." She tapped her chin. "A marquess is higher in ranking than an earl, is it not?"

Weston's growl intensified.

"Do you have something in your throat?" she asked innocently. "Perhaps a nip of brandy might help."

"Miss Thorncroft," he bit out through gritted teeth, "has anyone ever told you how *incredibly* vexing you are?"

"Not Mr. Bridgeton. He thought I was…what were the words he used…" She pursed her lips. "That's right! Now I remember. 'Delightfully charming, astonishingly beautiful, and virtuous beyond reproach.'"

"A regular Alfred Tennyson, your Mr. Bridgeton," Weston sneered. "If he was so bloody perfect, why didn't you marry him?"

"Because I–oh, Lord Hawkridge, look!" On a gasp, Evie drew attention to a small, bleating lamb that had just come into view over the top of the hillside. "It's in trouble. We have to help it."

"It's a sheep in a field filled with sheep," he said pointedly. "I am fairly confident it does not require the assistance of two people, one of whom is–Miss Thorncroft, where the *hell* do you think you're going?"

Much later, Evie would look back on her actions and feel nothing short of humiliating, cheek-burning embarrassment. But in that moment, with her mind still pleasantly numb and her emotions running high, all she saw was a lamb calling out for its mother. As she knew the sting of losing a parent all too well, how could she *not* help?

Never mind that she didn't even *like* animals.

Especially of the smelly farm variety.

But while piles of dung would have been of utmost concern to sober Evie, intoxicated Evie barely noticed as she bunched up her skirts, climbed through the fence, and dashed off up the hill.

With alarmed bleats, woolly white sheep scattered in every direction. But the lost lamb didn't move. And it wasn't until she'd reached the frantically bleating baby and caught a glimpse of what was laying at the bottom on the other side of the hill that she understood why.

"Close your eyes," Weston ordered, materializing as if out of nowhere to grasp her waist and spin her away from the gruesome sight. He wrapped his arms around her trembling frame, holding her in a protective embrace against his chest as her stomach rolled in protest at what she'd seen.

"That poor thing," she cried. "It was…it was…"

"Dead," he said flatly. "Killed early this morning, if I had to guess."

"What could do such a thing? Wolves?"

"There haven't been wolves in England for hundreds of years. The sheep was butchered by poachers, most likely, as there's no natural predator large enough to take down a full grown ewe. At least nothing that would leave behind its lamb."

"The lamb!" Slipping out of Weston's hold, Evie crouched beside the distraught baby and gently ran her hand across its back. It couldn't have been older than a few days, a week at the most. She'd never seen one this size before. It had large, liquid brown eyes, velvety ears that stuck straight out the side, and long, spindly legs that were knobby at the knees. The lamb was as adorable as it was pitiful, and Evie could not conceive abandoning it where it was to either slowly starve to death or be picked off by some sort of creature. She gazed beseechingly up at Weston. "We have to bring it with us."

"Bring it…no," said the earl with a curt shake of his head. "Absolutely not."

"Why?" she demanded. "It's all alone. It needs us."

"There's easily five dozen sheep standing right over there. They can take care of it."

"Well they're not doing a very good job, are they?" Resolute in her decision, Evie carefully placed one hand on the lamb's chest, another under its belly, and scooped it up. It weighed less than a bag of feathers, and was in such shock that it didn't even raise a fuss, but instead pushed its head in the crook of Evie's elbow. Within moments, its rapid breathing had steadied, and the lamb fell fast asleep.

"This is stealing, you know," Weston commented as they made way out of the field and onto the road. But he reached for the lamb to lift it over the fence without Evie having to ask, and as she climbed between the wooden boards, she would have sworn his mouth curved into a shape that suspiciously resembled a smile.

Giving her skirts a good *thwack* with the palm of her hand to clear them of dust, she straightened her hat as best she could and tucked a limp strand of hair behind her ear. She must have looked like a positive fright but, for once, Evie didn't care about that. Her first concern was the slight, vulnerable animal being so tenderly held in the arms of the gruff, surly Earl of Hawkridge. Except no one, not even Weston, could look gruff *or* surly when they were cradling a lamb.

"We'll find the farmer and pay him fairly for it," she said dismissively. "No harm done."

"We're not *buying* anything," Weston said. "We're returning it at the first opportunity. I already have one uninvited houseguest to deal with. I'm not adding another."

"Shhh," Evie said, frowning. "She'll hear you."

"*She?*"

"Yes. Doesn't she strike you as a girl?" It was likely the lingering effects of the brandy, but Evie felt a distinctive maternal tug as she reached out and stroked the top of the slumbering lamb's head.

Strange, as she'd never been particularly aware of any mothering instinct before.

As a child, she hadn't played with dolls as much as she'd used their hair to practice braiding. When she grew older and her friends began to discuss how many children they were going to have, she'd been more concerned with keeping pace with the latest fashion trends coming in from Paris via the *Boston Women's Quarterly* which was at *least* four weeks behind than using the petals of a daisy to dictate whether she was going to have two boys or three girls.

All that to say, Evie knew she'd have to have children someday if she wanted to marry well, as the production of an heir was all but written into the contract. But she'd never given much consideration into what kind of mother she wanted to be.

Or what kind of father she wanted for her children.

Wealth and prestige were *much* more important factors in determining a suitable husband. At least, they had been until Weston absently rubbed the lamb's ear and Evie's heart did an odd *pitter-pat* inside of her chest.

"We should call her Posy," she whispered, glancing up at him from beneath her lashes.

"Posy the lamb," he snorted quietly. "How original."

"What would you name her, then?"

"Nothing. I am calling it nothing, because we're giving it back."

No, she thought silently as she watched Weston unknot his cravat and drape it over Posy so that the lamb's delicate pink nose wouldn't be burned by the sun, *I really don't think we are.*

IF SOMEONE HAD bet Weston fifty pounds that he would soon find himself responsible for a beautiful American and an orphaned lamb while stranded in the middle of the countryside, he'd have laughed and ordered the poor sot to hand over the money outright.

A fool's bet, he would have called it.

As it so happened, *he* was the damned fool.

He never should have agreed to travel with Evie to Hawkridge Manor. Not that they were anywhere near their destination, and were now actively walking *away* from it as they'd veered off the road onto a private, tree-lined drive that led to a cottage with a crumbling stone wall behind which several sheep grazed, indicating they'd found whom the lamb belonged to.

A line of geese temporarily halted their progression as the feathered fowl marched across the drive in an orderly row, chests puffed and orange beaks proudly held aloft. Once the parade had waddled past, he and Evie proceeded to the front door.

He knew by her stiff gait and the mutinous set of her lips that she wasn't pleased with his decision to return the lamb. But what did she expect him to do, willingly abscond with stolen livestock? He was an earl, not a thief. An earl who was beginning to question his own sanity with every minute that passed and he *didn't* leave Evie and her lamb behind to find their own way home.

Weston was no gallant knight devoted to safeguarding helpless maidens and defenseless animals. No one would think differently of him if he said to hell with it and left his charges on this very doorstep. Brynne wouldn't be pleased, but if Evie eventually made her way to Hawkridge Manor, what was the harm? He didn't owe this American anything. Certainly not any more of his valuable time than he'd already given. But neither could he bring himself to abandon her. It was an...unexpected conundrum. One he'd never faced before, as he made it a point to keep everyone at arm's length where it was easier to remain impersonal and indifferent.

Even his own mistresses were not privy to his undivided attention. Chosen strictly for their discretion and skills in the bedchamber, his intimate partners were informed at the beginning that there was to be no emotional attachment. And if that were to ever change (as it inevitably did, much to his general annoyance), they would be relieved of their position immediately. For if there was anything Weston's childhood had taught him, it was that it was better to be the person withholding love and affection than to be the one constantly craving it.

Vulnerability was another weakness, and a man was never so vulnerable than when a woman held his heart in the palm of her hand. Which was why he'd ensured that his heart was too cold to touch a long time ago.

But since having Evie forced upon him, he had felt anything *but* cold.

The woman infuriated him, and with fury came heat.

With heat came fire.

And with fire came desire.

The kind of desire that would lead a man to traipse through the countryside carrying a sheep because a raven-haired minx who heated his blood like no other had insisted they save the damned thing.

"This is for the best," he told Evie as he knocked on the door. "The farmer needs to be told there are poachers after his flock, and with this many sheep about I'm sure he has a ewe who can take the lamb on as its own."

"And if he doesn't?" she asked, her damning blue gaze making him feel for all the world as if he were about to toss a puppy into a pit of crocodiles.

Before Weston could reply, the door swung inward to reveal a young man with freckles across his cheeks and a shock of red hair sticking out beneath a flat brown cap.

"Can I help ye?" he asked, his curious gaze flicking from Evie to Weston before centering on the lamb.

"Yes," said Weston. "We were walking past your field–"

"Walking?" The lad scratched the back of his neck. "Where's yer carriage?"

"An excellent question," Evie interceded with a glare at Weston.

"A broken axle back by the Three Crossings," he explained, returning her glare. "We left the driver to tend the horses and set off on foot. Whereupon we found this fellow here"–he held out the lamb, which gave a worried sounding bleat–"and its dead mother. Butchered for her meat, if I had to guess."

"Aye," said the lad. "We've been having trouble with trespassers."

When he didn't say anything else, Weston bit back a curse of frustration (could *nothing* about this cursed journey be simple?) and said, "Can you take the lamb, then? Or direct us to someone who can?" He glanced past the boy into the house. From what he could see, it was sparsely decorated, but freshly swept. "Is your father or mother here?"

"They're gone. Won't return until tomorrow." The lad shifted his weight from side to side. Then his face brightened. "I can give it to my sister. She's just in the kitchen. Gertie!" he yelled, turning his head. "Gertie, I've another lamb for ye!"

Weston felt a tightness on his arm. He glanced down to see Evie had her fingers curled around his wrist.

"Why would you bring Posy into the kitchen?" she asked, her pretty brow creasing. "To warm her up?"

"Warm her up?" the boy said, visibly confused. "Ye mean when we put her in the stew?"

Evie blanched. "The *stew*? You're going to *cook* Posy?"

"I am sure that is not what he meant," said Weston. Having eaten his fair share of lamb and mutton stew, he knew that was exactly what the boy meant, but why alarm Evie any more than she already was? A pot of boiling water wasn't the ending he'd foreseen for poor Posy, but then life was often cruel and unforgiving. If that lesson had somehow escaped Evie thus far, it was better she learn it now than later.

"Aye," said the lad. "What else would we do with it?"

"Lord Hawkridge, you cannot mean to allow Posy to be turned into stew!" Evie cried. "Tell him we'll pay for her. Whatever price he wants. Please!"

"The lamb's yers for fifty pounds." Wiping her hands clean on an apron, a stringy beanpole of a woman with the lad's red hair and none of his youthful naivety sauntered up to the doorway and gave a shrewd smile. "Fifty-five, and we'll toss in a ribbon to go round its neck."

Weston almost choked on his own tongue. "*Fifty* pounds? It's worth half a shilling, if that."

"It is worth what someone will pay for it," said Gertie.

She wasn't wrong, but Weston would be damned if he spent a fortune on a *sheep*. Then he made the mistake of looking at Evie. A single glimpse at her heartbroken countenance, complete with a wobbling bottom lip, had him reaching into his pocket.

"I can give you ten now, and have the rest sent later." Given the recent rise in highwaymen scouring the roads for easy victims, Weston had stopped carrying large quantities of money on his person several months ago.

"The price is fifty," said Gertie, jutting out her chin.

Weston resisted the urge to grind his teeth. "I am the Earl of Hawkridge. Here, this is my family signet." He extended his left hand to show his gold seal ring with the family crest engraved on the top. "I can assure you that I am good for it."

"Fifty," Gertie repeated. "Or the lamb goes in the pot."

"As I told you, I do not have that sum currently, but I can easily acquire it once I reach my estate." Beside him, Evie tensed. Without giving much thought to what he was doing, he reached across the front of Posy and gently covered Evie's hand with his own. His fingers intertwining with hers, he gave a reassuring squeeze. It was, to his knowledge, the first time he had ever deliberately sought to give a woman comfort.

"Surely we can come to a mutual agreement," he said, speaking with the calm assurance of an entrepreneur accustomed to striking any manner of deals. Following a ten-hour negotiation, he'd leveraged his money and reputation to gain a position on the board of the Midland

Railway Company at a time when investors were divesting themselves of railway shares as quickly as possible.

Within half a year, Weston had secured enough private land leases to build a new railway from London to Bath. The more direct route had undercut their top competitor's time by nearly two hours, leading the Midland Railway Company to buy them out and become the second largest railway in all of England.

If he could accomplish *that* (no inconsiderable feat), then surely he could negotiate the simple sale of a lamb.

Except it appeared Gertie had no intention of negotiating.

"Tom," she said, her brown eyes hardening to chips of rock, "get Pa's pistol."

"You are being utterly unreasonable." Weston frowned as the lad obediently scampered off.

Gertie arched a scrawny red brow. "Ye've come to *my* parents' house, and ye stole one of *our* lambs, and I'm being unreasonable? Count yerself lucky I didn't have my brother shoot first and ask questions later. How do I know ye aren't the poachers that've been after our flock?"

"We did not steal anything," Evie cut in with a sniff. "We saved Posy. You should be thanking us." She gave Weston a hard nudge with her elbow.

"What was that for?" he snapped.

"I *told* you we shouldn't have come here."

Tom returned swiftly with the item his sister had requested, and gingerly handed it over.

Without hesitation, Gertie drew back the hammer and pointed the pistol at the ceiling. "Give my brother the lamb," she said threateningly. "Or else."

Had Weston been by himself, he would have tossed Posy over directly. He was a stubborn sod who didn't like to lose, but he wasn't an idiot, and he sure as hell wasn't about to get shot over a sheep.

But there was Evie and her wobbling lip to consider.

Along with the fact that he'd left his own pistol with his driver in case any passersby got it in their heads to help themselves to the contents of the town coach.

"No one puts Posy in a pot," he growled.

He looked at Evie.

She looked at him.

"Run," he said grimly, and that's what they did.

Down the steps, around the stone wall, and back to the road while Gertie, who likely belonged in a mental asylum for the lamb stew obsessed, fired bullets into the air.

Weston could have sworn he felt one fly over his shoulder, and he shoved Evie in front of him into a thicket of overgrown bushes. They huddled together, with Posy pressed between them, as their breathing slowed and steadied...but all it took was a quick measure of how close Evie's hand was to his groin for Weston's pulse rate to accelerate all over again.

Bloody hell.

What was he *doing?*

Then Evie started to adjust her position but lost her balance and used Weston's leg to regain it, her fingers burning through his trousers like an iron brand as they splayed across his upper thigh. She jerked her head up, and their eyes met, and all he could think as the air vibrated with delicious tension was what the devil were *they* doing?

Neither of them spoke. There was no need for it. Even if they weren't supposed to be in hiding, the mutual lust in their gazes said more than any words possibly could.

He leaned towards her, his thumb gliding along the edge of her jaw as he swept a tendril of hair behind her ear.

God, but she was gorgeous. He had strolled through London's ballrooms with some of the *ton's* Great Beauties on his arm and all of them, every last one, paled in comparison to Evelyn Thorncroft.

It wasn't just her sapphire-blue eyes or the soft pink of her lips. It wasn't all that black, silky hair or those thick, sooty lashes. It wasn't her high cheekbones or the tiny, almost invisible freckle to the left of her nose that he wanted to nip.

No, what made Evie exquisite–what made her *truly* incomparable–was the intimate knowledge that she possessed of her own beauty and stunning self-worth.

Even with her hat all askew, and dirt on her face, and her dress wrinkled nearly beyond repair, she exuded confidence. She flaunted grace. She held her chin as high as any queen's, and her small, catlike smile all but dared him to try and steal her crown.

For Weston, passion had invariably been about necessity. He used it to fulfill a need, nothing more. But Evie...Evie, he wanted to savor. Like a fine glass of port or a good cigar, he wanted to linger over her until the sun faded to black and the stars scattered across the heavens.

He wanted to lick, and taste, and nuzzle.

He wanted to hear her moan, and gasp, and cry out.

He wanted to watch those blue eyes glaze over, and her head fall back, and her body arch beneath his.

He wanted all that, and more.

So much more.

But for now...for now, he'd settle for a kiss.

And pray it was enough to satisfy this acute, feverish ache inside of him.

He cupped her chin, this siren whom he desired every bit as much as he despised.

Her eyes widened with awareness, but she did not pull away.

He slowly lowered his head, and...she licked his face.

No, not Evie, he realized as he pulled sharply back and swiped the cuff of his coat across his damp cheek. That hadn't been the sweet, seductive flick of a woman's tongue, but rather the wet, rough slurp of a...

"Posy!" Evie scolded, wagging her finger at the lamb. "That's quite forward of you."

Weston, the Earl of Hawkridge and heir apparent to the Dukedom of Caldwell, had been kissed by a sheep.

To add insult to grievous injury, Evie had witnessed it.

And she was laughing at him.

It really was too much to be borne.

"Get up," he snarled at her, all but tossing Posy into her lap before he surged to his feet. "We've yet a long way to walk if we want to reach the inn by nightfall."

"Yes, my lord." Blue eyes sparkling with merriment, Evie gave the lamb an affectionate pat behind its floppy ear before she set it on the ground and stood up, brushing bits of grass and leaves from her skirts. She started to step out of the thicket but stopped short, biting her bottom lip as she glanced at him over her shoulder. "Do you think Gertie and her brother are waiting for us?"

Weston looked at her mouth. He couldn't help himself. It was just *there*, all plump and tempting and his for the taking, but for the untimely lamb kiss he'd received.

Not to say that a lamb kiss should ever be considered timely.

Jaw clenching, he averted his gaze and deliberately took a step into the open. At this point, he'd almost welcome a bullet. But none was forthcoming, and after ascertaining that the way was safe and clear, he motioned for Evie to follow him out onto the road.

Side by side, the beleaguered earl and the amused American set off once again, with Posy scampering along behind.

CHAPTER FIVE

A S LADY BRYNNE'S carriage rolled to a halt in front of Hawkridge Manor, she found herself overwhelmed by a myriad of conflicting emotions.

She'd always preferred the rolling fields and forests of the countryside to the bustling streets of London. The natural light was better, for one. And as an amateur painter with secret dreams of grandeur, light was everything.

She also enjoyed the sheer openness. Comprising more than ten thousand acres, Hawkridge Manor was the largest estate for miles around. She could wander for hours with only her own thoughts for company. In the city, she couldn't walk out her own front door without being approached by a familiar face or jostled by a stranger.

But then, there was the heaviness. The invisible weight she felt whenever the trees parted and the manor came into view. Sometimes, it was so crushing she could hardly breathe, and other times it sat on her shoulders with such lightness that she could almost, if she tried hard enough, ignore it completely.

Unfortunately, as she departed from the brougham and pulled on her gloves (she'd taken them off during the long ride in order to sketch the passing scenery), the pressure concentrated in the middle of her chest felt anything but light.

If not for the house party and the dozens of guests that were about to descend upon the estate like locusts falling on a virgin field of crops, Brynne might have been tempted to climb right back into her carriage and demand the driver return to London with all haste. But of course she couldn't do that. For she was nothing if not an obedient daughter, and a dutiful sister, and whatever else it was that everyone required her to be.

Besides, Brynne reminded herself as she climbed the marble steps to the sprawling portico with its towering ivory pillars and menacing stone lions, she *did* enjoy having the manor overflowing with life and laughter. Such a stark difference from the chillingly still and silent backdrop it had provided when she was a child fearfully tiptoeing through the vacant halls.

She also liked the various activities that comprised the month-long event, many of which she had a hand in planning as the unofficial hostess. From rousing games of whist with the ladies in the drawing room to a grand stag hunt with hounds on the second to last day, there was nary an hour that went by when there was not something to do. Which was also a problem, as it did not leave an adequate amount of time that she could devote to her painting unless she woke early in the morning or stayed up late into the night.

"Careful," she cautioned over her shoulder at two footmen as they used a pulley system comprised of ropes to slide her numerous trunks off the roof of the brougham. "Those supplies are more valuable than gold."

Perhaps she'd overpacked just a bit, Brynne admitted to herself with a wry twist of her lips as one of the footmen staggered beneath the weight of a trunk. But while the chalk she used to mix her paints was readily available in London, it was remarkably more difficult to come by this far outside of the city, and she'd been reluctant to leave so much as a single brush behind.

"Thank you," she said sincerely, stepping out of the way as the servants wrestled their heavy burden up the stairs and into the foyer with its white walls and white ceiling. Even the oak floorboards had been stained with a milky finish and sealed with beeswax. Everything, for as far as the eye could see, was white. And all the colder because of it.

Brynne had never understood why Weston had made *this* property his main residence when there were so many others to choose from. Her brother was fantastically wealthy, and could have had any unentailed estate from here to Manchester. Any number of *entailed* states, for that matter, as the traditional aristocracy were a dying breed in desperate need of an influx of monetary funds to keep them afloat. But when their great-grandfather had passed, and the line of titles had shifted, Weston had immediately laid claim to their childhood prison.

She refused to call it a home. A home implied happy memories. And there'd been no happiness to be found here after her twin had gone off to Eton, leaving her behind in this mausoleum of marble and morosity.

The only place she despised worse than Hawkridge Manor was Cheltenham Ladies' College, but she dared not reflect on her time spent there. Not unless she wanted to find herself spiraling down a rabbit hole of misery. And she couldn't do that, because she had a house party to prepare for.

"Mrs. Grimsby," she said, greeting the estate's head housekeeper with an affectionate smile. The eldest daughter of the previous housekeeper, a draconian woman who had incited terror wherever she'd gone, Mrs. Grimsby was a bouncing ball of energy and joy. "You are looking well. How are your boys doing? And your new grandson? Richard, isn't it?"

Her round face folding into a smile, Mrs. Grimsby's mob cap bounced up and down as she nodded her head with enthusiasm. "Little Dicky, as we've taken to calling him. And he's as fine as can be, Lady Brynne. Getting bigger by the minute, but then children are wont to grow too fast. Especially when they're babies."

"I am glad to hear it," said Brynne. "Have all the rooms been read-ied? There's no telling when guests will begin to arrive."

The house party was slated to begin tomorrow afternoon with a grand reception in the solarium, but the nobility was notoriously fickle when it came to keeping a set schedule. Brynne wouldn't be surprised if some people arrived in the next few minutes, while others might straggle in closer to the end of the week.

"Every last one," Mrs. Grimsby confirmed. "And a few extra, just in case."

"And Miss Thorncroft's room?" Brynne asked. "I know she was a last minute addition."

"I readied her chamber myself, and have placed her across the hall from Lord Hawkridge, as you requested." The housekeeper's brow furrowed. "Are you sure that is where you wanted to put her? Normally, all of the unmarried ladies are allocated to the East Wing. If I misunderstood–"

"No, no," Brynne said quickly. "That is where I want her to be. If my brother questions it, as he most likely will, you may tell him that all of the other rooms were already taken and there was nowhere else for Miss Thorncroft to go."

"All right," said Mrs. Grimsby in a slow, drawn out tone of some-one who *didn't* think it was all right, but also knew better than to argue. "I'll see that is where she is sent when she arrives, then."

Brynne was taken aback. "My brother and Miss Thorncroft haven't arrived?"

"No, my lady, I am afraid not."

"But they left at least an hour before I did." Concerned, she glanced at the longcase clock in the far corner of the foyer. "It's going to be dark soon, and it isn't like Weston to be late. I hope nothing has happened."

"I can have a rider sent out to look for them."

"Yes, please. As soon as possible."

Mrs. Grimsby snapped her fingers and a maid stopped what she was doing and hurried over. There was a whispered exchange, and the maid rushed off in the direction of the stables.

"I am sure it's nothing serious," the housekeeper said soothingly. "They've probably stopped for a bite to eat, or to exchange horses."

"Maybe," Brynne said, but she was doubtful. Given Weston's unfounded animosity directed at Evie, she did not think he'd do anything to purposefully delay their arrival. It was much more likely they'd gotten into some kind of contentious disagreement. Or they'd been set upon by highwaymen.

Given her plans for the couple, she almost hoped it was the latter. As long as they weren't seriously injured, perhaps the time together would do them some good. It *was* said that peril brought people together. And that's precisely where she wanted Evie and Weston.

Together.

It wasn't that Brynne *didn't* like Lady Martha, who was due to join them tomorrow along with her mother, Lady Smethwick, and sister, Lady Anne. It was just that she didn't particularly *like* her, either.

Similar to a fine tea, Lady Martha was pleasant to consume and easy to forget. There wasn't anything wrong with her. Quite the contrary. She was everything a future countess should be: beautiful, polite, and soft spoken.

Weston would be bored silly before the first month was out. Which was what he *thought* he wanted. That was to say, a wife who would require all the emotional investment of a turnip. Someone he'd get on well enough with when they were together, and forget when they were not.

But Brynne knew better.

She knew what her brother really needed, even if he did not.

They were twins, after all.

And what Weston needed–even though he'd never admit it–was a wife who challenged him. Who provoked him. Who made him commit to love and marriage instead of just going through the motions.

As their father had done.

And his father before him.

And his father before him.

The siblings had never met their mother. She'd died on the day they were born. Which meant they'd never had the opportunity to see their parents interact. But they'd heard the way the Marquess of Dorchester spoke about his late wife. On the rare occasions he'd ever bothered to mention her at all, it had been with a certain apathy. The sort of respectful indifference one might assign to a favorite chair they no longer possessed.

Brynne didn't want that for her brother.

Nor did she want it for herself.

Having suffered a broken heart not so very long ago, she was determined to avoid the entire matrimonial mess by remaining alone. A choice afforded her as a woman who was fortunate enough to be supported by an apathetic father and benevolent brother. But Weston, as the sole male heir to various titles and properties, including a dukedom, *had* to find a bride. Which was why he'd summoned the Smethwicks to Hawkridge Manor.

Everyone knew it.

What they didn't know–but Brynne did–was that Weston was choosing the wrong wife.

And she was determined to correct his mistake before it was too late.

"When my brother *does* deign to bless us with his presence, could you please tell him that I'd like a word?" she told Mrs. Grimsby. "There's a matter of...seating I should like to discuss with him."

"Yes, my lady." The housekeeper paused. "In consulting the guest list, I noticed there were some names missing from gatherings past. Should we be expecting Lord Farnsworth again?"

"No." The train of Brynne's traveling habit swished across the floor as she went to a circular table in the middle of the foyer. Usually, the table held a bust of her grandfather, the Duke of Caldwell. But in preparation for the house party, the bust had been replaced with a crystal vase overflowing with yellow roses and various glass bowls filled with sugary treats. Selecting a pair of silver tongs set out to the side, she helped herself to a handful of hard ginger candies. "Lord Farnsworth has sent his regards, but he is on holiday until the end of the month. India, I believe."

"A lovely place, so I am told. What about Lady Hilcox? Will she be joining us?"

"Lady Hilcox is expecting her fourth child, God bless her, and is on bed rest."

"God bless indeed." As the mother of eight children, Mrs. Grimsby clucked her tongue in empathy. Then her warm brown eyes crinkled slyly at the corners. "And will we being seeing Lord Campbell?"

The silver tongs fell to the floor with a loud clatter as all of the blood drained from Brynne's face. For a moment, she couldn't think. She couldn't even *breathe*. Grasping the edge of the table, her willowy frame trembled as she struggled to regain control.

Lord Lachlan Campbell was a name she'd *never* wanted to hear again.

Not after the way things had ended between them.

Gulping in a mouthful of air, she turned to face the housekeeper.

Weston wasn't the only twin whose gaze could turn to frost in the blink of an eye. As ice poured into her veins, Brynne fixed the housekeeper with a glare that was cold enough to turn the entire Serpentine River into a glacier. "If Lord Campbell sets foot upon these grounds, I want him shot on sight. Is that clear?"

"Yes, my lady. I–I apologize, my lady. I shouldn't have said any-thing." Realizing she'd overstepped boundaries, there was nothing for Mrs. Grimsby to do other than make a hasty retreat.

As the housekeeper scurried away, Brynne felt a twinge of regret for the way she'd spoken to the kindly woman. But not the words she'd used. After what he had done to her, a bullet was exactly what Lachlan Campbell deserved.

Now where the *hell* were her brother and Miss Thorncroft?

"WHAT ARE YOU grinning at?" Weston demanded, the heel of his boot kicking up a plume of dust as he stepped down with unnecessary force.

The earl, Evie had come to observe, stomped when he was angry. And stepped as light as a cat when he was furious. An important distinction she'd already tucked away in the back of her mind, along with all of the other habits she'd quietly observed during their time together.

Like that she had never heard him laugh. Not once. And that when he smiled–*really* smiled, which was exceedingly rare–there was the faintest hint of a dimple in his left cheek. And that when he gazed at her as he had in the thicket, all smoldering passion and carnal promises, he had the ability to make the earth tilt beneath her feet.

"You called her Posy," she said, casting a sideways glance at the lamb who had, once again, fallen asleep in Weston's arms. Her short legs had begun to falter after less than a mile, and with a suffering sigh–just loud enough to ensure Evie heard it–the earl had picked her up.

Baby sheep, it seemed, were not meant to travel long distances. And grumpy noblemen looked very charming when they carried them.

Stomp. Stomp.

Even if they were doing their best to appear menacing.

"The devil I did," Weston grumbled, shooting her a glare.

"You said, and I quote, 'You're not putting Posy in a pot'."

"That doesn't sound like me."

Stomp. Stomp.

"Then who do you propose it was?" Evie asked, rolling her eyes at him. Somewhere between drinking Weston's brandy (or was it cognac? She still wasn't sure) and being shot at, she'd abandoned any pretense at flattering sweetness.

The earl muttered something undecipherable.

"What was that?" Taking any excuse for a rest, Evie stopped short. She couldn't remember the last time she'd walked such a distance, if in fact she ever had. While her lithe frame and natural balance lended itself to a certain amount of athletic prowess, she generally limited her physical exertions to meandering strolls through the park and quiet rides on a docile mare. Activities that did *not* result in excessive perspiration. "You've taken to mumbling."

Swinging to face her, Weston set Posy on the ground between them and crossed his arms. He was sweating as well, a line of it trickling down his throat and disappearing beneath the collar of his shirt. He hadn't retied his cravat, and had even gone so far as to remove his jacket and roll up his sleeves, revealing forearms bronzed from the sun. His hat was gone. Lost, she presumed, during their mad dash away from Gertie. Disheveled, his hair fell away from his forehead in inky waves of obsidian while a few damp strands clung to the sides of his temple.

Ordinarily, Evie preferred her gentlemen to be just that. Gentlemen. Properly dressed in jackets lined with satin and crisp white cravats and boots that gleamed. But there was something undeniably attractive about Weston's state of undress. Something...*virile.*

She wet her dry, parched lips. When Weston had leaned towards her in the thicket, she hadn't just invited his kiss. She'd craved it. There was a part of her that continued to crave it. Which was also out of the ordinary.

Evie had been kissed before. Once by Evan behind a gazebo at a picnic, and a few other times by other suitors who had since gone on to marry women whose families weren't in financial ruin. She hadn't *dis*liked their kisses. But she also hadn't found much to like about them, either. As a whole, she'd found them to be...bland. Like going to Mr. Green's frozen ice cart in the village square and asking for peach ice cream, only to discover all he had left was vanilla.

Vanilla wasn't bad, per se.

But it also wasn't peach.

Then Weston had looked at her with that ravenous glint in his eyes and without kissing her, he'd given her peach. And strawberry. And peppermint. A single searing stare, a promise of what was to come, and she had tasted every flavor there was to be had.

If a gaze could do all that, what might a real kiss do?

Evie was almost afraid to find out.

"You're welcome to take your new pet and be on your merry way at any point," said Weston, his large hands anchoring themselves to his hips as his brows pinched together over the bridge of his nose in a hawkish scowl. All he needed was an eyepatch and he'd make a splendid pirate.

"Where on earth would I go?" she asked, tilting her head. "There's no one around!"

Which was the problem.

They'd been walking for what felt like hours and hadn't come across a soul. Not to mention the tavern Weston was leading them to. With the sun beginning to set in the west and a cool breeze blowing in from the east, Evie was beginning to experience her first genuine flickers of concern.

When she and Weston had first set out, their task had been simple enough. Walk two miles to the nearest town, find someone to fix their damaged axle, and be back on their way to Hawkridge Manor in no time at all. Then two miles had turned into three, she'd gotten drunk off brandy, stolen a sheep, met the *most* disagreeable woman of her entire lifetime, and now...now she didn't know what they were doing. But she did know one thing for certain: she could not, under any circumstances, spend the night outside in a *field* somewhere.

She was meant for the ballroom, not the bushes. Joanna was the one who had insisted that the sisters sleep out under the stars every summer. And Evie was the one who had retreated inside before the first firefly lit up the night sky.

No, what she required was a bed with a real pillow, not the straw stuffed monstrosities at Lady Privet's Boarding House. And a bath to soak in. With soap. Lots of soap. Enough soap to scrub every last layer of grit and grime from her skin. Then she wanted a dress. A lovely, fashionable dress like she'd seen the ladies in London wearing. With a bodice lined with ivory linen, and a plaited flounce trimmed in wide velvet ribbon, and beads made of real glass instead of painted tin.

"The tavern should be just around the bend," said Weston.

Evie huffed out a breath. "You said that three bends ago."

His mouth twisted in a humorless smile as he swept his arm out to the side. "By all means, take the lead."

"Why would I do that, if you know where we're going?" Something in his expression immediately roused her suspicions. "You *do* know where we're going, don't you?"

He scratched under his ear. "Almost definitely."

"*Almost–*" Evie cut herself off as a warm flush crept up her neck and spilled across her cheeks. "Do you mean to say we've been walking aimlessly for hours? I have blisters! Not to mention the irreparable damage the sun has caused to my complexion. I could get *freckles*." She shuddered at the thought. "I am going to have to soak my face in lemon water for a week."

"You were welcome to remain behind in the carriage."

"Which I would have gladly done, if I had known you had all the directional sense of a blind turtle!"

A muscle ticked in his jaw. "If you hadn't gone running after that lamb–"

"Don't you dare blame this on me," she interrupted, jabbing her finger at him. "Or Posy."

"*Not* blame you?" he said incredulously, taking a step towards her. "This entire debacle has been your fault from the very beginning!"

They were inches apart. Close enough for her to see the throb of his pulse and the tiny flecks of gold in his stormy gray irises that she'd never noticed before. Like slivers of lightning slashing across the sky in the midst of a terrible tempest.

"I haven't done anything." She tilted her chin, although in invitation or challenge, she couldn't be sure. Her entire body hummed with anticipation; a bowstring drawn taut and just waiting to be released.

"Liar," Weston said hoarsely as his hands slid into her hair, dislodging whatever pins that remained so that her mane tumbled down over his wrists in a spill of black satin and her breath caught at the flash of raw hunger she saw in his gaze. He was staring at her as if she were a tasty rabbit...and he was a starving wolf intent on devouring her whole. "You've done something to me."

"W-what?" she whispered.

His hand glided down her neck, over the slope of her shoulder, and around to the small of her back. A coaxing nudge, and they were together, her legs cocooned between his powerful thighs and her breasts pressed against the hard, flat plane of his chest. He gave a tortured groan.

"I've no bloody idea." Lowering his head, he kissed her, his mouth warm and surprisingly soft on hers.

Evie's previous kisses had taught her to anticipate a bit of fumbling. Noses that bumped and teeth that clicked and, in one unfortunate instance that she'd like very much to forget, the invasive taste of salmon.

But with Weston, there was no awkwardness.

Kissing him, being kissed *by* him, was...effortless. Just like when they'd danced together, their bodies instinctively knew what to do even without the strains of Beethoven's *Fifth Symphony* to guide them.

She latched on to the front of his shirt, her nails digging into the smooth fabric when he changed the angle of their kiss, demanding more of her as his tongue slipped boldly between her lips. She responded in kind, her desire driven by all of the angst, and the anger, and the frustration she'd experienced since they'd left London. Since she'd left Boston, really, for that was when it had all started. An untold number of decisions heaved upon disappointments that had served to lead her to this moment, with this man. This arrogant scoundrel who enticed as much as he enraged.

Weston's short, rough side-whiskers scraped against her sensitive skin as he began to trace a fiery path along the slender line of her throat. On a keening sigh, her head rolled back, liquid heat spilling into the secretive garden of curls nestled between her thighs as he nipped her earlobe and then soothed the bite with his tongue, suckling for what felt like an eternity of sweet anguish before his mouth resumed its wicked path across her flesh.

She gasped when he drew her nipple into the hot, slick cavern of his mouth. The layered texture of the damp fabric of her bodice rubbing against the swollen nub was almost too much to bear. Her knees wobbled, and she might have collapsed in a pool of passionate disbelief if not for the hand splayed across the middle of her back. Weston held her securely as he continued to lavish attention on her breasts, his seduction as slow and unhurried as waves lapping against the shoreline.

Any more, and Evie feared being dragged under the water. But it was a good type of fear. A *delicious* type of fear. The kind that pushed people to do any manner of impossible feats. Like being the first to race across the Arabian desert on horseback. Or bravely setting sail for a new world. Or being ravished senseless on the side of a road by a devilish rogue in earl's clothing.

True, one of those things wasn't quite like the others.

But what was abandoning all inhibitions, if not stepping off a cliff into the unknown?

Evie had never given much consideration to being *ravished* before. She'd assumed she would be, of course. Most likely on the night of her wedding, as she wasn't about to endanger her chances of marrying up by being caught down with some nameless ne'er-do-well who promised her gold and gave her cheap brass instead. But while Weston was undoubtedly a rogue–the *things* he was doing to her body!–he was also a nobleman. A nobleman she still had every plan to marry.

Surely there was no harm in sampling the goods before buying the product.

In fact, some might call it a sound business decision.

Evie's lashes stirred, her gaze unfocused as she opened her eyes. She saw the top of Weston's head as he bent over her breasts, and she started to thread her fingers through all that thick, luxurious hair before something darted across her peripheral vision.

Something white and fluffy.

Something that appeared suspiciously like a–

"Posy!" she cried, wrenching free of the earl's embrace as the lamb went bounding off across a field of late blooming yarrow. "Oh, you have to get her before she goes too far. I don't want her to become lost!"

Weston cursed. Yanking off his coat, he threw it on the ground at Evie's feet before he took after Posy, stomping through the sea of pink and yellow flowers with all the finesse of a bull in the proverbial china shop. At first, Posy seemed to think it was a game, and she ran two circles around him before he managed to grab hold of the lamb and tuck her under his arm.

Hands clasped beneath her chin, Evie anxiously awaited their return.

"At least I know what we'll be eating at the house party," Weston grumbled as he emerged from the field and set Posy on the road. Picking up his jacket, he gave it a good shake, releasing a plume of dust into the air.

"What's that?" Evie asked absently, crouching down to receive the lamb as she bounced happily over, pleased to once again be the center of attention.

Weston glared at Posy. "Mutton."

CHAPTER SIX

B EFORE DARKNESS COULD wrap them in her obsidian embrace, Weston and Evie finally stumbled upon a tavern.

It sat directly on the edge of the road, a jumbled pile of stone and wood with a slate roof that sagged in the middle and front steps that creaked ominously beneath Evie's feet as she followed Weston inside.

"Are you certain it's clean?" she asked, her nose wrinkling as she took in a dimly lit interior that smelled of stale meat and sweat. All of the rooms for rent must have been on the second floor. For down below, a narrow hallway led directly into a rectangular pub with a bar on one wall, a stairwell on the other, and tables in the middle, of which more than half were occupied.

"No one is troubled by the fact that you're holding a farm animal," Weston replied. "So I am confident in saying it is anything *but* clean. You're welcome to keep walking if you think you can find something better."

As she watched a grizzle-faced patron shovel stew into his mouth with his fingers, Evie suppressed a shudder. This place made Lady Privet's Boarding House look like Kensington Palace, but she wasn't about to separate herself from Weston. Like it or not (and after their knee-wobbling kiss, she was leaning heavily towards the "like it" category), they were in this together.

Whatever "this" entailed.

"I'm sure the lodgings will be adequate for one night." Tightening her grip on Posy, she clung to the earl's coattails as he navigated his way through the tables to the end of the bar where an older man, his stringy white hair tied in a tail at the nape of his neck and a damp rag slung over his shoulder, greeted them with a shuttered expression.

"How can I help ye?" he asked, swinging the rag off his shoulder and onto the bar with enough force that Evie jumped.

Reaching blindly behind him, Weston caught her around the waist and pulled her snug against his side. "My wife and I would like a room for the night."

Her lips parting, she stared at him in amazement, only to clamp her mouth closed when he gave her a meaningful jab with his elbow.

"Is that right?" the barman said, gazing directly at her.

"That's–that's right," she stammered, for once finding herself at a complete loss of words.

"Second floor, all the way to the end, last door on the left. Pay before ye leave. It'll be an extra shilling for the sheep."

Weston gave a clipped nod, and then ushered Evie up the stairs, his grip tightening protectively when a catcall pierced the noisy din.

"Keep walking," he snarled in her ear, and she hastened to obey, lifting the hem of her skirts and taking the narrow steps two at a time until they'd reached the landing.

Logically, she knew that if the riffraff in the tavern were to overwhelm them, there was little Weston could do to keep her safe. But she knew, somehow she just *knew*, that he'd sacrifice his own life before he allowed anything despicable to happen to her.

Weston Weston was a man who protected what belonged him.

Savagely, if necessary.

And whether *he* liked it or not, she was in his care until they reached Hawkridge Manor…and far beyond, if Evie had her way.

"Your wife?" she said, coquettishly fluttering her lashes at him once they were in their room. If the box with a straw-stuffed mattress on the floor and a single window could be described as a room. A candle flickered feebly on the sill, casting a dull circle of light. There wasn't a washbasin or even a chest of drawers, not that Evie had anything to be packed away. All of her belongings remained in a trunk sitting on top of Weston's carriage.

"Would you have preferred I called you my mistress?" With a loud *click*, he shut the door.

As her eyes struggled to adjust to the murky lighting, Evie found herself grateful for the curtain of shadows that separated her and Weston, as it disguised the hot blush that filled her cheeks and trickled down the front of her chest until it pooled in her breasts, causing her nipples to swell into aching buds of secret longing.

Weston's mistress.

There were worse things to be, she supposed, than an earl's lover.

Especially an earl that looked as this one did.

Leaning against the door with his thighs spread slightly apart and his arms loosely draped behind his back, he was the very picture of rakish nonchalance. As if he'd just strolled out of a billiards room after taking the game in eight instead of a hundred-mile walk through the desert.

Well, maybe not a *hundred* miles.

And the green fields hadn't contained a speck of sand.

Still, it might as well have been a trek through the Sahara for all that she'd wilted in the heat. Whereas Weston could not have been more relaxed or at ease. Only his piercing stare betrayed the tension that constantly simmered just beneath the surface. That, and the solemn set of his mouth.

Heavens, but did the man *ever* smile?

She wanted him to, Evie realized.

More than that, she wanted to be the reason he did.

And that…that wasn't part of her plan.

"As I am neither your wife nor your mistress, you might have just told the truth." Setting Posy down to explore their meager accommodations, she lowered herself onto the edge of the bed and began to remove her shoes, needing *something* to focus her attention on other than the potent allure of Weston's wolfish gaze.

Desire was all well and good, but she wouldn't let it distract her. Her goal was marriage. Not kisses on the side of the road. And she wasn't going to let anything, or *anyone*, keep her from achieving her *raison d'être*.

Especially not Lord Hawkridge.

Lust and love had their place. Her sister, Claire, was quite taken with the local butcher's son and was blissfully happy about it. But Evie didn't want to fall in love. She wanted to be a countess. And she had only to look to her mother's affair with Lord Dorchester to see that love was a detriment when it came to marriage, not an advantage.

Anne Thorncroft could have stayed in England and been a *marchioness*. Maybe one day even a duchess. Instead, she'd fled back to America and married Evie's father while pregnant with the marquess' child. She had given up everything for the sake of *love*. And Evie couldn't even ask her mother why she'd done such a ridiculous thing, because she had died when her middle daughter was barely old enough to remember the smell of her perfume.

Evie did not begrudge her mother her choice to return to Somerville and marry her childhood beau. Had she not done that, Evie would never have been born. But try as she might, she couldn't make sense of her mother's decision. Given the same choice, Evie would pick being a lady over being in love every time.

It wasn't even a question.

"Wife was simpler than the truth," Weston drawled as he shrugged out of jacket and waistcoat, then tossed the wrinkled garments into the corner for lack of a chair. "It should also ensure our privacy, and make us no less memorable than any other wedded couple passing through." His brow arched. "Unless you'd like to tell the barman that you're really the insufferably annoying sibling of my illegitimate half-sister who has imposed herself on my good graces."

Having removed her ankle boots, Evie leaned back on her hands and lifted a brow of her own. "From what I've witnessed, you do not possess any good graces. And you did not find me 'insufferably annoying' when you had your tongue between my–"

"That was a mistake," he interrupted.

Ignoring the twinge of hurt his words invoked, she made herself nod. Weston was right. Ultimately, their kiss *had* been a mistake.

But not in the way he meant.

Any passion between them had to be carefully supervised and meticulously controlled, or else it posed a serious threat to how she wanted Weston to perceive her. Which was not as a potential mistress, but a wife. *His* wife. For real, not pretend. Because it was common knowledge that men bedded the women who tempted them, and wedded the woman who did not.

"For once, we concur," she said.

"Furthermore, I do not want to–we what?" he said blankly.

"We concur," she repeated. "Our...encounter was a mistake. A combination of impulsivity and sun-induced madness, if I had to guess. It shall not happen again."

"Then...we're in agreement."

"Indeed. Should we find a bowl of water or some milk for–"

"But to be clear," he cut in, "*I* am choosing not to have any further...encounters with *you*."

The mattress rustled as Evie stood. Nudging her shoes aside so as not to trip on them in the dark, she bit back an impatient sigh when her stomach, completely empty save for the dregs of brandy she'd foolishly imbibed, gave a pitiful grumble. "I am hungry. I'm sure Posy is thirsty. Does it really make a difference who is choosing to end encounters with whom?"

"Yes." In the shifting shadows, his eyes gleamed like polished granite. "It does."

Obstinate rogue. Was there any battle, large or small, he wasn't determined to win? The sensible side of her acknowledged that it would have been better, and most likely wiser, to simply allow him this minute victory. But Evie heralded from a family of strong women. Strong women who did not understand the meaning of surrender. Which meant even if she wanted to, she had no white flags at her disposal.

"Does it bring you pleasure?" she asked, moving away from the bed.

A floorboard creaked beneath the weight of his boot as he took a step towards her. Once again, they found themselves within inches of each other, trapped in a room that had shrunk to the approximate size of a teacup.

"Does what bring me pleasure?" he asked.

"Arguing." Thick lashes skimmed across the top of her cheekbones as she lowered her gaze, then lifted it to regard him with a bemused smile even as her heart slammed against her ribcage. "I've never met a man who argues as much as you do."

"And I've never met a woman who–" He stopped short.

"Yes?" she prompted.

Another creak. A slow inhale of breath. Gray eyes burning into hers. Fingers trailing down her arms to encircle her wrists.

"Who entices me as much as you do, Evelyn." Weston's voice was velvet wrapped around the edge of a knife. He gave a tug, and despite her better judgment, despite her all-important *plan*, she fell into his embrace without resistance. Because there was a part of her that had always been falling. Ever since she first saw him in that crowded ballroom. Her avenging knight charging in to rescue her from mayhem…only to drag her straight into madness.

"We just agreed to no more encounters," he rasped, his angular countenance a tortured blend of temptation and torment.

"I won't tell if you won't." Slipping her arms free, she wound them around his neck, rose up on her bare toes, and pressed her mouth to his.

HE WAS KISSING her.

Again.

After he'd just vowed–after *they'd* just vowed–that they weren't going to. His idea, by the way. Which made both of them liars. But if Weston was going to the devil, at least he'd be in good company.

Weston had dined on the nectar of Evie's lips less than an hour ago. How was it that he already craved more? That he already *needed* more? He felt as if he'd been staggering about in the sweltering heat for days, months, years. His entire life, really. And she was his only source of cold, fresh water.

Except there was nothing cold about Evelyn Thorncroft.

Fire licked across his skin as his fingers dove into her coiffure and his tongue plunged between her lips. Their first kiss that started gently had been slowly building to a promising crescendo before the damned lamb had ruined everything. This one began right where they'd left off, pitching them straight into a passionate inferno.

His hands swept down across her body, seeking out her luscious curves through her traveling habit. He touched her breasts, enjoying the weight of them in his palms, their delightful feminine fullness, before his thumbs strummed across her nipples and the muscles in his abdomen clenched to already find them hot and erect and pushing against the confines of her chemise.

Weston understood ardor in all its many intricacies. He had a healthy appetite for carnal pleasures, and had sated that hunger with any number of mistresses, chosen as much for their discretionary nature as their abundance of skills in the bedchamber. But there had always been something...deliberate about the act. Something shrewd in all that sin. Something he'd held back.

With Evie, he felt no such inhibitions.

Their kiss deepened, pulling them both into a place that defied reason or explanation. A place neither of them wanted to leave. Not yet. Not until they'd explored a little further. Tasted a little more. Danced a little closer to that perilous edge from which there would be no easy return.

He felt the sharp prick of her nails digging into his shoulders as she pressed herself wantonly against him, her soft, rounded edges providing a delicious juxtaposition to all his hard, lean angles. He nipped her bottom lip and rolled her swollen nipples between his fingers, a deep, possessive snarl emanating from the depths of his throat when she arched her spine in response.

Her head fell back as he kissed his way down her neck and across her shoulder, pulling her bodice as he went so as to expose all that creamy satin skin to his ravenous mouth. With a tearing sound, the stitching finally gave way, and with the unparalleled eagerness of a young man about to see his first pair of breasts, Weston yanked the dress off her arms and it fell to the floor in a crumpled pile of cotton and crinoline.

"Let me look at you," he rasped. "I *have* to look at you."

It was like gazing at a priceless painting. In the glow of the candlelight, Evie was nothing less than a work of art. In varying shades of white and the palest yellow, her undergarments accentuated the sumptuous body of a goddess while her ebony curls framed the face of a siren. He had never seen her equal, and he knew he never would again, for lightning never struck the same place twice. And surely some sort of divine power had been at work to place such splendid beauty on earth.

Heavy lidded with desire, her blue eyes boldly met his stunned stare, a coy smile flirting with the corner of her mouth as his tongue threatened to follow her gown all the way to the ground. With a stern mental shake, Weston reminded himself that he wasn't some green lad flummoxed by the sight of tits, but an experienced lover who knew all the wicked ways a man could bring a woman to ecstasy.

He kissed Evie again, a long, liquid pull of passion that ended with him on his knees and his mouth on the inside of her thigh, venturing as far up as he could go before fabric impeded his journey towards her coiled thatch of dark curls and all the honeyed sweetness they were guarding.

She gasped when he yanked impatiently at the satin ribbon holding up her drawers. The undergarment fell to her knees and he guided her out of it, delighting in the way her legs quivered as he lifted first one ankle and then the other, fingers gliding along the curve of her calf.

It occurred to Weston, almost in passing, that perhaps he ought not to do…well, what he was about to do. Not the act itself, for which he was historically somewhat fond, however he couldn't ever recall a time where he'd looked forward to it with such fervor. But rather, the implied intimacy of such an erotic display. Did he *want* to step off this ledge? Then Evie's hands burrowed in his hair, and a mewling cry of desperation spilled from her lips, and it wasn't a matter of want, but of when.

He cupped her bottom, palms fitting perfectly around her arse as his head slipped beneath her chemise. Trimmed in lace, it bunched around his shoulders as her feet slid apart. The intoxicating scent of her unique fragrance invaded his nostrils, an earthy mixture of arousal and jasmine that nearly caused him to spend in his trousers.

The first lick, the first heavenly taste, was all but his undoing. He wanted to throw back his head and howl like a bloody wolf. He wanted to pick her up and take her against the wall. Or the bed. Or the floor. Anywhere. He'd take her anywhere, and everywhere. Once more, and once more, until they were both too sated to move.

Instead, he contented himself with the luscious banquet laid out before him. Using only his tongue and his mouth, he drove Evie to a ruthlessly fast release, wrenching a cry from her lips as her thighs contracted around him and her arms slid bonelessly to her sides.

"*Again*," Weston growled, and this time it was a vow that he kept.

CHAPTER SEVEN

M EN WERE PECULIAR creatures.

After Weston had nearly made her weep with pleasure, he left without a word, leaving Evie to lean weakly against the windowsill and wonder what in heaven's name had just *happened*.

Bliss was the simple answer.

Pure, unadulterated bliss.

The sort she had never imagined possible, because she'd never imagined…whatever it was that Weston had done to her.

Kissing, she told herself as she padded barefoot across the room to where her poor traveling habit lay in a heap on the floor. It had just been kissing. Very, very *private* kissing.

Picking up her dress, stained with dirt and dust and whoever knew what else from their long walk, she held it out and gave it a shake, but couldn't make herself put it back on. Not that it would have been suitable even if it had been clean, as she vaguely recalled, through her haze of lust-induced euphoria, that Weston had nearly torn the bodice in half in his eagerness to divest her of her clothing.

The fierce possessiveness in his gaze as he'd stared at her…with an involuntary tremble, Evie folded her gown in half and laid it on the bed before she went to the corner of the room, where Posy had made a nest of Weston's coat, and sank down beside the sleeping lamb.

No man had ever looked at her like that before.

Oh, she'd been openly admired.

Leered at, even.

But no one had ever made her nipples harden with a glance. Or scorched her flesh without laying a finger upon her skin. Or made her body yearn to be touched with such intensity that she'd felt a trickle of moisture between her thighs.

No one…

Until the Earl of Hawkridge.

Because it *had* been more than just kissing.

The emotions he'd wrought from her body…the things he'd made her feel…it defied description. Which was fitting, as *he* defied description. Hot one moment, cold as ice the next. Not that she'd been expecting any proclamations of undying love after their second…*encounter.* But a smile would have sufficed. Or even allowing a few minutes to pass before he bolted out of the room as if his damned pants had caught fire.

On the bright side of things, she'd forgotten all about how hungry she was. Temporarily, that is. Now, however, as the proverbial dust settled and the candlelight began to wane, Evie's stomach was alive with grumbles and gurgles and all sorts of mortifying sounds. It almost made her glad Weston had left, as men ought never be privy to any sight or sound or unpleasant smell that might make them believe a woman was actually human.

With a sigh, she curled up beside Posy and closed her eyes.

WHEN EVIE WOKE, it was morning. A gray, drab, dreary morning with a sky spitting rain, but morning nevertheless. Wincing, she sat up and lifted her arms in a long stretch that helped work some of the aches and pains from her muscles that came from spending the night on the floor with a lamb.

The irony of it did not escape her, and as she rose, her mouth twisted in a mirthless smile. Here she was, finally in the company of an honest-to-goodness earl. An earl with a fortune rumored to be *so* large that it boggled the mind. Yet for all that, they'd traversed the country-side on foot, been shot at by a crazed farmer because Weston hadn't thought to carry any money on his person, stumbled upon a tavern filled with questionable patrons, and slept on the ground. At least *she'd* slept on the ground. There was no telling where Weston had laid his head.

Or when he'd be returning for her.

Maybe...maybe she'd made a mistake in choosing the Earl of Hawkridge as her future husband. Even though she hadn't chosen him so much as the ring had. A particular turn of fate that had brought them together, for better or worse. As Evie stepped onto something squishy and lifted her foot to reveal a present left behind by Posy (not the good kind), she grimaced and acknowledged that this was almost *certainly* the worse.

"Disgusting," she muttered aloud, searching the room for some-thing to clean herself off. There was no washbasin. Not even a towel. But there was her traveling habit. Her only traveling habit, as it so happened, but given that it was already torn and soiled, what was a little lamb excrement to finish it off?

"I need to take you outside and find us both some food and water." Hands on her hips, she watched Posy frolic on top of the mattress. With a happy bleat, the lamb leapt off the side and went skidding across the floor, her tiny hooves scrambling for purchase on floor-boards worn smooth from decades of heavy use. Chuckling, Evie scooped up her pet and carried her over to the window. Faces pressed together, they peered out through the grimy glass in unison, Posy searching for a patch of clover and Evie searching for any sign of Weston.

"There he is," she said, relief flowing through her when she spied the earl walking around the side of the tavern, his powerful stride and broad shoulders unmistakable, even in the rain. He was carrying something under his arm. A bag or a package, she couldn't tell for certain. As he headed for the front door, Evie set Posy down and ran her fingers through her hair in a desperate attempt to make herself look presentable.

Loose and tangled, it was knotted on the one side and drooping on the other, with pins snarled in between. Her bonnet was gone, plucked from her head sometime between their arrival and this morning. She suspected Posy had eaten it, but the lamb wasn't talking.

Without a comb, Evie made do with an embarrassingly simple braid. And here she'd thought her beauty regimen was restrictive when she and Joanna had shared a room at the boarding house! She missed her creams. Or potions, as her sister referred to them. She missed the bucket of warm water they'd been allotted each day. She missed gazing at her reflection in the mirror, searching for imperfections with the ruthless scrutiny of a surgeon examining his patient. She missed the beautiful gown she'd worn to the Countess of Beresford's ball.

And she knew it was vain, and small, and petty, these things that she missed. There were children going hungry. Men losing their lives in pointless wars. Women selling their bodies to put food on the table. But in a life that had felt beyond her control ever since her father died, Evie's appearance was the one thing she *could* control. The one thing she could take pride in. The one thing no one could take away from her.

Unlike her childhood home, and her treasured belongings, and her beloved school, and her so-called friends.

All snatched away, like a dream in the morning.

The only things she and her sisters had left were each other and their mother's ring.

And then that, too, had been taken.

By *him*.

Weston Weston, the Earl of Hawkridge. The heir to a dukedom,

Joanna's half-brother, and the only man to ever make her knees wobble.

She'd never known knees could do such a thing before he had kissed her.

Wobble, that is.

Joanna and Claire were the ones who believed in such ridiculous notions as love and happily-ever-after. For her part, Evie held a much more practical view of courtship. It was a means to an end. A straight road to take her where she wanted to go with no time for stops or detours along the way.

But then Weston, in all his dark, brooding glory, had made her weak in the knees.

And he'd kissed her.

Down *there*.

If that wasn't a detour, she didn't know what was.

Worse than that, she hadn't the faintest idea what to do about it.

Hair styling and dresses. Mixing the perfect shade of eye paint to bring out the blue in her irises. Flirting not for the fun of it, but for the sole purpose of attaining what she wanted. Those were contrivances that Evie was familiar with.

These growing *feelings* she had for Weston were decidedly...not. And without her potions and a pretty dress and an air of calculated frivolity to hide behind, she felt helplessly exposed. As if by kissing her, Weston had done more than make her legs wobble. He'd stripped away a layer of the stone wall she had built around herself. A wall whose rough edges she'd disguised with coy smiles and fluttering lashes and a cavalier demeanor...so that no one would ever guess how much hurt she'd buried beneath it.

Evie startled when the door swung open and Weston entered the room without so much as the courtesy of a knock.

"I could have been naked," she said, a belated prickle of self-consciousness causing her arms to cross over the front of her chest.

Even without her traveling habit, she still wore several layers of clothing. But she'd never stood before a man covered only in her unmentionables before.

At least, not in the light of day.

"Which is why I've brought you a new gown." Dropping a cloth bag on the floor (the object she'd seen him carrying), Weston removed a plain gray dress made of wool and held it out her. "Here you are. To replace what I...ah..." He cleared his throat. "What was accidentally torn."

Evie just stared. "I cannot wear *that*. It's almost as hideous as what you're wearing." Her nose wrinkled as she took note of Weston's change in wardrobe. Gone was his crisp white cravat, tailored jacket, and trousers specifically cut to fit his long, muscular legs. Instead, he wore a brown coat with sleeves that were much too short, a coarse linen shirt, and a pair of breeches that hadn't been in style since before Queen Victoria took the throne. "What *are* you wearing?"

"I attempted to tell the barman who I was." His brow creased in irritation. "But it appears travelers to this particular tavern often attempt to barter their good name in exchange for an evening's stay, only to never make good on what they owe."

"You mean to say the upstanding citizens who would choose to frequent such a splendid establishment lie about who they are in order to get free lodging?" Evie said dryly. "How shocking."

"I realize this is not the Langham Hotel–"

"The understatement of the century."

"–but I didn't see *you* offering up another solution."

Her braid slid over her shoulder as she gave a belligerent toss of her head. "My solution would have been to never travel that awful excuse for a road in the first place. If we'd gone the same way as Lady Brynne, you wouldn't have had to trade your clothes because we never would have found ourselves here to begin with."

"The main post road would have taken twice as long and been

cluttered with traffic."

"And this is better?" she said incredulously, eyeing the potato sack he was holding. "That thing is probably crawling with lice."

"The hag I got it from seemed very clean."

Evie blinked. "Did you...did you just tell a joke?"

For an instant, it almost looked as if Weston was going to smile. The edges of his mouth pulled back. The corners of his eyes crinkled. Then his almost-smile gave way to an all too familiar scowl and he tossed the dress at her before stalking to the window. "Wear it or not, I could care less. I've arranged a growler to take us the rest of the way to Hawkridge Manor. It should be here momentarily."

Catching the dress before it hit the floor, Evie draped it over her arm and tried not to shudder. It didn't even have a stich of ornamental lace, let alone a proper bustle. But it was better than arriving to the house party in her chemise and drawers. Knowing that she would already be under intense study as both an American and Joanna's sister, whose identity was flying through the *ton* like wildfire, she wanted to make a positive first impression on the other guests. Not make them reach for their smelling salts by showing up in her unmentionables.

"A growler?" she asked Weston, the term unknown to her.

"A carriage for hire," he said, his steely gaze pinned to the glass. "Slightly larger and quicker than the hansom cabs in London. If the rain does not increase, we should arrive at Hawkridge Manor right after luncheon. Before that happens, I should like to discuss our..."

"Encounter?" she suggested when he hesitated.

Finally, he turned to look at her, his eyes as gray and impenetrable as the cloudy sky behind him. "We both know that was more than an encounter, Miss Thorncroft."

"Apparently not enough of one for you to start calling me by my given name." She'd meant it as a quip; an attempt to bring levity to a situation that suddenly felt as heavy as the wool dress she was holding.

But there was no humor to be found in Weston's sober countenance.

"What we did...what *I* did to *you*..." A dull flush began to spread beneath the shadow of bristle that had gone unshaven since their departure yesterday. "I lost control, and my behavior was inexcusable. I apologize."

"I do not accept your apology," she said coolly.

He grimaced. "Miss Thorncroft–"

"I do not accept your apology, because you've nothing to apologize for." Her chin lifted. "If you lost control, Lord Hawkridge, then so did I. And I am not sorry for it. Neither should you be. Had I wanted to stop, I've a voice that works, and I would have used it. But I did not, because I found our encounter to be extremely enjoyable."

She could tell he didn't know what to make of that by the way he gripped the nape of his neck, fingers digging deep into taut, coiled muscle.

Her lips twitched.

"Have I thoroughly shocked you with my admission, my lord?"

"You're an American," he said flatly. "Your entire country is wholly uncivilized. Nothing you could say would shock me."

"Even if I said I wanted to do it again?" she asked, genuinely curious as to what his response would be. She knew that she was testing waters best left alone, at least for now. But provocation was its own source of power, and Weston wasn't the only one seeking to regain control. In this ongoing battle of wills, there was room for a single victor, and Evie was determined it was going to be her.

Before...whatever it was they'd done last night (encounter did not begin to cover it), she'd thought to keep their physical interaction to a bare minimum. But since the only time Weston let his guard slip was when they were wrapped in a passionate embrace, she would surely be remiss if she didn't use their tangible attraction towards each other as a means to achieve her ultimate goal.

She even toyed with the idea of going a step further. Given Weston's strong sense of responsibility, as shown by his refusal to leave her or Posy behind, he would feel obligated to marry her when...that was to say, *if* they had intimate relations.

The sort that ended in a bed, not with Weston storming out of the room.

But while Evie was desperate to make a good match and retrieve her mother's ring in the process, she wasn't yet *that* desperate. The British author Francis Edward Smedley may have claimed that all was fair in love and war, but what he'd failed to mention was that there were unspoken guidelines. And tricking a man into marriage by nefarious–albeit pleasurable–means was largely frowned upon.

Not to say that she *wouldn't* ruin herself with the earl.

But surely it was best kept as a last resort.

Besides, if she had to choose, she'd rather a man marry her out of some sort of emotional attachment (it didn't have to be love; a mild affection would suffice) instead of a sense of forced responsibility.

In short, she wanted Weston to propose not because he *had* to, but because he *wanted* to. A distinction that was notable only because she hadn't bothered to make it before she and the earl had set out on their misguided adventure.

"No, Miss Thorncroft, we will *not* be doing that again," said Weston, speaking with the absolute certainty of someone who had just declared the sky was blue and the grass was green. "If you'll recall, we both agreed that our first kiss was a mistake. The second was no different."

"That's all right." Unfolding the dress he had given her, Evie held it up for closer inspection. "I am certain there will be plenty of eligible bachelors at the house party who would be more than happy to...strike up a conversation with me."

"I hadn't realized you were so free with your charms," Weston said caustically.

Evie slowly lowered the dress to meet his stare over the hideously square neckline. "Are you jealous?" she asked with a coy flutter of her lashes. "I assumed that was the purpose of house parties. For young women seeking a husband to mingle with young men seeking a wife. Or am I mistaken and everyone *really* attends for the lemonade and the parlor games?"

"Is that the real reason you're going, then?" His face expressionless, Weston leaned back against the windowsill and crossed his arms. "To find some pitiful bloke either too stupid or miserable enough to marry you?"

A flash of angry pink bloomed high on her cheeks at the blunt insult. "If you must know, yes, that is *precisely* why I am going. And you're right, my future fiancé is both stupid *and* miserable."

Weston's eyes narrowed. "Then you've already selected him?"

Her laugh cut through the air like the slash of a whip. "I fail to see how that is any of your concern."

"Because he is my guest. And as I consider all of my guests to be acquaintances, if not friends, I'd like to give the fellow fair warning before you sink your claws into him."

"*I* am your guest," she pointed out. "Does that make us friends, Lord Hawkridge?"

Now he was the one who laughed; the harsh sound containing no more humor than hers had. "If I had friends like you, Miss Thorncroft, I'd have no need for enemies."

"Do you kiss all your enemies?" she taunted.

Angry black storm clouds rolling across a clear blue sky would have been less menacing than the dangerous glint in Weston's gaze. Pushing away from the wall with the heel of his boot, he stalked over to her. "Careful, Miss Thorncroft."

"Or what?" Evie had three sisters. An arrogant earl did not intimidate her in the slightest.

"Or you won't like the consequences."

Her chest rose on an angry intake of breath, breasts straining against the rigid boning of her corset. "Is that a threat, Lord Hawkridge?"

He smile darkly. "That is a promise. Now get dressed and meet me downstairs, or find your own way to Hawkridge Manor."

HE WAS LOSING his mind, Weston decided as he waited for Evie to join him out front of the tavern. Or maybe he'd already lost it. That would explain his behavior over the past day and a half, as nothing else did.

A misting rain fell, coating his hair and shoulders. He closed his eyes, welcoming the touch of the cool water on his skin and hoping it would help to calm all this heat inside of him. Bursts of sparks and flame that Evie, damn her, had ignited with that first sultry glance across the ballroom.

And he'd been burning ever since.

But Weston wasn't a man who ran on fire. He preferred the cold, emotionless sheen of ice. And he'd rather a thousand winters than one hot, sticky summer night filled with the scent of wisteria and the flickering glow of fireflies and Evie, dressed only in moonlight and sin.

Bloody hell.

He ran a hand down his face, palm catching on the rough stubble that clung to his chin and jaw. He needed a shave and a shower bath. A fresh set of clothes. A proper cravat. Maybe then he'd feel more like himself and less like this...this love-struck dandy who couldn't get out of his own way.

If he wasn't furious with Evie, he wanted to kiss her. And when he didn't want to kiss her...all right, he *always* wanted to kiss her. Which was the damned problem, wasn't it? This...this *fever* he'd contracted. Where the only cure was Evie's lips.

When he'd seen her this morning, her eyes heavy with sleep and her mouth swollen from his, it had taken every ounce of self-restraint he possessed not to take her in his arms and complete what they'd started the night before.

After he'd left her alone in the room–after he'd *had* to leave, or else Evie would not have awoken as an innocent–he had walked off his throbbing arousal before drowning himself in cheap ale. He'd the pounding head to pay for it today, but he'd prefer that over the alternative...and while a hard chair had made a poor bedfellow, at least he still had his pride.

What was left of it, anyway.

Bollocks, but the woman cut him to the quick A minute in her company and his nerves were raw and exposed, his heart a skip away from doing something he'd sworn it would *never* do. Which was why he'd spoken so sharply to Evie before he'd stormed out to soak in the rain...and his own guilt for being harsh with her.

He would apologize for that, Weston decided. They may not have been friends, but if they were to survive the house party without tearing at each other's throats for the duration, he needed to restore some semblance of civility to their relationship.

Not passion or anger, but cordial apathy. The sort he held for Lady Martha.

Yes.

That was it.

As the answer presented itself, Weston straightened.

He needed to make himself feel for Evie what he felt for his almost-fiancée.

God knew he had never pictured Martha bathed in moonlight. He'd never even kissed her on the mouth, let alone dropped to his knees and pleasured her with his tongue until she wrapped her pillowy thighs around his head and cried out in ecstasy...thrice.

No, he'd never done anything like that with Martha. Truth be told, he probably never would. Because she was a proper lady, and aside from the fact that she'd most likely swoon at the mere mention of such a wickedly sensual act, that was what mistresses were for.

A wife for a smoothly run household and a male heir.

A mistress for entertainment and sexual gratification.

That was the way the Weston men had conducted their marriages for generations. Who was he to upend tradition? He'd already set himself apart by choosing to give a damn about his sister, and had no interest in pursuing further ostracization by committing the unpardonable sin of being in love with his own wife.

Weston men didn't fall in love. Or if they did, it ended badly. He had only to look to his father for confirmation.

The Marquess of Dorchester had made a splendid match in Weston's mother, Lady Felicia, whom Weston knew only through portraits, the most coveted of which was a miniature by Brynne's own hand. By all accounts, the late Marchioness of Dorchester had been a lovely woman. Gently bred, perfectly mannered, and well versed in all feminine pursuits, Felicia was the obvious choice for a gentleman of the marquess' ranking and wealth.

But then she'd died, and Jason Weston had gone and lost his heart to his mistress, an American debutante who never had any intention of remaining in London once the Season was over. With a baby growing in her belly, she'd returned to Boston to marry another man and by all reports, the Marquess of Dorchester had never been the same since.

While most young boys grew up idolizing their fathers, Weston had come to use his as an example of what *not* to become. He'd no interest in having his heart broken and living the rest of his life as a shadow of the man he had once been. Bully on that. Weston was going to do what his father *should* have done.

Marry a lady, take on an experienced mistress, and keep his damned heart to himself.

Such an endeavor left no room for the likes of Evelyn Thorncroft, which was just fine with him. As soon as they reached Hawkridge Manor, he was going to distance himself as far from the tempestuous beauty as the seventy-two room estate permitted. When their paths did intersect, he'd conduct himself with the utmost chivalry. From this point forward, for all intents and purposes, Evie was just another guest. There'd be no more arguing. No more taunting. No more admiring her bottom when she wasn't looking.

And, most importantly, there would be absolutely *no* more kissing. On the mouth…or otherwise.

CHAPTER EIGHT

THE REST OF the journey to Hawkridge Manor passed without incident. Riding in the growler, while a far cry from the resplendent luxury of the town coach, was much more preferable than walking. Especially given the distance they'd yet to go. At least nine miles, Weston had told Evie in a clipped tone when she'd inquired. An arduous task on foot, to be certain, but much easier to accomplish when being pulled along behind a horse.

Inside the growler that smelled heavily of floral perfume with a hint of cigar smoke, Evie and Weston sat facing the same direction. Posy dozed on the floor between them, snuggled into the bed Evie had constructed using the remnants of her traveling habit.

While the lamb slept, the human occupants of the carriage were careful to avoid any motion that might possibly be conceived as an acknowledgement of the other. They hadn't spoken a word since boarding the growler, which was just fine with Evie. After the way Weston had treated her at the tavern, she did not have anything to say to him. At least nothing of a complimentary nature.

Thus they traveled the remainder of the way in brittle silence, each lost to their own brooding thoughts as the road sloped down and then up again in a winding path that carried them over a clear babbling brook and along a stone wall covered in moss.

Despite the tight knot of tension in the middle of her chest, Evie couldn't help but be charmed by the natural beauty unraveling in all directions like a spool of ribbon let undone. The landscape reminded her of the fields at home, all soft and green and glistening with raindrops that had since given way to clear blue skies and sunshine. There were more forests in Somerville; the land wasn't nearly as developed as this. But there was something undeniably magical to be found in the hills and valleys of England's sprawling countryside.

If only she could say the same of her traveling companion

Tongue darting between her lips, Evie dared a sideways glance at the earl. And was startled to discover him looking straight her, heavy brows drawn in an expression of vague perplexity, as if he were studying at a puzzle whose last piece was proving elusive.

"What?" she said, self-consciously brushing a curl behind her ear. She knew that between her braid and the wool dress, she held all the appeal of a peasant. But Weston didn't have to point it out by *staring*. "Do I've something on my face?"

He shook his head. "We've been on the grounds of the estate for the past mile. Before we reach the manor, I think it wise that we discuss our behavior these past two days, and how we might conduct ourselves going forward."

Evie's eyes widened in surprise. Everything surrounding them–the meadows, the brook, the stone wall–was Weston's? There must have been thousands of acres. It was nearly unfathomable that one man could lay claim to such an enormous expanse of land. But even in a plain, ill-fitting jacket and sans vest or cravat, there was no mistaking the earl for a commoner. He wore his nobility like a second skin. No matter what clothes were on his person, he could not change the regal composition of his countenance or the bold assurance with which he carried himself.

Of *course* all of this belonged to him.

Evie had seen the noblemen who felt the need to prove their superiority with checkered trousers and neck cloths of flamboyant green and swallowtail coats that cinched at the waist. Rather like male cardinals showing off their feathery red plumage.

But Lord Hawkridge was not some twittering songbird.

He was a hawk.

Fierce and imposing.

"What more would you like to discuss?" she asked, tempering her tone to reveal none of the anger or the raw, restless attraction she felt for the man seated beside her. "I believe you made your opinion quite clear before we left the tavern. A she-devil just waiting to sink her claws into someone, wasn't it?"

He didn't even have the good grace to look away, but instead met her accusatory stare without blinking and said, "I never called you a she-devil."

She gave a derisive flick of her wrist. "I am sure you've thought it."

"Yes. I have." Now he sat back and directed his gaze to the passing scenery outside his square window partially obscured by a drape steeped in dust. "You're a difficult woman, Miss Thorncroft. In any manner of ways. I say that as a compliment," he added when her nostrils flared. "Not an insult. The ladies I am acquainted with do not have nearly so many...layers as you do. You're like an onion."

"An onion," she repeated. "And you are *not* trying to insult me?"

"Onions are strong, solid stock. They can be used in any variety of soups, broths, and salads. They're excellent sautéed in garlic and served alongside liver." He glanced at her, saw her expression, and frowned. "I can see I am not making myself clear."

"Oh, as clear as liver," she said sweetly.

"What I am trying to say, Miss Thorncroft, is that you...you are much more than what you appear on the surface. Like an onion–"

"I believe this would go better for all parties involved if you stopped comparing me to a root vegetable."

A wry grin settled upon his lips, like the first layer of snow falling on the ground. The sort that made you look twice, because you couldn't believe it was really there. "You're probably right, Miss Thorncroft. I…what?" Now he was the one who ran his fingers through his hair. "Do I've something on my face?"

"No, it's just…I finally understand why you scowl with such frequency," she said in a choked little voice, her gaze transfixed by the roguish tilt of his mouth.

"And why is that?" he asked.

"Because you are absolutely devastating when you smile." Her eyes rose. "It's unfair, really. That such a grumpy, cantankerous man should be in possession of such a mesmerizing grin."

"Grumpy and cantankerous?"

"You called me an onion and said I'd pair well with liver," she reminded him.

The earl winced. "Not my best attempt at flattery."

"Is *that* what you were trying to do?" Her head tilted in amusement. "Pray tell, do you tell Lady Martha Smethwick she has hair like carrots and eyes that look like broccoli florets?"

When his smile abruptly faded and his gaze shuttered, Evie could have kicked herself. Weston hadn't earned himself any favors by comparing her to an onion of all things, but bringing another woman into the conversation was even worse. *Especially* when that woman was someone Weston had an interest in marrying.

Evie did not know very much about Martha Smethwick. No more than what Brynne had told her, which was that the lady was pretty, and polite, and dreadfully boring.

"She'll be at the house party with her mother in tow," Brynne had shared with all the enthusiasm of someone who had just sucked on a lemon. "While my brother hasn't formally declared his intentions, it is only a matter of time. He is not getting any younger, and Lady Martha is impeccably bred. She will make a splendid countess, albeit a dull sister-in-law."

"You make it sound as if she's a prized thoroughbred," Evie had said, to which Brynne sighed.

"Isn't that exactly what we are?"

Over the past two days, Evie hadn't allowed herself to dwell on the impeccably bred Lady Martha Smethwick. She really didn't know why she'd brought her up now, except that there was a part of her that had wanted to see Weston's reaction to the mention of his not-yet-formally-declared fiancée. Especially since they would soon all be at Hawkridge Manor together. A merry family comprised of a surly earl with the smile of an angel, a perfect lady with the bloodlines of a horse, and the most versatile of all root vegetables.

How splendid.

"Lady Martha's hair is blonde, not orange, and I don't know what color her eyes are." Weston's fingers drummed along the windowsill in an impatient *rat-a-tat-tat*. "Miss Thorncroft, I want to–"

"You don't know what color her eyes are?" Evie interrupted. "I was under the impression you and Lady Martha were going to...that is, you plan to propose."

"I do," he said and to her credit, Evie did not flinch. "But I fail to see what a marriage proposal has anything to do with eye color. Miss Thorncroft, before we reach Hawkridge Manor I'd like to take the opportunity to establish some–"

"What color are mine?" she asked, pinching her eyelids together.

"What are you talking about?" he said irritably.

"My *eyes*." Were they open, Evie would have rolled them. "What color are my eyes?"

"This is ridiculous."

"Just answer the question. Unless you can't," she challenged. "In which case, I shall graciously permit you to admit defeat."

"Blue," he snapped. "Your eyes are blue."

"There. Was that so–"

"Except when you are angry, and then they're the color of velvet midnight. Or when you're happy, and looking at you is like gazing at a cloudless sky on the first day of spring when the air smells like honeysuckle and the soil is ripe with possibility."

Evie did not know what to say.

For the first time in her life, she found herself rendered completely and utterly speechless.

It was a strange feeling. Almost as strange as the sensation of tumbling backwards even though her feet were planted firmly on the floor of the carriage. But maybe that was what falling in love was meant to be like. Not a falling in the literal sense, as that would be far too messy. But rather an abrupt loss of all common sense that left the mind inwardly flailing for balance. For surely there was nothing logical about being in love with Weston. There was nothing logical about love, period. But it was especially nonsensical when it involved a man whose concept of adulation revolved around a *scallion*.

And yet...

"We're here," he said brusquely, and Evie's eyes flew open.

The growler was passing beneath an arched section of the stone wall that was just barely high enough to accommodate its sloped roof, leading her to conclude they were accessing the estate via a side entrance. She craned her neck, seeking an unfettered view of the main house through the bushes and the brambles that had become as much a part of the wall as the stone itself.

They crested a short knoll and then there it was, Hawkridge Manor. Her initial impression was that it was smaller than she'd anticipated, but then the carriage continued on past the front and she saw, with wide eyes, that the gray sandstone extended far beyond the initial footprint to include a rambling addition, a solarium made almost entirely of glass, and a multi-tiered terrace with its own spiral staircase spinning up out of an artfully designed garden of roses.

The roof was slate with peaked dormers and matching brick chimneys on either side. Ivy crawled along the walls, making it difficult to discern where the stately house ended and the gardens began. Wide marble pathways, meticulously groomed and gleaming white in the afternoon sun, cut through all the greenery like pearl ribbons stitched to the hemline of an emerald gown.

There were several fountains, the biggest of which sat in the middle of the circular drive and sprayed water out of the pursed lips of a playful cherub, nude save for the granite cloth draped around its round hips.

For Evie, who was accustomed to sturdy colonial architecture, the romanticism of Hawkridge Manor was marvelously endearing. She couldn't wait to see what the interior held. Specifically the ballroom, and the parlor, and her bedchamber. Oh, to sleep in a real bed again! With proper pillows stuffed with goose down and a mattress filled with wool and horsehair. It was going to be *wonderful*. And if not for the house party, she might have been tempted to disappear into her room for at least a week, rather like a bear seeking a cozy den for its hibernation.

But there *was* the house party to contend with. She could see the tents sprawled across the back lawn from here, colorful flags waving in the breeze as a herd of servants moved hastily about setting up chairs and tables and unrolling carpets so that the ladies' heels wouldn't sink into the grass.

"How many guests are you expecting?" she asked, slanting a peek at Weston out of the corner of her eye as the growler lurched to a halt underneath the dappled shade of a large elm tree and the driver came round to open her door.

"More than I'd like," said Weston curtly. "The housekeeper, Mrs. Grimsby, will know what room you're staying in if my sister is not readily available. Should you require anything during your stay, you may defer to her.

"If the town coach has preceded us here, your trunks should have already been brought upstairs. If not, I'll see that they are delivered with all haste once they arrive. Meals are generally served in the solarium or out in the tents, the exception being the official receiving dinner which will be held tomorrow night in the formal dining room after all of the guests have arrived. If you are so inclined, you may also have platters brought directly to your chamber. Do you have any questions, Miss Thorncroft?"

"Yes," she said, as annoyed with the rigid formality of his welcome address—one he'd doubtless delivered a hundred times before—as she'd been with his barbed cruelty at the tavern.

How can you be a wordsmith one minute and an emotionless cad the next?

How can you kiss me senseless and still look at me as if I were a stranger?

"Miss Thorncroft?" Weston prompted.

"Never mind." Making use of the stepping crate the driver had thoughtfully placed beneath the door, Evie descended from the carriage with all the graceful aplomb of a young queen. She may have worn the attire of a common scullery maid, but that did not mean she had to perform the part. Similarly, she may have been losing her heart to the earl, but that did not mean she had any obligation to act on her feelings. Not until she'd managed to regain some of her balance, at least.

A bath, a nap, and a change of clothes, she decided. That would help return her to her old self and steer her away from this bewildering, doe-eyed debutante who suddenly fancied herself in *love* just because Weston had said her irises reminded him of velvet midnight and honeysuckle.

"I shall see you at the receiving dinner, my lord." Chin held high, she reached into the carriage, picked up Posy, and sailed off towards the house in search of Mrs. Grimsby.

WESTON WAITED UNTIL Evie was out of sight before he dismounted from the growler and flagged down a passing footman dressed in navy blue livery.

"See that this man is paid," he said, nodding at the driver. "Include an excess of eight pounds to close an account I've opened at the Penn Street Tavern, and see that any personal belongings I have there are returned to me."

"Right away, my lord." The footman hurried away to find the butler, Mr. Stevens, who was the only other individual on the estate aside from Weston who had access to the coffers. While the vast majority of Weston's wealth was tied up in land and investments, with nearly all of his liquid assets held in London at the Bank of England, he kept several thousand pounds readily available. Whereas his peers relied on notes to extend their credit, often far exceeding the balances in their accounts, he preferred to pay for things outright. Debt–of any sort–had never set well with Weston.

That task accomplished, he set out to complete the next item on his list.

Confronting Brynne.

He found his twin where he'd expected she would be: in a gazebo behind the solarium, partially obscured behind a wall of evergreens. She was painting, her arm moving in fluid strokes across a canvas considerably larger than the one she'd been working on in London.

"Something new?" Weston asked, resting his foot on the bottom step of the gazebo.

With a gasp, Brynne dropped her brush and clasped both hands to the middle of her chest. "You shouldn't sneak up on people like that!" she accused, leaning in her chair to glare at him around the edge of the painting. "You nearly frightened me half to death."

"And you shouldn't be so free to spread family business," he said mildly.

She picked up her paintbrush and dipped the bristles in a clear glass half-filled with water, releasing a cloud of red pigment. "What are you talking about? And where have you *been*? I've already dispatched two outriders and was going to send a third if I hadn't heard from you by dinner. Is Miss Thorncroft all right?"

He lifted a brow. "*I'm* well, thank you for asking."

"Obviously, or you wouldn't be standing here."

When had it become his lot in life, Weston wondered, to be surrounded by belligerent females?

"Miss Thorncroft is fine. We were delayed due to a broken axle. And a sheep," he added belatedly.

"Oh, did you hit one crossing the road?" Brynne said in dismay. "They're not the brightest, are they? The poor thing. I do hope it didn't suffer."

He crossed his arms. "You do realize you've just displayed more concern for a stranger and a *sheep* than your own brother."

"Miss Thorncroft is not a stranger. And sheep are very sweet. Unlike *someone* I know."

The caustic note in Brynne's voice had Weston lifting his other brow. While his sister was never afraid to speak her mind, she generally tempered her opinion with a more mild tone.

"Have I done something to offend you?" he queried.

"Yes," she said. Then she buried her face in her hands. "No. *No.* You haven't done anything. It's...it's this place. Being back here. You know it puts me on edge." She lowered her arms. "I still fail to understand why you would have ever wanted it."

"Because it's mine. Would you prefer it had gone to ruin?"

"Yes." Her hazel eyes flashed. "Yes, that is *exactly* what I'd like to happen...and exactly what this place deserves."

"I am sorry," he said gently. "But you know I cannot do that, sweetling."

Weston was well aware of his sister's feeling regarding Hawkridge Manor. He knew that while he saw it as his birthright, she looked at the plaster walls and saw a prison. While he and Brynne were not in the habit of keeping secrets from each other, she'd never told him of the years she'd spent confined here while he was away at Eton. He knew her time had been a misery only because of how much she detested returning. But she had never given him any specific details, even when he'd pressed.

"I know," she muttered, reaching for her brush. After wiping it dry on the cotton apron she wore over her dress, she dabbed the tip of the bristles in a vat of crimson paint and resumed her work. "At least the light is better here than in the city. It's so much clearer, and the days last longer without all the building and factories to block out the setting sun."

He nodded in agreement. Brynne may have despised Hawkridge Manor, but he'd invariably found a sense of solace here amidst the wandering streams and thick forests and undulating hills. He could hop on his favorite mount and ride for hours without running out of room, a freedom that did not exist amidst the crowded streets of London.

"What did you mean when you said I was spreading family business?" Brynne asked, her fair brow creasing in concentration as she focused on the middle of the canvas. Weston had no idea what she was painting, and he knew better than to ask. His sister was one of the kindest people he knew, but she'd happily scratch out the eyes of anyone who dared look at her artwork before it was finished.

"My pending engagement to Lady Martha," he said.

Brynne's brush hovered in midair. "What about it?"

"You told Miss Thorncroft."

"I didn't realize it was a secret."

"It's not."

"Then what is the issue?"

"The *issue* is that my private affairs are none of Miss Thorncroft's concern!" His shout was loud enough to startle a collection of sparrows in a nearby tree. Tiny wings flapping madly, they swooped low over the gazebo before vanishing into the heavy thicket of evergreens.

On a sigh, Brynne began painting again. "I may have mentioned, in passing, that you were considering a proposal. It was not a main topic of conversation, and I certainly was not 'spreading family business' when you and Lady Martha are all but public knowledge. Unless something between the two of you has changed, that is. You *are* still planning on getting down on bended knee before the house party concludes, aren't you?"

"Yes," he said, ignoring the sharp twinge in his gut.

"That's a shame. I was hoping your time spent with Miss Thorncroft may have...altered your perspective on what you want out of a marriage. Not to mention given you the opportunity to reflect on our little chat before you left."

Weston snorted. "The only thing my time spent with Miss Thorncroft has done is convince me that I don't want to spend any further time with her. The woman is...is..."

"Is...?"

How to summarize Evelyn in a word?

"Exhausting," he concluded after taking a moment to think about it. "Miss Thorncroft is *exhausting*."

Brynne smiled. "Americans do have their own unique source of energy, don't they? I find it refreshing, myself."

"I do not," he said sourly.

"That much is apparent." Her smile widened. "I am glad to hear that your little venture with Miss Thorncroft went well, and you've both made it to Hawkridge Manor no worse for wear. Although I would be remiss if I did not comment on your choice of apparel. That jacket does not suit you at all."

"Well? *Well?*" he repeated, incredulous. "It was a bloody disaster from start to finish!"

"Now that you mention it, you *do* seem a tad flustered."

The Earl of Hawkridge?

Flustered?

Preposterous.

"Don't be absurd," he said, raking a hand through his hair. "I'm just…weary."

"Weary," Brynne said skeptically.

"Indeed. I did not sleep well."

"Where *did* you sleep, by the by? On the side of the road, or at an inn, or–"

"A tavern with rooms above."

"A tavern! How very…rustic. Did you and Miss Thorncroft happen to have separate rooms, or–"

"Separate," he said through gritted teeth. "Most definitely separate."

"That's good," she said with a sage nod. "Wouldn't want any pesky rumors swirling about. Not with you about to become engaged to another woman, that is. Think of the scandal."

"Ah, yes. I'm sure that is what you were doing when you invited the sister of our father's hidden by-blow to Hawkridge Manor to mingle with our closest friends and family for a month. Thinking of the *scandal*."

"We don't *have* any close friends or family, which is why I invited Miss Thorncroft." Rising from her stool, Brynne removed her apron and hung it neatly on a hook pinned to the side of her easel. "I will admit, I did not anticipate that you'd have such a strong reaction to her."

Weston's foot slid off the step. "I am not–I am not having a *reaction*."

"Stuttering as well," his sister said sadly. "It's an unfortunate thing to see."

"Enough," he snarled. "That is enough. Enough with the endless litany of questions, and the thinly veiled suggestions, and the talk of marriage proposals. Do you think I don't know what you're doing?"

"I'm not doing a thing," she protested, even as a damning smirk betrayed her. "But if I *was* doing something, it would only be because I have your best interests in mind." She sobered. "You cannot seriously ask Lady Martha to become your bride, West. She is wrong for you."

"And I suppose you believe Miss Thorncroft is right?" he asked with a harsh laugh.

"Given she's managed to chip through that infamous icy exterior of yours in less than two days, then yes, I *do* think she's right for you. At the very least, she's a sight better than Lady Martha. Butter would not melt in that woman's mouth. And I don't mean that as a compliment." Brynne took a breath. "Wouldn't you want to be with someone you could love instead? Someone who was capable of loving you in return?"

"We are not having this conversation again."

"But–"

"No." It was not a request, but a command. "That is the end of it, Brynne. I've done you the favor of allowing Miss Thorncroft to attend the house party, but I am not inclined to indulge any more of this absurd dialogue. For the duration of this event, I do not want to hear any further mention of engagements, or weddings, or"–he winced just to say it aloud–"love. Not even a *hint* of romance. Is that understood?"

"You're an arrogant prat, Weston Weston," said Brynne, not without affection.

"So I've been told," he said dryly.

"You could always be a bachelor for the rest of your days. Gamble away the family fortune and sink into a life of excess and debauchery."

He pinched the bridge of his nose. "Don't tempt me."

WESTON SPENT THE rest of his afternoon inspecting the new aqueduct system being installed on the eastern, crop-rich edge of the estate to ferry water to the western side where drier conditions had yielded poor returns for over a decade. When he finally returned to the manor, just shy of sunset, he was informed that he had a visitor waiting for him.

"Sterling." Expertly concealing his surprise at seeing Sterling Nottingham, the Duke of Hanover, standing in the middle of his private study, Weston sat in a large leather chair and gestured for his unexpected guest to do the same.

The two men had met at Eton. They hadn't been best mates, per se, but they'd gotten along well enough and had extended their acquaintanceship beyond their school years, occasionally meeting up at a gambling hell or attending a race together. It wasn't difficult to maintain a casual friendship with Sterling. As amiable and charming as Weston was cold and reserved, the duke was highly regarded by all who knew him.

"I did not think I'd be seeing you until the Season started," Weston continued. "I wasn't aware you'd accepted your invitation, or that you'd be here this early."

"Wasn't going to," Sterling replied, remaining on his feet as he perused Weston's large collection of liquor kept in a glass case trimmed in mahogany. "House parties aren't my usual source of entertainment. No offense."

"None taken," Weston said dryly. "I am not overly fond of them myself."

"Your sister has outdone herself with the decorations, as usual. I especially enjoyed the little soaps molded into hearts. Very sweet."

Heart soaps.

Brynne hadn't mentioned any heart soaps.

Given that he had deliberately stated he wanted to see nothing over the next few weeks that could possibly be perceived as romantic, Weston could only assume the soaps were an oversight. One that needed immediate correction.

For an instant, during his long, solitary ride back to the manor, he had let his mind wander…and it wasn't soon before his head was filled with images of Evie, dressed only in a sliver of red satin.

The things he'd done to her on that ride...it was wicked incarnate. And the last thing he needed was anything that might intentionally provoke his ardor...or hers. For while he may have initiated their *encounters*, Evie certainly hadn't shied away from them.

She was as passionate a female as any he'd ever kissed, and while she lacked the finesse of a mistress skilled in the art of seductive practices, she more than made up for her inexperience with raw, unbridled enthusiasm.

Kissing Evie...being kissed *by* Evie...was like touching the sun. It was bright and beautiful. But getting that close to something so hot was not without consequence and, if given the choice, Weston would always prefer the familiar, emotionless touch of cold against his flesh instead of heat.

Fire was unpredictable.

Uncontrollable.

Untenable.

And he didn't need damned *soap hearts* floating around to remind him how much he had loved the lick of the flame.

"Where are they?" he demanded.

"In the receiving baskets in our rooms. Along with a miniature flask of champagne–quite clever, that–and chocolate in the shape of–"

"Let me guess," Weston bit out. "Hearts."

Sterling nodded. "It appears to be the running theme. Am I to assume we are preemptively celebrating your engagement to Lady Martha Smethwick?"

Martha. The woman he *should* have been daydreaming about, if he was to dream of any.

Instead, she was the furthest thing from his mind.

"I wasn't aware I'd made my plans to propose public," he said.

"Come now. You should know better than most that there is no such thing as a secret in the *ton*. Which is why I'm here." Finally settling on a bottle, Sterling twisted off the cork on a circular bottle of scotch and carefully poured the amber liquid into two glasses. Carrying one over to Weston, who accepted it gladly, he kept the other for himself and took a sip. "Excellent vintage. Scottish?"

Weston nodded. "You've a good palate. That was a gift. One of the last batches of whisky ever made at Glenavon Distillery."

Sterling pursed his lips and whistled. "I've been after one of these for years. Can't find them anywhere. And that's saying something, given my connections. Who gave it to you?"

"Lord Lachlan Campbell."

"How do I find him?"

"Devil if I know," Weston shrugged. "Our fathers attended Eton together. Lachlan was as close a friend as any I had growing up, and then last year he disappeared. He was here, for the house party, and then he left early without a word. Haven't heard from him since."

"Tall fellow?" asked Sterling, holding a hand several inches above his not-so-inconsiderable height of six feet. "Auburn hair? Bellowing laugh?"

"That's him."

"Hmm. Shouldn't be too hard to track down an enormous red-haired Scot. Speaking of disappearances..." Topping off his glass, Sterling sat across from Weston and tilted his head to study his whisky. "You've heard the news by now, I assume."

"That you killed your mistress in cold blood, chopped up her body, and tossed it in the Thames to be devoured by sharks?" Weston lifted a brow. "I heard something to that effect, yes."

"Bloody *sharks?*" Sterling scowled. "Next it'll be Nile crocodiles."

"I thought it was a little farfetched myself."

"Then you don't think I did it."

Not bothering to deign such an absurd statement with a response, Weston just gave a snort and sipped his whisky. "That's why you're here, then. To avoid the gossip running rampant through London."

"Aye. The private detective I've hired believes it would be best if I laid low for a while. Let the attention shift elsewhere and all that before the House of Lords reconvenes."

That gave Weston pause. "You cannot seriously believe you'll be brought before us on real charges. You're the Duke of Hanover, for God's sake."

"And a murderer, if public opinion counts for anything."

"By the start of the Season, everyone will have found some new piece of salacious gossip to entertain themselves with, and doting mothers will once again be shoving their daughters in your path like sacrificial lambs."

Sterling looked up from his glass. "Speaking of lambs, do you know there's one in the parlor?"

"I'm well aware," Weston said through gritted teeth. "Her name is Posy, and she belongs to Miss Evelyn Thorncroft. I've high hopes that both the lamb, and Miss Thorncroft, will be departing shortly."

"Thorncroft...Thorncroft...why does that sound–I know." Sterling snapped his fingers. "I've met her sister. The red-haired one. Ah...Joanna. She's working for the private detective I've hired to clear my name. Thomas Kincaid. Nice fellow. You'd like him."

"You mean she *was* working," Weston corrected. "Joanna was working for Mr. Kincaid, and now she's on her way back to Boston." *With Evie soon to follow in her footsteps,* he added silently.

"Boston? No, not unless she's a doppelgänger I don't know about," Sterling said cheerfully, oblivious to the sudden tension in Weston's jaw. "Just saw her yesterday afternoon. It seems she and Kincaid have taken up with each other. Never seen him happier." The duke drank his whisky. "Shouldn't you know all this? Joanna's *your* sister, not mine."

"Half-sister." Throwing back the remainder of his drink, Weston rose to pour himself another. "Joanna Thorncroft is my *half*-sister. And I want absolutely nothing to do with her. Or Evelyn."

Especially Evelyn.

"Inviting her to be your guest for a month is an odd way of show-ing your dislike."

As the tension in his jaw traveled down into his shoulders and arms, Weston gripped the crystal decanter with such force he wouldn't have been surprised if it had shattered in his hand. "Brynne invited her, not me. She has some nonsensical idea about wanting a close friend. For my part, I'd just as soon never see Miss Thorncroft again."

"Is that the sister you're not related to, or the one that you are? Sorry," Sterling chuckled when Weston uttered a curse. "With the way things have been going lately, if I didn't have fun at your expense, I'd have no fun at all. Relax, mate. I've never seen you this flummoxed over a skirt before."

"I am not *flummoxed*," Weston growled.

Sterling nodded sagely. "Exactly what someone who is flummoxed would say."

"You're a right bastard. You know that, don't you?"

"So I'm told." Sterling stretched his legs out in front of him. "Do you think you'll really do it, then? Propose to Lady Martha."

"Why wouldn't I?" Having topped off his glass, Weston pivoted to face the duke and notched a brow. "I have to marry someone. We all do, yourself included. It's the price we pay for the titles hanging round our necks, and Lady Martha will make as fine a countess as any."

"A tad boring, isn't she?"

Why did everyone keep saying that? True, there was nothing that made Lady Martha Smethwick particularly interesting. But that was what he liked most about her. Pretty and predictable was far better, in his opinion, than captivating and capricious.

A wife was meant to be a dependable means by which to keep his house in order. Not a distraction or, worse yet, a temptation.

Again, he thought of Evie.

Wrapped in silk.

Her tongue peeking out to wet her lips as she sank to her knees before him and–

"Lady Martha is a young woman of distinction," he growled, swiping Evie from his mind with all the testiness of a bear swatting at a bee that persisted in buzzing around its head. "She has impeccable manners, her family has never suffered so much as a hint of a scandal, and our political interests align. I cannot imagine a more suitable wife."

Sterling yawned. "As I said, boring."

"When are *you* going to take a bride?" he asked pointedly.

"Why the hell would I go and do that?"

"Because you're a duke, and you need a proper heir."

A shadow of grief rippled across Sterling's countenance as he raised his glass to his mouth, a stark contrast to the cheerfully roguish persona he generally exhibited. "Sebastian was the duke," he said, referring to his eldest brother who had been killed in a duel. A duel Sterling had jestingly urged him to participate in, never imagining in his worst nightmares that it would cost Sebastian his life. "I'm just the spare pretending to take his place."

Weston did not know what to say. What words would bring comfort to a man who felt responsible for the death of his brother? A man who was about to be put on the trial for the murder of his mistress.

"Here," he said gruffly, reaching for the decanter of scotch. He filled up Sterling's glass, then struck his against it. "To Sebastian, may he rest in peace."

"To Sebastian," said Sterling bleakly.

Together, they drank.

CHAPTER NINE

E VIE FELT LIKE a new person.

After sending her wool dress monstrosity away to be burned, she'd soaked in an honest-to-goodness porcelain tub with a hand carved wooden rim polished in beeswax. As if that wasn't luxurious enough, the water had been hot–not tepid, not warm, but *hot*–and scented with rose oil. Bubbles had floated on the surface, so thick and plentiful that Evie hadn't even see her own limbs beneath the frothy concoction of glycerin soap and sugar.

It was the first real bath she'd had since leaving Somerville, and even then, the round metal tin she'd shared with her sisters and grandmother with water pumped directly from their well (which was so cold it took nearly an hour to boil, and then there were the long treks with heavy pails up and down the narrow stairs) hardly qualified.

After emerging from the tub, she had taken a nap, and slept through the afternoon into the evening. Dinner in her room, and then back to bed, whereupon she'd floated off into dream until morn-ing...and nearly wept with joy when she found *another* bath already prepared and waiting for her.

This time, she stayed in the water until the bubbles had all but dissipated, and when she was ready to emerge, all she had to do was a ring a bell and her appointed lady's maid, a beaming brunette named Hannah, bustled in carrying a Turkish towel that was nearly as tall as

Evie herself.

"Here you are, Miss," said Hannah, holding the towel wide and politely averting her gaze as Evie emerged from the tub. "How was your bath?"

"*Wonderful*," she said with feeling. "Just what I needed."

She wrapped herself in the thin, flat cotton, mindful not to slip on the ivory tile beneath her bare feet. Her bedchamber was *so* large it included two entirely different types of flooring! Wide oak boards beneath the brass bed and accompanying furniture, which included a wide velvet lounge she couldn't wait to take a nap on, and glossy marble squares that distinguished the bath from the rest of the room, along with privacy panels draped in pale yellow silk to match the wall hangings.

"Very good, Miss. I had your trunks brought up and unpacked your belongings while you slept, along with a few other things that Lady Brynne wanted you to have during your stay with us at Hawkridge Manor. I hope you don't mind–I was afraid I might wake you, but you're a *very* heavy sleeper."

"Don't *mind?*" Evie said with a delighted laugh as she crossed the room and flung open the doors of a towering armoire to reveal half a dozen dresses she'd never laid eyes on before. "Hannah, I could kiss you!"

The maid blushed. "I am pleased that you are pleased, Miss. Lady Brynne indicated that you are an extremely special guest, and that I am to take excellent care of you."

"I could kiss her as well," Evie said fervently, running her fingers down the sleeve of a lavender walking dress with double-breasted buttons and chenille fringe.

Even though I'd much rather kiss her brother.

The unbidden thought stilled her in her tracks. As her cheeks suffused with hot, splotchy color, she kept her head tucked behind the door of the armoire and took her time sorting through the colorful sea of gowns that Brynne had graciously allowed her to borrow.

There were narrow-sleeved jackets in crisp taffeta, peplum skirts with long trains, a stunning morning dress in floral printed silk, and an evening gown that stole her breath with its cascading layers of flounces and striped tulle bodice, all in a splendid canary yellow that was certain to draw attention for miles around.

Deciding to save the yellow gown for the receiving dinner, she settled on a white day dress with pagoda sleeves, red satin trim, and rosettes piped in black lace. Hannah helped her get ready, and even styled her hair in an elegant coiffure with curled tendrils that framed the sides of her face. A pair of modest pearl earrings that had once belonged to her mother, and Evie was prepared to greet the other guests and rub shoulders with British nobility.

Her heelless slippers made nary a sound as she descended the master staircase into the middle of an empty foyer, a grandly sized room that was notable if only because there was nothing about it of note.

Plain white was the dominating color, with nary a picture or a rug or even a tapestry to break up the monotony created by such a lack of pigmentation. Given the natural, almost fairytale-like beauty of the manor's exterior, Evie had been expecting the inside to be...well...*more*. Certainly she hadn't anticipated this blank slate of ivory. But maybe she should have, considering the estate's principle occupant.

If Weston had designed a house to reflect his personality, he'd succeeded and then some. The cold, emotionless man who'd all but shoved her out of the growler paired perfectly with this frigid, icy backdrop. Rather like French wine and Italian cheese, but without the delicious aftertaste.

"Miss Thorncroft!"

Evie automatically turned at the sound of her name, and smiled when she saw Lady Brynne Weston hurrying over. The two women exchanged pleasantries, and then recused themselves to an adjoining parlor with views of a pond that Evie hadn't noticed upon her arrival. A pair of swans floated across the calm surface, their arched necks forming half a heart as they paddled in leisurely circles.

"Are they tame?" Evie asked, nodding at the fowl.

"The swans? They were raised here on the estate, but I wouldn't call them tame." Brynne gave a rueful shake of her head. "Just make sure that if you ever go over to the pond that you've plenty of bread crumbs with you, or else you'll need shoes that are equipped for running. Tea?"

"Thank you." Accepting the delicate cup made of bone china and embossed in gold, Evie added a swirl of cream and then sat down across from Brynne. "I also wished to thank you for your generosity," she said, stroking her skirt with all the loving adoration of a parent embracing their newborn child. "I shall endeavor to do your clothes justice, and I absolutely must have the name of your modiste."

While Evie couldn't afford so much as a new handkerchief at the moment, she was already looking forward to when cost was no object and her husband's allowance permitted her to buy whatever she desired. She needn't wear the same gown until the stitching became threadbare ever again. Or get blisters on her feet from hand-me-down shoes that were a size too large because they'd been made for Joanna's enormous rabbit feet. Or feel that awful prickle of embarrassment at the nape of her neck when she walked past her peers in their fashionable dresses designed straight from the pages of *Journal des Dames et des Modes*.

"Think nothing of it." Brynne gave a dismissive flick of her wrist. "I am fortunate to have more clothes than I could wear in a lifetime, and you'll fill them out better than I ever could. Please consider everything a gift."

Evie's jaw dropped. "Oh, no. I couldn't possibly keep–"

"You can," Brynne said firmly. "And you will."

"All right." Why object further, when it was clear this was what

Brynne wanted? She didn't want to be *rude*. "I should like to get you something in return, though."

"Tell me about you and your sisters." Brynne smiled encouragingly over the rim of her teacup. "That is the only present I require."

Evie often liked talking about herself. Honestly, what wasn't there to like? But she failed to see any facet of her life that might possibly be of interest when compared to the gorgeous gowns and glittering ballrooms and lavish house parties that made up Lady Brynne's world.

As the sister of an earl, the daughter of a marquess, and the grand-daughter of a duke, she had doors available to her that Evie could never dream of. Doors that would have opened, at least partially, for Joanna as well...*if* she'd decided to stay instead of following in the footsteps of their mother and sailing back to Boston.

Evie did not understand her sister's decision any more than she did her mother's. Who would want to leave all *this*? It was like giving a bird wings and then telling it not to fly. Or entering a horse in a race and then not allowing it to run. As for herself, Evie couldn't imagine leaving England. And not only because her last sailing expedition had begun and ended with her head in a bucket.

From the second she stepped onto British soil, she'd felt a sense of belonging. Of recognition. Of coming home, even though she'd never traveled further than Boston.

But then, England *was* in her blood.

Her grandmother, Mabel Ellinwood, had been a lady. The second-born daughter of the Viscount of Clarencott, who had fallen in love with a visiting American scholar by the name of Joseph Pratt. They would go on to marry, and have a daughter of their own...Evie's mother, Anne.

By Evie's calculations, that made her a quarter-British. It wasn't as good as Miss-Joanna-my-secret-father-is-a-marquess, but surely it was better than nothing. And it also helped explain her innate love of the country's architecture, and its fashion...and its earls.

One earl in particular, but who was keeping track?

Certainly not Evie.

Not after the way Weston had treated her.

As if she were just any other guest. As if she were no one of importance. As if she were *ordinary.*

And for Evie, who prided herself on her exceptionalism (even under the most dire of circumstances), there was no greater insult to be had.

"What would you like to know?" she asked Brynne, mustering a smile that was tight at the edges, like a stocking too small for her calf.

"Oh, *everything,*" Brynne gushed, her hazel eyes lighting. "What was it like growing up with two sisters? I've only a brother to compare, and, well, you've met Weston. He can be…difficult."

To put it mildly, Evie thought as she raised her tea to her lips.

"Although I'd be remiss if I did not say that there are times he is so sweet-natured and thoughtful you could just kiss him. Don't you agree, Miss Thorncroft?"

Evie almost spit her mouthful of tea back into her cup. "I…er…I don't believe I've gotten to know that side of him."

"Haven't you?" Brynne said innocently. "That's a shame."

She knows, Evie realized. Maybe not everything, but Weston's sister knew *something.* At the very least, she suspected.

Pesky things, suspicions.

They could either prove to be helpful…or hurt Evie's plan in any number of ways. One thing was for certain: until she knew where Brynne stood in regards to her brother marrying an American, it was best to steer their dialogue towards safer waters.

"Growing up with two sisters was very…loud," she said, deliberately inserting good cheer into her voice despite the constrictive band wrapped around her throat. "Joanna and I invariably find ourselves at odds, whereas Claire, the youngest, can do no wrong. But when Joanna isn't throwing a shoe at my head, we're really very close. Our disagreements stem from being *too* much alike, I fear. We're both obstinate and opinionated, whereas Claire is as gentle as a kitten."

And she missed them both terribly.

The sisters had never been apart before. Not like this. Which was why she'd been doing her best not to think about it. Something she had managed to do during the chaotic trip from London to Hawkridge Manor, but now that she was here and some semblance of normality had returned (at least, she liked to *think* that porcelain tubs and marble tile and floral printed silk was her new normal), the ache of their absence had started to settle in.

"How fascinating," Brynne breathed. "And you never knew? About Joanna's unique...history? I am sorry to ask such a personal question. But given the connection between our families, I see no reason to purposefully ignore the large elephant in the room. I've found they tend to start stampeding when you do that."

The edges of Evie's mouth twitched. "We wouldn't want stampeding elephants."

"No, not until all the tents have been taken down, anyway."

"Naturally."

They exchanged a grin, and Evie's discomfort began to melt away. Whereas she felt the need to be on her toes around Weston (both figuratively *and* literally, at least when they were kissing), she was very comfortable with Brynne. There was a certain ease between them. A developing camaraderie that usually only came after years of knowing someone. Their habits and their eccentricities. Their strengths and their flaws. Even then, you couldn't trust that person not to turn their back the instant you fell upon difficult times.

Just like all of Evie's "friends" had done to her.

Women she'd known since childhood had turned up their noses as soon as it became public knowledge that the once mighty Thorncroft family had fallen off their pedestal. Women she'd laughed with, and shopped with, and stayed up late into the night sipping watered champagne and giggling over Mrs. Waterman's feathered hat at Senator Bridgeton's annual ball.

Evie had never thought much of that laughter.

How cruel it was. How much pain it could cause.

Until it was directed at her.

Because her friends had never *directly* stated they wanted nothing to do with her. Oh, no. That would be much too straightforward. But they'd hosted parties and invited everyone but her. They'd gone shopping for new dresses and not bothered to include her. They'd deliberately crossed the street to avoid crossing her path.

And they'd giggled.

Mercilessly.

Joanna and Claire had never noticed. Or if they had, they didn't care. But *she* had noticed. And *she* had cared. And she had promised herself that there would come a time when no one laughed at Evelyn Thorncroft ever again.

"Are you all right?" Brynne asked, her gaze both sympathetic and searching. Reaching across the serving table, she gently clasped Evie's cold, still hand. "You look pale. If this subject is too difficult, we can talk of something else."

"No, I..." Swallowing with some difficulty, she took a drink of her tea in the hopes that the lemon infused water would help wash away unpleasant memories best left undisturbed. Which was why she'd taken such care to keep them locked in a box where they couldn't bother her. A box where she kept everything else she didn't want to face.

Such as the grief she still felt over her father's death. And the anger at her grandmother for not telling the truth sooner. And the trickling fear that no matter what she did, or who she married, or how much wealth she regained, it would never be enough to fill all this emptiness inside of her heart.

"I am fine," she said, summoning her biggest, brightest smile as she slammed the lid closed on the box and kicked it into the furthest corner of her mind. "A tad weary from my travels, perhaps. Nothing that cannot be fixed with an afternoon rest before dinner. But to answer your original question, no, my sisters and I never had any reason to believe that we might have different fathers. It wasn't even a consideration. Maybe if Claire and I looked the same, and Joanna was the proverbial sore thumb...but we all inherited our appearances from various family members. I've my father's dark hair, Claire is as fair as a sunbeam, and Joanna is the mirror image of our mother."

Brynne sat back in her seat. "How *did* you find out, then?"

"The ring." In this, Evie knew she had to proceed with caution. The ruby ring, now in Weston's possession, had come to mean so many different things to so many different people.

For Brynne and Weston, it was a priceless heirloom to be passed from one generation to the next through marriage, and their father never had any right to give it away to his American mistress as a parting gift.

But for Evie and her sisters, the ring was one of the last physical connections they had to a mother they could barely remember. It was also a means to financial freedom, should they choose to part with it. Two conflicting ideas that she hadn't yet reconciled...and if her plan went accordingly, she'd never have to. Because if she married the Earl of Hawkridge, the ring would pass to *her*, thus circumventing the need to sell it...or steal it, which was Joanna's solution.

All things considered, Evie liked her idea the best.

Being a countess was vastly preferable to being thrown in an English prison. Newgate, she believed it was called. And her complexion would *never* recover from being locked in a cell without any natural light.

"After my father died in the war between the states," she continued evenly, her composure returned now that the box containing all of her unwanted feelings had been successfully closed, "we found ourselves burdened by financial strain. The ring, which Claire found in the attic, was the only thing we had of any value. It wasn't until it was…taken that our grandmother revealed its significance, and told us that Joanna was really the daughter of a British lord."

"You mean when the ring was stolen," Brynne said wryly. "It's all right. You needn't dance around the truth for fear of offending me. Just like you and Joanna, my brother and I often find ourselves at odds. Were it my decision, I would have given the ring back to you and your sisters straightaway. Weston, unfortunately, is of a slightly different opinion. But then, he is a man, and men are beholden to what they believe is rightfully theirs, whether it be a crown, or a country…or a ring."

"Lord Hawkridge *has* been very reluctant to discuss any means by which the ring might be returned to us," Evie acknowledged.

"What a nice way to say that my brother is a bullheaded dunce."

She laughed. She couldn't help herself. "I wouldn't dare incur your annoyance by disagreeing."

Placing an arm around her ribcage, Brynne propped her elbow on her wrist and her chin in the palm of her hand. "I like you, Miss Thorncroft."

"I like you as well," said Evie and, to her surprise, she meant it. She *did* like Brynne. Immensely. What had begun as a means to get closer to Weston was rapidly developing into a friendship. The first that she'd entertained in years.

When a flicker of guilt nudged at the edge of her conscience, she pushed it aside.

It wasn't as if she were taking advantage of Brynne. All right, maybe she had at first. Just to get herself an invitation to the house party. But now that she was here, she could foster a genuine relationship with Weston's sister. One that would help fill the void left behind by Joanna and Claire. And if she wasn't being *completely* forthright in her intentions regarding Weston…well, surely that wasn't the same thing as lying.

Was it?

When a frown threatened, Evie deliberately relaxed the muscles around her mouth. She wasn't doing anything wrong. If anyone should feel guilty, it was Weston. *He* was the one who had put all this in motion when he'd taken the ring.

Stolen, she reminded herself, using Brynne's own term.

When he'd *stolen* the ring.

In doing so, he had cast a rock into a pond, creating an untold number of ripples. How far and where those ripples might travel remained to be seen, but Evie knew one thing with absolute certainty: no matter how rough the water became, she was *not* going to let her boat to sink.

"I'd like to thank you," she told Brynne impulsively.

"For what?" asked Weston's sister, smiling.

"For this," she said, gesturing around the room. "For welcoming me here. For being so accepting of the skeletons my family has unknowingly harbored in our closet." She paused. "Not to say your father is a skeleton."

"He has been called much worse, I can assure you."

"W-will the marquess attend the house party?" For the first time, Evie considered that she might actually meet Joanna's birth father before Joanna. It was an uneasy thought, made increasingly more so by the fact that she hadn't the faintest idea of what she would say.

"Hello, Lord Dorchester...how nice to make your acquaintance...no, I'm not the illegitimate daughter you conceived with my mother out of wedlock and kept a secret for two decades. I'm the other one–the one that intends to marry your son."

Oh, yes.

What a splendid introduction *that* would make.

"Who knows whether my father will grace us with his presence or not?" Brynne said lightly. "To the best of my knowledge, he is in Scotland. Or maybe it's Spain. My father is very fond of traveling.

Attending house parties, not as much."

Evie's brow knitted. "Is he aware that…?"

"That his long-lost daughter and her sister came to London? I haven't any idea, to be honest. When he does find out, if he hasn't already, I'm certain he will be quick to make things right. Which is to say, he will settle an obnoxiously large sum of money on your sister and wish her good health and good fortune before he heads off to another part of the world."

"I don't know what Joanna will think about that," Evie said honestly. "She may not be a…*willing* recipient of his generosity. At least, not anything of a monetary nature. I could be wrong, but I believe she mostly wants to learn more about him. Specifically, the time he spent with our mother. What she was like. What they did. Where they went. That would truly be of value to her. To both of us, really."

Brynne's smile lost some of its warmth. "Alas, I regret to tell you that his attention is the one commodity my father is in short supply of. Wouldn't Joanna like to become an heiress? There are those who'd attempt to take advantage of her newfound wealth, of course. But from what you've shared, she strikes me as an intelligent, independent woman who is more than capable of fending off would-be fortune hunters. And from personal experience, I can tell you that being an heiress *does* come with its own unique set of benefits."

"You needn't convince me," Evie said with a laugh. "Were I in her position, I'd have no such qualms. But that is an area where my sister and I differ. Not to say that she absolutely would not accept such a boon were it freely given. But I'm familiar enough with how her mind works to know that she wouldn't want to feel as if…as if it were merely a transaction, or a debt to be paid."

Brynne nodded. "I understand."

They sipped their tea.

"Would you care for a walk around the grounds?" Brynne asked after an uncomfortable pause. "There's a garden I'd like to show you, along with the stables. We've just had a foal born. Late in the season, I'm afraid, but she's a strong little lady. You can help me come up with a name, if you'd like."

"I'd *love* to." Grateful for the opportunity to leave their heavy conversation behind, Evie rose from her chair and followed Brynne out of the parlor.

WESTON'S MORNING RIDE over hill and dale on a fresh, frisky mount had done him good. Not only had it helped to clear his head from the lingering effects of drinking too much with Sterling the night before, but it'd given him a way to expend his energy.

Outside of the bedroom.

Hopefully, the gallop, coupled with the cold bath he'd taken upon waking, would alleviate any lingering fantasies he'd been nursing of Evie since their last kiss…and ease the throbbing between his thighs that was a constant reminder of how badly he wanted to kiss her again.

Everywhere.

Anywhere.

All at once, and then so slowly that she screamed out his name.

He wanted to hear her say it.

Weston.

Weston.

Weston.

His name would spill from her lips as he suckled at her breasts, alternating between the soft ivory globes before he kissed his way down her ribcage to her navel, and then lower still until he used his tongue to part her sweet curls and–

Bloody hell, he cursed inwardly.

So much for that ride.

He dismounted outside the stables. Giving the gelding a hearty slap on its lathered neck–it wasn't Luther's fault that his owner was a walking cockstand–Weston discreetly adjusted his breeches and then strolled into the barn.

Like any nobleman worth his salt, he maintained a modest breeding operation that encompassed half a dozen broodmares, all retired racers, and Bold, a three-year-old colt out of Doncaster, winner of the Epsom Derby. He was pleased with both Bold's superior confirmation and sensible temperament, and planned to stud him out at the beginning of next year.

The faint, but pleasing scent of leather and straw welcomed Weston as he made his way from one stall to the next, greeting each horse standing inside the roomy wooden boxes with more affection than he generally gave most people. But then, horses weren't selfish. They kept no secrets. And short of death, which came for both man and beast eventually, they would never break your heart.

He'd just exited the last stall on the row when he heard it.

Or rather, when he heard *her*.

The sound of Evie's husky laugh was as unmistakable to him as rain on a window. Or the boom of thunder in the midst of a storm. Or the chirp of crickets heralding in that first warm spring evening after months of winter.

Her laughter was instantly identifiable because *she* was instantly identifiable.

Even without having her in his line of vision.

Then he stepped around the corner and there she was. Glowing like a beacon in a white dress that accentuated every curve and line of her delectable little body. Her hair was pinned back from her face, allowing him an unfettered view of her blue eyes framed with long, sweeping lashes, plump mouth highlighted with some sort of gloss that made the muscles in his abdomen stretch hard as a drum, and that narrow chin that tended to jut whenever she was angry with him.

But she wasn't angry now.

As she placed her arms over the top of the foaling stall and peered within, her entire countenance radiated pure joy. And Weston experienced an unexpected surge of jealousy because *he* wanted to be the one to bring her such happiness. He wanted her to gaze at him with the same delight in her eyes. He wanted to be the reason she smiled.

Which was so utterly absurd, he wondered if he wasn't suffering some sort of acute swelling in his brain. Especially since there was swelling in other, similarly sensitive areas.

"Miss Thorncroft. Brynne." His voice was louder and harsher than he'd intended, and both women jumped before they whirled around.

"*Weston,*" his sister gasped. "What did I say about sneaking?"

"What are you doing here?" Ignoring Brynne, he asked the question directly of Evie, who frowned at his accusatory tone.

"Lady Brynne wanted to show me the new filly," she said, adjusting the crimson shawl draped over her shoulders. "I was not aware the stables were off limits."

"They're not," Brynne interceded, rolling her eyes at him. "My brother is being an arse. As usual."

"You know I don't like guests wandering unsupervised around the barn," he said. "Or have you forgotten the time Lady Gibberson tried to feed my prized colt champagne?"

"That happened *once*. And if I recall, he quite liked it."

"That is beside the point."

"Then what *is* the point?" said Brynne. "For 'tis obvious that Miss Thorncroft is neither unsupervised nor wandering. We just wanted to see how the foal was faring."

"Yes, it seems Miss Thorncroft has a particular fondness for baby farm animals." He glared at Evie, who returned his stare calmly, prompting him to demand, "Where *is* Posy, anyway?"

"Who is Posy?" Brynne asked. "I don't recall that name on the guest list."

"She is a lamb that Lord Hawkridge and I rescued after we discovered that her mother had been killed by poachers." Evie smiled pleasantly at Weston. Were it not for the sharp glint in her gaze, he would have almost thought she meant it. "As to her whereabouts, I gave her to a footman to be bathed and fed."

"That's not what my footmen are for." Even without his sister telling him, Weston knew he was being an arse. Had Brynne brought anyone else into the stables, he wouldn't have given them more than passing greeting. But Evie wasn't anyone else. She wasn't like anyone he'd ever met.

A second in her presence and all of his self-control, all of his carefully constructed emotional barriers, were stripped away, leaving him helplessly undefended against her natural allure. If he didn't snap at her, he was going to kiss her. And since he very well couldn't do *that*, his only alternative was to disguise his lust with loathing.

"He did not look busy," she countered, lifting a dark brow.

"Two dozen members of the *ton* are about to descend on this estate at any moment," he growled. "Every single maid, servant, and livery boy is busy. And none of them have time to bathe a damned sheep!"

"Three dozen, actually," Brynne corrected. "But who is counting?"

"I am. *I* am counting." Incredulous, he raked a hand through his hair. "*Thirty-six* guests? Bloody hell. Why would you ever invite so many? Where are we going to put them all?"

"We've enough bedrooms to accommodate twice that amount. And if anyone is to blame, it's you."

"Me," he said flatly. "This ought to be good."

Brynne shrugged. "After Lady Smethwick made it known that she and her daughter would be attending, I was fending off callers day and night. Everyone wants to say they were present when the Earl of Hawkridge and Lady Martha became–"

"Did you pick a fabric for the chairs?" he interrupted.

"What?" she said, blinking in confusion.

"The chairs." He threw his hand in the air. "The dining room chairs that you wanted to reupholster in green but the fabric wasn't available. Did you ever select another color?"

Staring at him as if he'd suddenly sprouted a second head, she nodded slowly. "Yes, as a matter of fact, I decided on the eggplant. I didn't realize you were actually listening to me."

Neither had Weston, but he'd needed *something* to stop Brynne from going on about his engagement plans, and dining room chairs in need of reupholstering was the first thing that came to mind.

He hadn't any idea why discussing Lady Martha Smethwick in front of Evie was so innately repulsive to him. He only knew that it felt…wrong, somehow. Like discussing his wife in front of his mistress. Not that Evie was–or ever would be–his mistress. For even if he *was* inclined to make her his (which he definitely wanted to, but also absolutely did not), she deserved more than some clandestine affair in a house tucked away on a side street that he visited in the dead of night.

Evie was far too proud for such an arrangement, and he'd never demean her by asking her to place herself in a situation where she was less than. Even if it meant having those luscious curves available to him whenever he desired. Kissing her for as long as he wanted. Loving her until the sun went down and then rose again, painting the sky in an endless streak of pink and gold as they finally collapsed beside each other in a slick, tangled heap of limbs.

Swallowing hard, he shifted his weight onto his heels and cast his attention into the foaling stall where the filly, still unnamed, slept soundly. "Brynne, I'd like a word with Miss Thorncroft. In private."

"Anything you have to say to me can be said in front of Lady Brynne."

He turned his head to stare at Evie, and were such things possible the heat blazing in his eyes would have ignited the pile of hay behind her. "No. I cannot."

"There's...there's a sitting arrangement I really must tend to," said Brynne, her gaze darting between them. "Have a lovely chat."

Off she dashed, leaving Weston and Evie alone save for the horses...and the tension simmering between them. Straw rustled as the broodmares moved around in their stalls. From somewhere out in the yard came the sound of a rake scraping across gravel. At the other end of the barn, Bold let out a shrill whinny.

Evie wet her lips. "Why are you looking at me like that?"

"Like what?" he said roughly.

"Like you want to ravish me."

"What if I did?"

"Want to ravish me?"

He gave a clipped nod.

"But at the tavern you said–"

"To hell with what I said." Three steps, and he was in front of her. Four, and she was in his arms. He grabbed her waist. Yanked her against him. Relished the quiver he felt go through her entire body. Craved the taste of her mouth like a man half-starved.

She tilted her head back. Her sooty lashes spilled across the tops of her cheeks, and then lifted to reveal blue eyes dark with smoke and sensuality. "Ravish away, my lord."

CHAPTER TEN

WESTON DID NOT need another invitation.

On a muffled groan, he crushed his mouth to Evie's and kissed her with the wild, wicked abandon of a man who was biting his thumb at the devil…and didn't give a damn about what consequences might come.

To hell with his vow.

To hell with yesterday and tomorrow.

To hell with anything that might keep him from *this* moment. From this woman. From this madness.

For that's what it was. Sheer madness, to want someone as badly as he wanted Evie. But he didn't care.

Tonight, he would. Tonight, he'd curse himself for his recklessness. Tonight, he'd drink, and brood, and make another vow. A better vow. A *stronger* vow. One that could resist this tumultuous storm raging inside of him.

But for now…for now, he was going to run straight into the rain.

Power and passion surged through him in equal measure when he backed Evie up against the barn wall, his arms braced on either side of her head as they devoured each other in a kiss that was raw, and primitive, and desperate.

He wanted, and so he took. She desired, and so she gave.

Their tongues tangled. Their teeth clicked. Their noses bumped.

It was messy and imperfect.

It was mania and impatience.

Combined, it was a tempest neither of them were able to control.

Evie's hands streaked greedily across his torso, nails scraping against his flesh as she found the edge of his shirt.

Weston palmed her breasts, then rolled her nipples between his thumb and finger until she arched her spine off the wood, her soft belly pressing against his hard arousal.

He could have taken her there. Against the barn, or in the hay. It didn't matter. He just wanted to thrust his throbbing staff into all that wet, clenching silk. And it wasn't until he held her skirts in his fists that he fully comprehended what he was about to do. What he *would* have done, if his common sense hadn't come rushing back with all the subtlety of a train clattering down at the tracks at full speed.

"Jesus." He dropped her dress before he staggered away, his breath whistling between his lips in a shocked exhalation of self-disgust. He'd been seconds away from taking Evie in a horse stable. On the bloody ground. Like a…like a rutting boar. No. Worse than a boar. The flea that fucked on the boar. *That's* what he was. A flea. And Evie, bright, beautiful, brilliant Evie, was…

Crying, he realized with a painful jolt.

She was crying.

And he was flea dirt.

"Miss Thorncroft–" Awkwardly he reached out, but she shoved his hand away.

"Don't," she choked before she fled past him out of the barn.

Stunned, he remained in the barn for less than five minutes before he went after her. After a quick search of the main house, he found Brynne in the dining room directing a small army of servants, but his twin had seen no sign of Evie.

"Losing a cravat is acceptable, Weston," she chided. "Not a guest. What did you do now?"

His chest heaving, he scowled and said, "Why do you presume *I* did something wrong?

"Because you're a man," she answered simply. "You've always done something wrong. And if you haven't done it yet, you're about to. Have you tried the stone garden? I showed it to Miss Thorncroft earlier, and she seemed taken with it."

The stone garden.

Without bothering to bid his sister farewell, Weston stormed out of the dining room with its eggplant chairs–the most hideously ugly color he'd ever seen–and veered left, using a delivery entrance to access a narrow, rarely used path that wound around the edge of the glass solarium and through a grove of silver birch before leading to a green labyrinth comprised of round boxwoods and tall hedges. Thin cut slices of granite rock, set directly into the ground, made a trail of stepping stones that eventually led to the middle of the maze where a statue in the likeness of the late Marchioness of Dorchester had been erected after her death, thus giving the garden its name.

When Weston and Brynne were children, they'd made a game of losing themselves in the labyrinth. With its many twists and turns, it wasn't difficult to do. But Weston was in no mood for frivolity, and he cut through the hedges with the ruthlessness of a scythe slicing through wheat.

He found Evie at the center, sitting on a bench beside the statue of his mother.

To see them together, one in stone and the other in flesh and blood, halted him in his tracks. He'd known these two women for such brief periods of time. His mother, less than an hour. Evie, less than a week. And yet they'd both had such a strong impact on him.

The Marchioness of Dorchester had given him life.

And Evelyn Thorncroft…Evelyn Thorncroft had made him *feel* it.

The anger. The passion. The frustration. The pleasure.

For so long, all of those emotions, all of those *feelings*, had been lying dormant inside of him. Shielded behind an impenetrable wall of ice. Until Evie strolled in with her chisel in hand and went to work.

The wall remained standing, but she'd managed to chip off enough pieces to create a deep crack that ran the length of his heart. And through the crack had slipped the tiniest amount of warmth…just enough to begin thawing the edges of all that cold.

"Miss Thorncroft."

She lifted her head at the sound her name, and he was relieved to see that her eyes were dry. But for the hint of red underneath, and the linen handkerchief crumpled in her right hand, she might have never been crying at all.

"Go away," she said frostily. "In case it was not clear, when someone retreats to the middle of a hidden garden, they wish to be left alone."

"It's called the stone garden, actually. That is my mother, there." He nodded at the statue. Set on a marble pedestal, it depicted Lady Dorchester in a standing position with her hands linked behind her back and her head raised to the sky. The folds of her gown were simple, as were the lines of her countenance. But the sculptor had skillfully captured her gentle grace and that, more than her face or dress, had been her defining characteristic.

Occasionally, Weston was given to wonder how his upbringing might have been different if his mother had lived. Would it have meant a childhood spent at dinner tables and family gatherings instead of his room, a place made even more isolating by the knowledge that no parent waited for him downstairs? Would it have meant praise for a job well done, and kind encouragement for when he could do better? Would it have meant an eagerness to return to Hawkridge Manor after being away at school, instead of the quiet dread that had grown louder and louder with every turn of the carriage wheel?

"Your sister told me who the statute was when we came here earlier." As Evie rose from the bench, the stern brackets around her mouth softened. "She was beautiful. Your mother. It must have been very hard to have never known her."

As his gaze shifted from the statue to Evie, it occurred to him, somewhat belatedly, that they had *both* lost a parent at a very young age. And it was because of that communal loss that they were standing here, together.

If Weston's mother had not died in childbirth, his father would have never fallen in love with an American debutante. For despite all of his flaws (which were numerous), the Marquess of Dorchester was a loyal man who would not have stepped out on his wife. And if he never had an affair with Anne Thorncroft, they never would have conceived a child, thus unraveling the thread that bound Weston and Evie together.

The marquess never would have given his wife's ring away.

Weston never would have had reason to go searching for it.

And Evie never would have come to London to get it back.

With all the people in the world, and an ocean between them, the odds of their paths ever crossing was so miniscule it was all but incalculable.

To have never known Evie...the shape of her smile, the light in her eyes, the smell of her perfume, the taste of her lips...it would be like looking to the heavens every night and never seeing a shooting star.

When his stomach twisted unpleasantly, as it sometimes did when he ate or drank to excess, Weston swiped a hand across his face. He needed to get ahold of himself. Any more melancholic thoughts like those and he'd begin spouting poetry or some other such nonsense.

Not meeting Evie would have been a bloody *blessing*, not a trage-dy.

Any ideas to the contrary were just further proof that he was los-ing his mind.

Or maybe he'd already lost it.

Either way, *she* was to blame.

This tempting minx who'd set his world on fire...and they were both burning with it.

"By all accounts, my mother's beauty was what first drew my father to her." Taking the seat Evie had vacated, he stretched his legs out in front of him and his arms along the back of the bench. "That, and the knowledge they'd make a splendid match. Which they did, until she passed within hours of my sister and me being born."

"I am sorry for your loss," Evie said softly. "And even sorrier that you never had the chance to meet her. Every child should have their mother, even if just for a little while."

"Do you remember your mother?" he asked. "I understand she died when you were very young, as well."

"Yes, she did. When I try to recall her face...the details of it..." An ebony tendril, loosened from their tryst in the barn, slid free of Evie's coiffure and tumbled across her cheek as she shook her head. "But I remember the scent of her perfume. Lilacs. She smelled like lilacs. And I remember the sound of her voice. When she was first stricken with fever, my sisters and I would all sit beside her in bed. She'd read to us for hours. Until her voice gave out. Or she grew too tired to speak. I think..." Evie's voice cracked, and Weston's heart ached in response.

He wanted to get up and gather her in his arms, but he didn't trust himself. How could he, after they way he'd nearly lost all control? Thus he remained sitting, his expression carefully stoic, and allowed her to finish without interruption.

"I think she was..." As Evie paused to take a breath, she cast her gaze heavenward, and her mouth curved. "I think she was trying to fit an entire lifetime of reading into that last month she had with us. I shall never open the pages of *Oliver Twist* without thinking of her."

"She sounds as if she were a wonderful mother," he said gruffly.

"She was. Patient, and kind, and loving. I realize you may have a different perspective, given the...the unique relationship between her and your father, but—"

"No." At that, Weston could not remain seated any longer. Rising from the bench, he went to Evie and gently took hold of her wrists, his fingers easily encircling the tiny bones as his thumbs came to rest on the fluttering points of her pulse. "I will admit that when I first learned of the affair, I was angry. Furious, even."

"You?" she said, blue eyes widening in exaggerated surprise. "Furious? Surely not."

He squeezed her hands. "Since I've had time to contemplate, I realize that the source of my fury stemmed not from the affair itself, but rather from learning twenty years after the fact that I have a half-sister my father never bothered to mention. I may have...*misplaced* some of that anger on you and Joanna. Given the timing of your arrival, I thought that you were here for the purpose of monetary gain through blackmail, or some other nefarious means. I can see now that I was...I was wrong."

It was the closest Weston had ever come to an outright apology. The closest he *would* come, banning some unforeseen natural disaster or a horrific form of torture. As a prideful man, and an arrogant one besides, it was difficult for him to admit that he'd jumped to a conclusion too hastily.

But not impossible.

He owed Evie this much, if not more, for suspecting the worst of her without taking the opportunity to get to know her first. She may have been many things. High-spirited. Argumentative. Stubborn to a bloody fault. But she wasn't a liar or a schemer, out to steal his family's fortune. The past few days in her company had taught him that, if nothing else.

There was a flicker in Evie's gaze. An undecipherable flash, there and gone again, like the blink of a firefly on a humid summer night. Then she smiled. Smirked, really. "You're right. You *were* wrong. We only came here to retrieve our mother's ring. And to find out the identity of Joanna's birth father. It was never our intent to make any demands of you or your family. We also didn't plan to create such a stir at the countess' ball."

"Two Americans set loose on the *ton*, one the illegitimate granddaughter of a duke and the other a raven-haired goddess, and you *didn't* think you'd cause a stir?" he said drolly.

A pleased blush enveloped her cheeks. "Is that how you think of me? As a raven-haired goddess? It has a nice ring, doesn't it?"

He quirked a brow. "What makes you believe I think about you at all?"

"That kiss in the stables, for one."

As he was reminded of their passionate embrace, and her response to it, Weston sobered. His behavior in the barn had been abominable from start to finish, and judging her too harshly before they'd even met wasn't the only thing he needed to apologize for.

"Miss Thorncroft, I–"

"If you are about to mention my tears, I'd prefer you didn't."

He frowned. "But–"

"No, thank you."

"I–"

"On *very* rare occasions, Lord Hawkridge, I succumb to…emotional distress. It was nothing you did," she said before he could speak. "I was just…overwhelmed by the moment we found ourselves in. I'd like to forget it happened, if it's all the same to you."

"The kissing or the crying?"

"Both, I presume, as one wouldn't have happened without the other." Her expression grew serious. "I am not a plaything, my lord. To be picked up and cast aside whenever the whim strikes you."

His grip on her wrists tightened imperceptibly, and then fell away as he took a step back and ran his fingers through his hair. "I know that," he said defensively.

"Do you?" she asked. "Because what occurred in the barn implied otherwise. Not to say I wasn't a party to it. Or that I did not enjoy myself. But I...I should like to know where I stand with you, Lord Hawkridge."

"Where you stand," he repeated, and even though they were out in the open with the grass beneath their feet and the sky stretching above their heads, he could have sworn he felt the walls closing in.

"Yes. What are your intentions in regards to our relationship?"

"Relationship."

A line of annoyance formed between her brows. "If you keep parroting back what I've just told you, I'm going to feed you a cracker."

"We...we do not *have* a relationship, Miss Thorncroft. You are...you are my guest. And, I suppose, in a distant sort of way, we may even consider ourselves family. Of a sort. Fifth cousins, thrice removed." He shoved his hands into the pockets sewn onto the rear of his breeches. "My lapses in judgment notwithstanding, that is where we stand."

"Oh." Her shoulders stiffened. "I see."

Bollocks.

This–this right here–was precisely why he *didn't* want a romantic entanglement with Evelyn Thorncroft. Brynne's opinion on marrying for love be damned.

Lady Martha would never dare question their relationship, or where they stood. She'd be happy enough just being his wife, and bearing his child, and joining him for tea on occasion. As it should be. As any man in his right mind would *want* it to be.

Except he wasn't in his right mind, was he? Hadn't been, ever since he'd glanced across the ballroom and seen the most magnificent creature that God had ever seen fit to create.

"I don't..." He paused. Took a breath. "I don't want to injure your feelings."

"Don't you?" Evie asked, canting her head to the side.

"No, of course not."

"Then you've an amusing way of showing it." Her eyes glittered. "Should we make a vow not to have another encounter, or save ourselves the breath?"

Impertinent vixen.

"What happened in the stables–"

"Shall never happen again," she finished. "So you've said before."

He scowled. "This time I mean it."

"I'm sure."

"I *do*," he insisted. "With the other guests soon to join us, these…er…"

"Lapses in judgment?" she said icily.

Not, he admitted, his best choice of words.

"Yes. I mean no." What was it about Evie that tangled his tongue in knots? "I mean–"

"You mean you wouldn't want your precious Lady Martha to catch you fornicating with an American." Her smile was sweet, and all the more sharp because of it. "I understand."

He gritted his teeth. "If you'd let me finish a bloody sentence–"

"It's growing late, and I have to change for the receiving dinner. I will see you inside, my lord." She brushed past him, and he didn't try to stop her.

He wouldn't have known what to say if he did.

CHAPTER ELEVEN

EVIE FELT HORRIBLY guilty. Or she *had* felt horribly guilty, until Weston had absolved her of all remorse regarding her deceitful plan to marry him by uttering four hurtful words she wasn't soon to forget.

My lapses in judgment.

That's all that kissing her meant to him, apparently.

A lapse in judgment.

A miscalculation.

A *mistake*.

And to think, she'd been on the brink of telling him that she *had* come to Hawkridge Manor with ulterior motives in mind. That she did want the ring, and his fortune, and his title, besides. That she did deserve some of the blame he'd just absolved her of.

The admission had danced on the tip of her tongue for the entirety of their conversation...right up until he'd compared her to a fifth cousin.

A *cousin*.

She wasn't his cousin, thrice removed or otherwise. There was no blood shared between them. But there was passion. At least, she'd thought there was. Until he had informed her that she was no more than a lapse in judgment.

The bounder.

She was of half a mind to gather her things and leave. But that would be tantamount to admitting defeat…which was something Thorncrofts simply did not do. It wasn't in her to give up, and thus she would keep going forward. All the way to the altar. Because she hadn't come this far, and gone through this much, to *not* become a countess.

The foyer was a bustling hive of activity as footmen and scullery maids alike rushed about, hurrying to complete finishing touches before the first wave of guests descended upon the estate. They filled vases with flowers and glass dishes with colorful candies. Rubbed a final layer of beeswax on any exposed wood to bring out its natural luster, and took care to polish each doorknob until it shone. The drapes were pinned back. Rugs were unrolled. Paintings were hung on the white walls with care and large potted ferns were given a fresh layer of topsoil before being strategically positioned to bring some color into the manor.

From the front drawing room came the random plinking of keys as the piano was tuned, and in the parlor the loud *pop* of a cork as sparkling wine was poured into glass flutes arranged on a long table.

Keeping her head down, Evie was able to slip unnoticed up the stairs and into her bedchamber.

She'd been looking forward to the receiving dinner with all the giddy delight of a child on Christmas morning, but her interlude with the earl had dampened her spirits.

Not the kissing part.

She'd thoroughly enjoyed the kissing part…even if she was mortified by her reaction. She had been so caught up in Weston's embrace that when he had pulled away without warning, the abruptness of his rejection had made her eyes well with tears.

He had kissed her, and she had *cried*, and then he'd called her his cousin.

Clearly, her plan needed a few modifications.

Slipping out of her shawl and kicking off her shoes, Evie flopped belly first onto the bed and buried her face in a pillow. She could not remember the last time she'd cried. When she and her sisters had received news of their father's death, perhaps, because she vividly recalled *not* crying at his funeral.

Claire had. From when they'd first entered the church to when they'd left, she'd sniffled quietly into a white linen handkerchief with pink roses embroidered on the corner. Joanna's grief had been louder, but then such was Joanna. Loud and vivacious in everything she did, even mourning. But Evie...Evie hadn't shed a single tear.

She had *wanted* to. She had tried to. But her eyes had remained dry for the entire service and even after, when they'd laid the wooden casket into the earth, she'd been unable to cry. Her lack of a reaction had garnered more than a few stares, some from her own family, but there was nothing she could do. In a desperate act of salvation, she'd taken all of the grief and loss and love that she'd felt for her father and bottled it up inside of a plain glass jar where it couldn't hurt her anymore. Then she'd sealed it shut. And in the years that followed, the jar had remained closed.

The loss of her childhood home hadn't opened it. Having to part with all of her beloved material possessions and the subsequent abandonment of her friends just made the lid tighter. As had the discovery of her mother's affair, and the subsequent loss of the ring. She'd wanted to give in to despair when she and Joanna were sailing across the ocean and her head was in a bucket, but she'd been so dehydrated from her sea sickness that the tears hadn't come.

Why, then, would she cry over Lord Hawkridge, of all people?

When she hadn't managed a tear for her own father.

Rolling onto her back, Evie stared blankly at the canopy draped over the bedposts. The answer, she feared, was obvious.

She wasn't just *falling* in love with Weston.

She'd fallen.

Completely.

And the lid on the glass jar that she'd poured all of her grief and hurt and heartbreak into had finally wrenched loose.

She supposed that it wasn't unexpected. The pressure had been building for days. A culmination of lust, and frustration, and longing. It only made sense that it *had* to be released, or else the jar–and Evie along with it–would have shattered into a thousand little shards of sorrow and splintered glass. And when Weston had kissed her, and then rejected her, yet again, the jar had finally popped open and her tears had fallen out...along with her heart.

Which Weston then stole.

The cad.

He had her heart, damn him! And she wanted it back. Immediately. Because while marrying the Earl of Hawkridge was part of her plan, being in love with him was not. If she couldn't trust *herself* to be kind with her own heart, how could she possibly trust Weston?

A soft knock sounded at the door; a welcome interruption from the dark turn her thoughts had taken. Quickly running the heel of her hands across her damp cheeks, Evie sat up on her elbows.

"You may enter," she called, assuming it to be Hannah come to prepare her for the receiving dinner.

But while a brunette stepped into the room, it wasn't her lady's maid.

"Rosemary!" At the sight of her cousin, Evie sat all the way up and swung her legs over the side of the mattress. "What...what are you *doing* here? Not to say I'm unhappy to see you," she clarified hastily when she realized how her words might be taken. "I'm just...surprised."

"I was, too, when I received Lady Brynne's invitation." Petite and curvy with a heart-shaped face that was perpetually wreathed in a smile and almond-shaped eyes that were a color somewhere between blue and gray, Rosemary Stanhope was their Grandmother Mabel's niece, twice removed. When Mabel married her American scholar and moved to Somerville, she'd left behind a sister, Dorothea, Lady

Ellinwood, who'd chosen to return to her maiden name after the death of her husband, Sir George Stanhope.

Lady Ellinwood and Sir George had one son, Gregory Stanhope, who eventually married and had a child of his own, before ultimately perishing in a tragic fire along with his wife, leaving their young daughter, Rosemary, to be raised in the care of her grandmother, Lady Ellinwood.

The Thorncroft sisters hadn't even known they *had* a cousin before Evie and Joanna came to London. Another secret kept from them, albeit a good one this time, as Rosemary was delightfully sweet...if a tad eccentric.

"You didn't bring Sir Reginald, did you?" asked Evie, referring to Rosemary's pet squirrel.

"I would have," Rosemary said in all seriousness, "but he's feeling under the weather. Too many acorns, you understand. I ordered him to remain at home and rest up."

"Probably for the best," Evie said solemnly.

"Indeed. Do you mind if I...?" Rosemary glanced at the bed.

"Please, make yourself comfortable." Scooting closer to the headboard, Evie patted the empty space beside her, and as her cousin climbed onto the mattress, a pang of homesickness caught her off guard.

Even though they'd three beds between them, she and her sisters had often sat just like this. Shoulder to shoulder, hip to hip, they had made some of their most important life decisions crammed together on top of the blankets. Like kittens in a basket, their grandmother had been fond of saying. An apt analogy, as it was never long before one of them started swatting at the other. But when they'd all gotten along, and their room had rung with the sound of their laughter, it had been nothing less than pure magic.

"Thank you." The crinoline beneath Rosemary's skirts rustled as she drew her legs up and wrapped her arms around them. Her dress was a medium tan, with a higher neckline than was fashionable and sleeves that extended all the way past her elbows and ended in a tuft of lace. It was a spinsterly garment; far too old for a young woman who'd not yet seen her twentieth birthday.

When they'd first met, Rosemary had mentioned that she was not a member of the popular set. Evie had assumed it was because of Sir Reginald, but now she suspected it had more to do with the way her cousin presented herself. The *ton* could overlook a squirrel *or* a severe hair part. But not both.

It was a shame, really. Underneath the voluminous gown and brown curls that had been slicked to the side of her head, Rosemary was very pretty. A softer hairstyle, a silhouette that helped flaunt her natural figure instead of hide it, and she'd be beautiful.

"I hope you do not mind my intrusion," Rosemary went on. "But when I arrived, and Lady Brynne shared that you were already here, I just *had* to come right up and see you. Isn't the estate marvelous? The sheer size is staggering! I've never been here before. When our invitation arrived, I had to retrieve my grandmother's smelling salts! We've you and Joanna to thank for that."

Evie's brow knitted in confusion. "For your grandmother fainting?"

Rosemary gasped. "No! No, I didn't mean...for the summons to come here. Grandmother claims it's because Lord Hawkridge has his eye on me, which is utter hogwash. The poor man probably still walks with a limp after our one and only dance last Season."

"You should have stomped on him harder," Evie muttered under her breath.

"What was that?"

"I said that you should not underestimate yourself. You have excellent bone structure, Cousin. And the color of your hair is divine."

Rosemary's shoulders hunched. "That is kind of you to say, but...it's just plain brown."

"It is mahogany," Evie corrected. "And chestnut, with underlying notes of caramel. I'd love to have such depth and dimension in mine." She absently touched her own coiffure, then grazed her fingertips across Rosemary's tightly wound bun. Her nose wrinkled. "Perhaps a little less bandoline."

Gummy in texture, and hard as a rock when it dried, liquid bandoline was a popular fixture. Evie had never liked it, herself. She found the smell distasteful, and even though it had never happened to her—heaven forbid–she'd once heard a story of a girl whose hair had *fallen out* because of it.

"Grandmother swears by the stuff," said Rosemary.

"I can see that." Evie hesitated. "Does your grandmother also select your wardrobe?"

"Down to the stockings," her cousin said ruefully as she lifted her skirts to reveal homely cotton hosiery with nary a shiny button or ribbon embellishment to be seen. "I know my attire is sorely out of date, but Grandmother believes that drawing unwanted attention upon oneself by one's wardrobe is in poor taste. I should win a man's favor with my feminine charm and wit. Never mind that I haven't any."

"Grandmother" sounded like a stodgy old schoolmarm with a penchant for wooden rulers.

"You needn't dress provocatively to be noticed," Evie allowed. "But your clothes should reflect your personality, and from what I know of you thus far, you're much more bright and beguiling than this gown would suggest."

Rosemary flushed. "Do you know, I believe that is the nicest thing anyone has ever said to me."

"I'm glad to hear it, but you shouldn't be receiving compliments from *me*. You should be getting them from your suitors."

"Suitors?" her cousin giggled. "Oh, I don't have any of those either. Unless Sir Reginald counts."

"He does not," Evie said firmly. "If you'd like, I can help you achieve a more modern appearance. It wouldn't hardly take any effort at all. We'd start by washing all of that awful bandoline out of your hair, and then making a few tiny alterations to your attire. That tan is doing nothing for your complexion." She smiled confidently. "You'll be turning heads in no time."

"I couldn't possibly ask so much of you, especially during a house party," Rosemary protested even as her eyes lit with thinly veiled excitement. "But it *would* be nice to feel fashionable for once. To have people look at me not out of pity, but because they actually think I am pretty."

"You *are* pretty. Beautiful, really. And to be honest, I'd prefer the distraction." Evie smoothed a wrinkle on the coverlet and sighed. "The house party hasn't exactly gone as I...anticipated it would."

"But it hasn't even started! Surely nothing too awful could have happened yet."

"You'd be surprised," she said wryly.

Rosemary patted her hand. "It'll be all right, now that we're together. I normally have to depend on the company of my books to keep me occupied at these sorts of social events. I cannot tell you have pleased I am to have you here with me, especially since I had to leave Sir Reginald behind. I *do* hope he's not too cross. Squirrels, as you know, are quite finicky."

Evie did *not* know, but since she had more or less adopted a lamb, she was hardly in a position to judge Rosemary for her unusual attachment to a rat with a furry tail.

From what she'd learned of her cousin thus far, it was apparent that Rosemary was lonely and kept mostly to herself. Which was understandable, given the ironclad way with which Lady Ellinwood yielded control over every facet of her granddaughter's life. But that didn't make it acceptable.

Evie and her sisters were raised from an early age to be independent, and to think for themselves. That upbringing had fostered a sense of self-reliance that had helped see them through the difficulties of the last few years, and Evie was loath to imagine what might have happened to them if they'd been forced to live trapped beneath their grandmother's thumb.

Certainly, she and Joanna would never have had the courage to travel halfway around the world. Although, in hindsight, she didn't know whether that decision was brave so much as it was foolhardy. Maybe she *would* have been better served to have stayed in the parlor with a pile of books. At least then she wouldn't have gone and fallen in love with an earl who considered her to be nothing more than a lapse in judgment.

The lout.

"Your grandmother came with you, I presume?" she asked in a deliberate attempt to steer her thoughts away from Weston.

Rosemary nodded. "She is just getting settled in. Traveling upsets her gout. Will Joanna be joining us today or tomorrow?"

"I am afraid she won't be joining us at all, as she is currently on a very large ship headed for Boston."

"That's strange. She did not mention she was leaving when we had coffee yesterday."

"You had coffee with my sister?" said Evie, startled.

"Yes, at a lovely little tea shop in Mayfair. Their cider cakes with spiced jam are positively divine, and the snowdon pudding is–"

"I'm sorry," Evie cut in. "But just to make sure I am understanding you correctly, you spoke with Joanna *yesterday*. As in, the day before this one."

"Was I not meant to? I'm sorry." Sliding off the bed, Rosemary wrung her hands together as she edged towards the door. "I have overstepped. I tend to do that. It's why I don't have many friends, I fear. Or any friends really, except for Sir Reginald. Who I *know* is a squirrel." She gave a slight, self-deprecating smile. "But he never mocks me, and he listens, and occasionally he even chatters back. Which is more than I can say for anyone else in the *ton*."

"You did nothing wrong," Evie assured her cousin. "I just didn't know that Joanna had decided to stay in London."

A letter would have been nice, she reflected with a pinch of annoyance. Which reminded her that she had letters to give out as well. Farewell notes, written by Joanna, to be distributed to Brynne, and Weston, and Rosemary. In the chaos of the last few days, she'd forgotten all about them. But if Joanna *was* still in London–and she had no reason to doubt Rosemary's account–then her sister could distribute them herself.

Joanna knew where to find her.

And Evie had an inkling of where she might find Joanna.

Her sister failing to get on that ship could only mean one thing...she and Mr. Kincaid must have reconciled their differences, and Joanna had finally found what she'd been searching for. Not the ring, or her birth father. She'd found those as well, of course, but Evie had always suspected that, deep down, her sister had come to England to look for something much more meaningful.

True love.

Which she'd finally discovered with a dashingly handsome British private detective.

And Evie wasn't *jealous*. That would be absurd. Kincaid didn't even have a title, for heaven's sake. But apparently that did not matter to Joanna. Why would it, when she was set to inherit a fortune? *If* she accepted the marquess' generosity, that is. Knowing how stubborn and perverse her sister could be, Evie wouldn't be surprised if Joanna refused to take a single penny from her birth father. Especially now that she had something worth more than all the money in the world.

Rising from the bed, she glanced at Rosemary. And frowned when she saw her cousin's crestfallen expression. The poor thing looked like a dog that had been ordered beneath the table after trying to sneak a treat. Ears back, tail curled, eyes down.

This wouldn't do.

This wouldn't do at all.

"Ignore whatever your grandmother and the *ton* says," she ordered as she crossed the room to rest her hands on Rosemary's shoulders. They were approximately the same height, allowing her to look straight into her cousin's anxious gaze. "You are intelligent, and witty, and charmingly different. If someone chooses to ridicule those traits which I so admire in you, then that speaks more to their character than to your own. Because you do have friends. Wonderful ones, if I do say so myself. You have me, and Joanna, and Claire. *We* are your friends, and your family, and you need never feel alone again."

"I...I am not sure what to say," Rosemary whispered, her blue-gray eyes glistening with unshed tears.

"You don't have to say anything at all. I–*oomph*," Evie grunted as Rosemary threw her arms around her in a tight embrace. She'd forgotten how much her cousin adored hugs. Gently extricating herself from Rosemary's strong grip, she retrieved her shawl and shoes. "Would you care to come find my lamb with me? I gave her to a footman to be bathed, and he should be finished soon if he isn't done already."

"You have a pet lamb? How dear!" Rosemary cried, bouncing on her heels in delight. "Oh, how I wish Sir Reginald had been up for the trip. He would have loved to meet her."

"Maybe next time." Linking arms, the cousins went off in search of Posy.

CHAPTER TWELVE

E VIE WAS NOT at the receiving dinner.

As discreetly as possible, Weston sipped his port and searched for her amidst the sea of familiar faces. He saw the Duke of Hanover, trapped in the corner between two starry-eyed mothers with a bevy of marriageable daughters between them. He saw Lord Ellis, notable for his long white mustache and wandering eye. He saw the Earl of Crancroft, an old friend of his father's who drank like a fish, and his wife, Lady Crancroft, a tall, shrewish woman with the staccato laugh of a hyena (which probably explained the earl's drinking). He nodded in his head in greeting at Mr. Henry Greer, the eldest son of a baron whom had recently joined him on the board of Midland Railway Company. And bowed politely when the Dowager Countess of Dunlop crossed his path.

But of Evie, he saw no sign, and when it was time for everyone to take their seats around the expansive dining room table, her chair was conspicuously empty.

For the duration of the seven-course meal, Weston engaged in small talk and even managed to stretch his mouth into something that vaguely resembled the shape of a smile when Lord Ellis shared an amusing story about finding a mouse in his boot. But his thoughts were far away, and it was only due to his well-known disdain for frivolous socialization that no one noticed he was particularly standoffish.

No one except for Brynne, that is.

"What is wrong with you?" she hissed, giving him a poke with her salad fork. She was seated directly to his left, the dowager countess was to his right. Sterling, as the guest with the highest ranking, had assumed the other chair of honor at the far end of the table, with all of the other guests filling in the space between. The mood was jovial and conversation flowed freely (as did the wine), but as the dinner dragged on, the storm cloud hanging over Weston's head had only grown darker and more ominous with each passing minute that Evie did not arrive.

"Not everyone is here," he said, keeping his voice low.

"We've more guests arriving tomorrow. The Smethwicks among them, if that is who you are concerned about. Did you see I invited Lady Ellinwood and her granddaughter, Miss Rosemary? We've not traveled in the same circles as them before, but given that Rosemary's a cousin of the Thorncrofts–"

"How nice," he interrupted. "Where *is* Miss Thorncroft?"

Brynne brought a bite-sized piece of asparagus to her mouth. Chewed. Swallowed. Dabbed at her mouth with a linen napkin. "Why do you want Miss Thorncroft?"

"I don't *want* her, I…" Scowling, he cut himself short. "Never mind. It is not important."

"It sounds important." She narrowed her eyes at him. "Did you and she have a row? Because if you cannot manage to be polite for a day, this is going to be a very long month."

Yes, it was.

But not for the reason his sister meant.

He should have been glad that Evie wasn't sitting at the table. Four days ago, he would have welcomed her absence. But that was before.

Before she'd made him smile.

Before she'd challenged him with her wit.

Before she'd tempted him with her lips.

He had hoped to settle things between them once and for all in the stone garden, but all he'd done was make an arse of himself and incite her anger. Well deserved, as he still couldn't believe he had actually referred to her as his cousin. An attempt, however poor, at tricking his mind into thinking of her as family. But the decadent things he wanted to do with Evie, to do *to* Evie, made her as far from family as she could possibly get.

What the devil would it take to purge himself of her?

Ignoring her hadn't worked.

Kissing her had only made everything worse.

He wouldn't disgrace her by making her his mistress...and marriage was out of the question unless he wanted to feel like this for the rest of his life, which he decidedly did *not*.

He could pay her to go away, as he'd intended to do originally. But that would only place her out of sight...not out of mind. A way to treat the symptoms while the virus ran rampant beneath the surface.

No, what he needed was a real solution.

A *permanent* solution.

As he drank his port and took a slow, measured glance around the table at all of the lords and ladies feasting upon his food and wine, the answer occurred to him.

Just like that.

He couldn't marry Evie.

But someone else could.

"By God, that's it," he murmured.

"What is it?" Brynne asked.

"Nothing," he said even as the wheels began churning in his head.

The only way to make himself stop obsessing over Evie day and night was to make her inaccessible to him. He wanted her now because there was nothing to keep him from having her. But if she was another man's wife...if she was another man's wife then he would be forced to stop this ill-fated pursuit.

It was a perfect idea. He didn't know why he hadn't thought of it sooner. And the house party was the perfect venue. Why, there are least three eligible bachelors sitting at the table right now. All he needed to do was make a few discreet inquiries, settle Evie with a modest dowry (not too much for fear of attracting fortune-hunters, but enough that she'd draw the attention of a nobleman of means), and choose the best of the lot.

Not Lord Markham. The viscount was in possession of both wealth and a title, but a worse scoundrel Weston had never met.

Lord Hendrickson was also out of the running, as his debts were as inflated as his ego.

That left Mr. Greer, who was a good candidate...but most of his investments were tied up with the railway and if that failed, how was he to adequately support a wife and children?

Weston drummed his fingers along the stem of his glass. More guests would be joining them on the morrow, and he was sure that one among them would be suitable. He needed a pleasant fellow. No disorderly rogues or rakes, but a gentleman who minded both his manners and his affairs. Certainly, he'd need to be patient. A tad boring. The male equivalent of Lady Martha, when it came right down to it. Surely that wouldn't be *too* hard to find.

As the cloud above him dissolved, Weston finished off his port and raised his glass to indicate he'd like another...to celebrate the end of all his American problems.

EVIE COULD NOT sleep.

She had tried.

For what felt like hours, she'd tossed and turned and then turned and tossed. But while her limbs were heavy, her mind was not. It was racing, in all directions, no matter how hard she tried to curb its frantic flight.

Just shy of midnight, she gave up and tiptoed from her room so as not to wake Posy. Full from a bottle, the lamb was sleeping peacefully in a basket beside the bed.

Slipping into a pair of flat, soft-soled shoes and drawing on a long wrapper with blue bows stitched down the front, she tied it closed at the waist and padded silently into the hall. From there she descended the main staircase and, using a candle and memory to guide her, made her way out to a stone terrace.

Formed in the shape of a half-moon, it offered a clear view of the pond. Silver light glimmered on the glassy surface, but there was no sign of the swans. They, along with everyone else, were undoubtedly resting, their heads free of an earl with piercing gray eyes.

She hugged her arms close to her chest as she went to the edge of the terrace and leaned against the railing. From somewhere across the lawn, she could hear the chirp of crickets and the trickling water of the fountains. It made for a soothing melody, and but for the fractious nature of her thoughts, she might have been lured into slumber.

A good thing she wasn't, perhaps, for then she would not have heard the creak of the door on its hinges followed by the drawl of a deep, unfamiliar voice.

"Either I've successfully drunk myself into a stupor and you are a hallucination, or else I am dreaming." Wearing the lopsided smirk of someone who had imbibed heavily in spirits, the handsome stranger shared Weston's dark hair and gray eyes, although his were lighter and far less solemn. He was larger as well; broader in both his face and his shoulders. Weaving an uneven line, he tottered over to her and bounced into the railing with a grunt. "Bollocks. Didn't see that there."

"It's very dark," she said, biting back a smile. While he was obviously foxed (if his slurred speech and stumbling hadn't given him away, the scotch on his breath surely would have), the man seemed harmless enough. And charming besides, especially when he swept off his hat and lowered himself into an exaggerated bow.

"You, my darling, must be Miss Thorncroft. Or else an angel sent from heaven above." His eyebrows wiggled suggestively. "Might I have a peek at your wings?"

"The last I checked, I hadn't any of those." She canted her head to the side. "How do you know who I am?"

"A lucky guess. And Weston told me you were here. Though he failed to mention you were even more gorgeous than your sister. Then, I've always preferred brunettes to redheads. Less prone to fits of temper." He scratched his chin thoughtfully. "But Kincaid seems smitten enough, so maybe I need to consider widening my horizons."

Evie was taken aback. "You-you know Joanna and Mr. Kincaid?"

"Aye. They're working on my case. Met with them right before I came here."

Had everyone known her sister was still in London except for her?

"Who *are* you?" she wondered aloud.

"Sterling Nottingham, Duke of Hanover, at your service." With a cheerful grin, he tossed his hat over the edge of the terrace. Then he frowned. "Did you see where that went?"

"No, I am afraid I did not."

"That was my second favorite hat," he said, peering over the railing.

Her lips twitched. "Then I'd advise you to be more careful with your favorite."

"You're probably right." With a sigh, Sterling crossed his arms. "Seems I'm losing everything these days."

"I'm not surprised, if you do to them what you just did to your hat."

His frown deepened. "I didn't toss my mistress over the balcony, if that's what you're implying."

Evie blinked. This was, she reflected, one of the most bizarre conversations she'd ever had. And it was only getting stranger by the second. "I'd never dare imply such a thing." She paused. "*Was* your mistress thrown over a balcony?"

"Last I checked, I dumped her in the Thames."

She started to laugh. Then her eyes widened. "You're serious."

"Yes. No," he corrected hastily when she started to slowly back away from him. "I mean, I don't know. What happened to her, that is. There was blood. Lots of it. And I was the last person to see her alive. Except for the killer, naturally. Whoever he is. But that's for Kincaid to figure out."

Evie considered his words. "I actually think I might have followed that. Maybe."

"I'm glad someone did." For an instant, the duke's countenance crumpled into misery. Then he cleared his throat, and flashed her another grin, this one even brighter than the last. "But enough about me and my misfortune. Tell me about yourself, Miss Thorncroft, and how it came to be that you're standing all alone on a terrace in the middle of the night."

She pulled her wrap more snugly around her shoulders. "I could not sleep."

"Fancy a nip?" Sterling asked, removing a flask from the inside pocket of his emerald green jacket. "Does the trick for me. Except when it doesn't."

As she eyed the flask, it occurred to Evie that this, right here, was one of the reasons she'd agreed to come to London in the first place. To find the ring and uncover Joanna's secret parentage, yes, of course. That was, without question, her main motivation for leaving Claire and her grandmother behind. But she would be lying if she didn't admit that she had also held out hope for a private rendezvous with a handsome duke. A rendezvous that would have blossomed into a courtship, and that courtship into a proposal.

Her Grace, Evelyn Nottingham…the Duchess of Hanover.

Now *that* would have set all of Somerville back on its heels.

If everything had gone as she'd first envisioned it, she'd be in a gown instead of a nightdress. With champagne in crystal flutes instead of scotch in silver flasks, and the strains of a waltz dancing on the air instead of chirping crickets. Most importantly of all, she wouldn't be standing in front of a duke…and secretly wishing he was an earl.

"I shouldn't," she told Sterling. "The last time I drank from one of those I found myself with a lamb."

Sterling chuckled. Tilting the flask to his lips, he guzzled down what remained and then returned it to his pocket. "Petunia, isn't it? I met the little fur ball yesterday. Never seen a sheep in a parlor before. Thought Weston had adopted a new breed of dog until it bleated at me."

"Posy," corrected Evie. "And she's very clean."

Sterling gave a jerk of his shoulder. "You don't have to convince me, darling. It's not my estate. What does our good friend Weston have to say about a sheep living in his house?"

As she turned to look at the pond, tension pulled her brows inward as if they were attached to tiny, invisible strings that automatically tightened whenever Weston's name was mentioned. "I do not care what his opinion of Posy is, and he is not my friend, good or otherwise," she said curtly.

"Well you can't stop *there*." After giving her a playful nudge with his elbow, Sterling rested his forearms on the railing and joined her in gazing out at the water. "What has he done now? If you've an especially heinous grievance to report, I can call him out for you. Pistols at dawn and all that."

If only it were that easy.

"While I appreciate your offer, I don't think a bullet would solve this specific problem."

"Maybe not. But surely it couldn't hurt to see him writhing in temporary agony."

Evie pursed her lips. "That's true."

"Alas, given my current reputation, I don't know if I'd be able to get anyone to stand in as my second. Besides, any bullet I fired would probably just bounce right off all that icy armor Weston wears and strike me instead." Sterling grimaced. "What if it hit this gorgeous face of mine? I'd be ruined."

"And dead, most likely."

"That, too." He contemplated the pond for a moment. "I like you, Miss Thorncroft."

"The feeling is mutual, Your Grace."

"None of that 'Your Grace' business. Hanover if you must, and Sterling if you'd prefer. That's what all of my closest acquaintances call me." A boyish grin teased the left-hand corner of his mouth. "And plotting the murder of our host has almost definitely made us close acquaintances."

"Sterling, then." What a shame, she thought silently, that she'd met him *after* Weston. Especially since the Duke of Hanover was everything that the Earl of Hawkridge was not. Amusing, charming, and kind.

She stole a peek at Sterling, willing herself to feel the same spark for him that she did for Weston. It didn't even have to be a spark. Just a flicker, really. But much to her annoyance, there was nothing. The duke may have exhibited all of the behavior that she knew Weston was capable of if he'd just lower that damned guard of his, but he *wasn't* Weston. Her traitorous heart, against the sound advice of her head, had made its choice. And now she had to live with the consequences.

"I believe I am going to return inside," she told Sterling. "But I'd like to thank you for the company."

"Happy to provide it." His grin faded. His eyes grew serious. "I've a question to ask you, Miss Thorncroft."

"Evie," she said lightly. "Call me Evie."

There might not have been a spark between them, but that did not mean she and Sterling couldn't be friends. She *did* like him. In an affable, companion sort of way. Although, given his inebriated state, there was a very good chance he wasn't even going to remember that they'd even spoken come morning.

"Evie." He pivoted away from the railing and took her hands in his. "Would you–is Evie short for something?"

"Evelyn," she said, struggling not to giggle at the sheer absurdity of the situation. Standing outside on a terrace holding hands with a drunk duke whom she had no romantic interest in because she had gone and fallen in love with an earl who was incapable of love.

If she *didn't* laugh, she feared she'd start to cry.

Again.

"Evelyn," Sterling declared with great dramatic flair. "I–what was I saying?"

"You were about to ask me a question."

"Ah, that's right. Evelyn, sweet Evelyn...would you like to be my mistress?"

Evie stared. "Your mistress."

"Indeed," he said cheerfully. "As it so happens, the position has recently become available. I wasn't looking to fill it straightaway, to be honest. But you're you, and I'm me, and us pretty people need to stay together. In bed. Without clothes. Don't you agree?"

For the second time in as many days, she found herself rendered utterly speechless. "I...I am incredibly flattered by your offer, but...but I have to decline. I am sorry."

"Is it because my previous mistress died under nefarious circumstances?" he said glumly, dropping her hands.

"There is that," she acknowledged. "But also because...I'm not sure how to say this, actually, but..."

"You're in love with Weston." Taking out his flask again, Sterling gave it a shake. "Did you drink the rest of my brandy?"

"No. Your Grace–"

"Sterling."

"Sterling, I…how do you know that?" she blurted. "That I'm…I'm…"

"In love with Weston," he repeated.

Her face heated. "Yes. I haven't told anyone. I've barely admitted it to myself. So how do you know?" Hope kindled in her breast, slight as the breeze created by a butterfly's wing. "Did-did Weston *say* something? Or do something to indicate that he…he may feel a similar way about me?"

"Not a thing," Sterling replied.

"Of course he didn't," she said, unable to keep the bitterness from creeping into her tone as her hope was extinguished. "Why would he? I am a *lapse in judgment*."

How she hated those words! Almost as much as she hated that she couldn't get them out of her head.

The duke snorted. "Is that what he told you?"

"Among other things," she muttered, glancing at the ground.

"Weston's a bloody idiot, especially when it comes to anything to do with love. Due to his father, I suspect."

"His father?" Evie looked up. "What did the marquess do?"

"More like what he did *not* do. Men don't discuss such things, you understand." Sterling gave her a stern look. "It is a threat to our masculinity. But as my odds of remembering this conversation are slim to none, I suppose it won't cause permanent damage to my exceedingly fragile manhood to tell you that the Marquess of Dorchester was, shall we say, apathetic towards his children. And that is putting it kindly."

Evie gasped in dismay. "You mean…you mean he beat them?"

"No, no, nothing like that. But it might have been kinder if he had, as that would have shown *some* emotional investment. No, Weston's father was simply…nonexistent. As much as I could tell, anyway. Weston and I were schoolmates at Eton, and never–not once in four years–did I see the marquess step foot on school grounds. For some reason, Weston still believed he would be there for our convocation. It was the most excited I'd ever seen him."

Evie's heart wrenched as she imagined a young, hopeful Weston, waiting to see his father's face in the crowd of proud parents. "But the marquess never came, did he?"

Sterling shook his head. "Sent his solicitor in his place. The cold-hearted bastard. Weston never said a word. Never complained. Never even got angry, as far as I could tell. But the next I saw him, he was…different. More contained. More reserved. As if he'd decided that by shutting himself off from everything and everyone, he would never have to be disappointed like that again."

"That's horrible," she whispered. But it did help to explain the earl's standoffish behavior. The way he could burn hot one second, and freeze her out the next. The internal battle he always seemed to be fighting.

She could barely remember her mother. But her father had helped shape her into the woman she was today. If he hadn't shown her compassion, or empathy…if he'd never wrapped his arms around her when she was feeling sad, or rested his hand on her shoulder when she needed support…wouldn't she, too, have become hard? Like clay left untouched when it should have been molded, and shaped, and loved.

"Maybe if the marchioness had lived…" Sterling shrugged. "Who is to say? All I know is that Weston is who he is, and barring some unforeseen miracle, that's unlikely to change. But if you should ever like to reconsider being my mistress, I remain at your disposal." He gave another bow, even more elaborate than the last, and nearly followed his hat over the railing.

"I should think it is time for both of us to seek our beds," said Evie, reaching out to steady him. "I am glad we had this opportunity to speak, and I am grateful to have made a friend. But to be clear, I will not be reconsidering anything."

Sterling slapped a hand over his heart. "A crushing let down, to be sure."

She bit the inside of her cheek to contain her grin. "I am fairly confident that you will not be lacking for attention over the next few weeks."

"That is true," he said, brightening.

They walked through the terrace doors together and stopped at the base of the staircase. She did not know for how long they'd been outside, but the sconces on the walls had sputtered down to their wicks, causing her to reach for the railing as a guide as she made her way up the steps with Sterling trailing behind.

"Goodnight," she told him once they'd reached the top.

"Sweetest of dreams, darling Evelyn," he mumbled, his eyes closing as he leaned heavily against the wall. "The one who got away."

Rogue, she thought with the same sort of mild affection she might have bestowed upon a brother. "Evie is fine, but I'd prefer Miss Thorncroft in public lest people be led to believe I entertained or even accepted your incorrigible offer."

A gray eye slit open. "Ah, but Evelyn is going to drive our good earl mad with envy."

Her ears pricked.

Oh it would, would it?

Ordinarily, she'd never consider deploying such petty means by which to gain attention. But when Weston had reduced their physical connection to a regrettable error, he'd thrown down a gauntlet. And having purged herself of self-pity and tears, she was ready to pick it up.

"Well, in that case..." she said, a coy smile stealing across her lips. "Evelyn it is."

CHAPTER THIRTEEN

"LATE NIGHT?" WESTON asked Sterling as the two men rode back to Hawkridge Manor after a brisk gallop through the neighboring fields and the duke delivered a jaw-cracking yawn. His fourth, by Weston's estimation.

"In fact, it was." Allowing the gelding he rode its head, Sterling slumped in his saddle and dragged a hand across his face. His eyes were bloodshot, his cheeks flushed. He'd stopped thrice to take a piss, and had been gulping water from his flask–Weston hoped it was water–like a damned fish. "I might have had a few too many nips of scotch last night."

"What gave you that indication?" Weston said dryly as they reached the stable courtyard and dismounted. Or rather, Weston dismounted. Sterling rolled off his horse like a potato sent down a chute and staggered for a bit before ultimately giving in to the demands of gravity and falling straight on his arse.

Handing his mount to a groom, Weston removed his gloves and tucked them into the waistband of his breeches before he held out his hand and hauled the duke back onto his feet, only to recoil in disgust as a very potent odor invaded his nostrils.

"Bloody hell, man. You've the stench of a distillery."

"Aye," Sterling agreed. "But it's a fine Scottish distillery."

Weston looked at the flask the duke was cradling against his chest like a precious babe, then back at Sterling. His eyes narrowed. "Is that the rest of my–"

"Glenavon scotch? Indeed." Sterling's grin was unrepentant. "As I said, it's an excellent vintage."

"You mean it *was* an excellent vintage," Weston grumbled as they walked towards the manor. "That was the last bottle I had."

"Then we'll just have to find Lord Campbell and get another. I've heard the Highlands are nice this time of year. Lots of buxom young maidens dashing about in plaid."

Weston lifted a brow. "Are whisky and wenches all you think about?"

"What else is there?" Sterling asked, appearing genuinely confused.

Ending a long day in the arms of the woman you love and waking up beside her in the morning.

The thought, as unbidden as it was unwanted, nearly caused Weston to stumble over thin air. As if *he'd* been the one who had spent the night drinking instead of Sterling. Something he would be hard pressed to do after the fact, given that the duke had polished off his best scotch.

"Let's just get you inside and cleaned up," he said shortly. "There's a breakfast this morning and a picnic outing planned for this afternoon. If I have to attend, then so do you."

"Shoot me now and be done with it," Sterling groaned.

Weston knew the feeling.

For a boy who had once yearned for companionship, it was the very height of irony that he had grown up into a man who despised it.

The loud noises, the socialization, the fawning attention from mothers who wanted nothing more than for their daughters to become countesses...if not for the obligation he felt to continue the tradition his grandfather had started, he would have ended the house party long ago.

At least Brynne enjoyed the planning and playing the part of hostess, for as much as it took her away from her painting. A role his twin would be subsequently released from once he was married to Evie.

No.

Not Evie.

Lady Martha, he corrected himself.

He was going to marry Lady Martha, whose carriage would be arriving within the hour. And Evie was going to marry a respectable nobleman of his choosing (which almost certainly ruled out Sterling, duke or not). They'd see each other occasionally at balls and at the theater, whereupon they would nod and smile politely, the time he'd brought her to rapturous release with the lap of his tongue and clutched her thighs as she trembled against him in tiny little aftershocks of pleasure all but forgotten.

Yes.

That was *exactly* what was going to happen.

He'd bet his last bottle of Glenavon scotch on it.

If he had a bottle of Glenavon scotch to bet with.

As Weston entered the foyer, he was relieved to see that it was blissfully quiet save for the rustling of servants as they dashed hither and yon, their arms filled with an assortment of linens and tea services. Given the early hour, all of the guests were either abed or preparing for the day that lay ahead. He didn't need to look at the schedule Brynne had given him, complete with dark lines and circles to emphasize the events where his presence was required, to know what was to occur. The first full day of the house party was invariably the same: a grand breakfast in the solarium, followed by a tour of the grounds and then a late outdoor luncheon on a hilltop with magnificent views of the entire estate. In the evening hours, the ladies and gentlemen would retreat to their respective corners, where they'd play whist or sip port and then retire to bed only to do it all over again on the morrow.

It was to be a long, repetitive month. The same as last year, and the year before that, and the year before that. The only difference of note *this* year was that when the house party concluded, he would have a fiancée. All he had left to do was pick how and when he wanted to propose.

Originally, he had planned to wait until the grand ball on the very last night. Take Lady Martha out to the gardens, compliment the way the moonlight shone in her hair or some other such nonsense, and get down on bended knee. She'd undoubtedly burst into tears of joy, he would slip his mother's ring onto her finger, and they would return to the ballroom to ringing applause.

It would be a perfectly suitable beginning to a perfectly suitable marriage.

Except...except he didn't know what color her eyes were.

How could he plan a proposal if he didn't know the color of her eyes?

He was fairly certain they were brown.

Or maybe hazel.

Gray?

He *did* know that Lady Martha's eyes weren't blue. Or if they were, they paled in comparison to Evie's vivid cerulean gaze.

And here he was, thinking about Evie once again.

"Bloody hell," he muttered, raking a hand through his hair. Damp with sweat from his ride, it nearly stood on end as he turned his attention to Sterling who'd gone into the adjoining parlor and, by all outward signs, had fallen asleep on a velvet settee.

"You're going to frighten the guests," he said, nudging the duke's boot as he walked by on his way to a sideboard that had been set with a modest assortment of breads, jams, fruit, and coffee for any early risers who might make their way downstairs in search of a bite to eat before the more formal breakfast was served.

Pouring himself a cup of dark, aromatic coffee, he added a splash of cream and then settled himself at a spindle-legged table across from Sterling who had begun to snore.

"Has the duke fallen ill?" Brynne queried some five minutes later when she swept into the parlor, looking as fresh as a daisy in a yellow dress trimmed with white.

"No, just the victim of a late night with a flask of my best scotch," Weston said with a disgruntled glance at Sterling. "You're up early."

"I am running nearly half an hour behind, actually. With the Smethwicks and Hodgesons due this morning before breakfast, and an unexpected guest to join us later this afternoon, it is going to be a busy day." Crossing briskly to the sideboard, she prepared a cup of tea before joining her brother at the table.

In unison, they sipped their collective beverages and stared at Sterling.

"If I stood accused of murder, I would probably be driven to drink as well." Brynne's nose wrinkled as a particularly loud sound erupted from the duke's nasal cavities. "Although I'd never snore as loud as that. Heavens, he sounds like a boar."

"A dying boar, maybe."

"Should we wake him?" she asked.

"I'd give him a few minutes longer," Weston said charitably. "Then call for a maid to dump a bucket of cold water on his head."

"He won't take kindly to that."

"No, most likely not."

Pursing her lips, Brynne blew a spiral of steam off the top of her tea. "Have you spoken to Miss Thorncroft?"

Coffee nearly sloshed over the rim of Weston's cup as his hand jolted. He quickly composed himself. "Why would you ask me that?"

"Because you were looking for her last night at the dinner," she reminded him. "I was just wondering if you'd found her."

"No, I haven't seen her. Who is the unexpected guest you mentioned?" He set his cup down to glare suspiciously at his sister. "It best not be Joanna Thorncroft."

One disruptive American under his roof was more than enough.

What the devil would he do with two of them?

"As much as I would like to have our sister here–" Brynne began.

"Half-sister," he interrupted.

She rolled her eyes. "You'll have to meet Joanna eventually. Sister or half-sister, she is our *sister* and I should like very much to have some kind of relationship with her, even if it is through letters sent across the Atlantic."

"A letter wouldn't be necessary. According to the Duke of Hanover, it seems Joanna has chosen to temporarily remain in London."

"Why, that's splendid!" Brynne cried. "You may not think so, West, but she and Evie never came here to do us harm. They wanted to find their family, and their mother's ring. You cannot continue to fault them for that."

"I don't," he admitted gruffly.

"You-you don't?" she asked with marked surprise. "When did you come to that realization?"

After I kissed Evie and the sun shone brighter, the air tasted sweeter, and my heart started to beat again.

He grimaced into his coffee. "I may have reacted...rashly when I first discovered our father's affair. I was angry with him, and I took that anger out on the Thorncrofts. Unfairly, it would appear."

"I've always found anger to be easier than acceptance," Brynne said quietly.

"Yes." Now it was he who looked at his twin with surprise. "Precisely. Now that cooler heads have prevailed, I've reconsidered my original position."

"Then we *can* host Joanna!" She clapped her hands. "How delightful. I'll send a carriage to collect her straightaway."

"No," he snapped. "Absolutely not."

By openly welcoming Joanna into his life and into his home, he'd be inadvertently extending the same invitation to Evie. And he wasn't about to go through all the trouble of finding her a husband just to have her waltzing back into his life whenever the mood struck.

It was one thing to tell a child they couldn't have candy and then put it up high on a shelf out of their reach. It was quite another to tell them it was forbidden and then dangle it right in front of their nose.

"Why?" Brynne inquired. "Joanna's sister is here, *and* her cousin. I can think of no better time to welcome her to Hawkridge Manor."

"Because…" As he couldn't tell his twin the truth, he struggled to find another reasonable excuse for not welcoming Joanna to the estate with all haste. "Because she is working for the private detective Sterling hired to exonerate him of murder, and I wouldn't want to distract her from such an important endeavor."

"Surely she can spare a *few* days," Brynne argued.

"Even if she could, do you really believe this to be the best environment in which to host a warm family reunion?" he asked with a sardonic tilt of his mouth. "The speculation and gossip incited by the sudden arrival of our father's illegitimate daughter would be all anyone spoke of for the duration of the house party. I doubt very much that Joanna would care to be the recipient of such attention."

Brynne frowned. "I hadn't thought of that."

"Once the Season commences and we're all in London, I will make it a point to extend an invitation."

"And if she's left England by then?"

"We'll send a letter."

Brynne raised her tea to her lips, then paused. "Your reluctance to have Joanna come to Hawkridge Mason wouldn't have anything to do with the *other* Miss Thorncroft, would it?"

"Nothing," he lied. "Why do you ask?"

"No reason. Other than you've been exhibiting strange behavior ever since you and Evie arrived. If I didn't know better…"

"If you didn't know better?" he prompted when she trailed away.

"I might start to suspect that you really *do* have feelings for her."

He pushed his chair away from the table. "We're not discussing this again."

"But–"

"Do not press me on this, Brynne. The matter has already been settled." Standing, he pointed his finger at her. "And don't think I wouldn't find out about the heart soaps."

"Those were all in good fun," she said with an airy flick of her wrist. "You needn't be so *serious* all of the time, West. It is going to give you indigestion."

"I'll be fine." He glanced at Sterling.

Good God.

Was that *drool* dribbling out of the side of the duke's mouth?

"What should we do with him?" Brynne asked, following his gaze.

"When will the Smethwicks and the Hodgesons be here?"

She rose to her feet. "In time for the breakfast, which is at half-past ten. You shall need to change out of your riding attire."

Weston nodded. "I'd planned on it. As for Sterling...we'll leave the poor sod him where he is for the time being. If he doesn't wake in the next hour, I'll send in a bucket. Meanwhile, we can direct the guests to the drawing room for coffee and tea."

The twins quit the parlor, making sure to close the door behind them.

"One final thing," he said absently as Brynne prepared to flit off to the solarium to ensure everything was being prepared to her exact specifications. "Sterling drank my last bottle of Glenavon scotch. Have you been in communication with Lord Campbell as of late? I know the two of you were close–"

The teacup his sister had carried with her out of the parlor fell to the ground with a loud *crack* and broke into pieces. On a gasp, she knelt and began to gather the shards until a maid rushed forward and took over the task.

"Are you all right?" Weston asked with concern. Taking Brynne by the elbow, he guided her to the foot of the staircase. "Did you cut yourself?"

Snatching her arm away, she curled it in tightly against her chest.

"No, I...I am fine. The cup slipped. That's all. To answer your question, I have not been in communication with Lachlan. Nor should I *ever* care to hear his name again."

With that, she hurried away...leaving Weston to wonder if his wasn't the only conflicted heart at Hawkridge Manor.

CHAPTER FOURTEEN

LADY ELLINWOOD'S GOUT had worsened overnight. An unfortunate turn of events for Evie's great-aunt (the condition was rumored to be quite uncomfortable), and an unexpected reprieve for her cousin, as it allowed Rosemary to sneak out from beneath her grandmother's thumb.

Taking full advantage of her cousin's temporary freedom, Evie had spent the early hours of the morning scrubbing, combing, and yanking all of the bandoline out of Rosemary's scalp. When she was finally finished, she was pleased to discover her cousin's hair were as beautiful as she'd suspected it would be. Soft and glossy with golden undertones, loose curls framed a face wide-eyed with astonishment as Rosemary stared at her reflection in the mirror.

Going through her various assortments of creams and powders, Evie had added a light dusting of rouge to define her cousin's cheekbones and a streak of kohl along her lash line to draw out the gray in her eyes. A thin layer of beeswax on the lips, and–

"I don't recognize myself," Rosemary breathed.

Inordinately pleased with the results she'd achieved, Evie met her cousin's gaze in the mirror and grinned. "Just wait until we get you into a dress from this decade."

When all was said and done, Rosemary no longer resembled a spinsterish wallflower. Instead, she absolutely shone in a gown of mint green silk with ruched sleeves and a scoop-necked bodice that flattered her bosom instead of hiding it, as if her natural curves were something to be ashamed of.

"You will have men fighting over you left and right," Evie predicted.

"Oh, I sincerely hope not," Rosemary said in dismay. "I wouldn't know the first thing to say to them. Usually, no one ever tries to speak directly to me if they can help it. I think it's because of Sir Reginald. For some reason, he makes people nervous."

"I can only assume it is because they are accustomed to seeing woodland creatures in the woods, not peeking out from your reticule. But you shan't have to worry about that presently, as Sir Reginald has remained at home. Here, put these on." Evie handed her cousin a pair of white kid gloves that extended up past the wrist and ended in lace. "There. As far as talking to men is concerned, all you need to do is smile and nod at whatever they say."

"That's it?" Rosemary said doubtfully.

"That's it," Evie promised. Returning to her dressing table, she dabbed a circular brush into a pot of pigmented chalk and dusted it beneath her eyes to disguise the dark shadows that loomed there courtesy of her late-night chat with the Duke of Hanover. "Most men like nothing more than to discuss themselves and their favorite hobbies in great detail, and if you give them the opportunity to do so, they will fill an entire conversation with the proper way to tie a fly for trout fishing."

"That sounds interesting. How *do* you tie a fly for trout fishing?"

"I haven't the vaguest idea. I don't actually *listen* to what they're saying. I just pretend to."

"And they never guess? That you're just pretending?"

Evie slowly lowered the brush. "Most of them don't, no."

"What about the ones who do?"

"They're rarely worth the trouble." She fixed a smile on her face.

"It's almost time for the welcome breakfast. Why don't you go, and save me a seat. There's one last thing I want to fix with my hair, and then I will join you momentarily."

"All right." Off Rosemary flitted, leaving Evie alone. Even Posy was gone, having been taken on a walk by Hannah.

Turning her palms inward and pressing them on the edge of the dressing table, Evie met her own stare in the mirror. She'd needed every bit of her talent with creams and potions to disguise the lack of color in her face and the drab texture of her skin. Losing her heart to Weston, it seemed, did not agree with her. Like coming down with a cold, or having an allergic reaction to a sting. If the poets *really* wanted to capture what being in love was like, they could start by being honest about it.

As she saw him
Standing there
Her heart galloped
And her skin glistened
With red hives
All over her body

Let Elizabeth Barrett Browning write *that* and then see how many women wanted to fall in love.

Evie was willing to bet the number would shrink considerably.

After all, why would anyone want to feel as she did?

Hopeful and anxious.

Excited and tired.

Happy and afraid.

If any more emotions tried to fit inside of her, she might burst!

And there'd be no amount of rouge in the world to fix *that* mess.

Her one bright spot in a sky of clouds was that following her unusual interlude with Sterling, she had a better understanding of Weston. And she was going to use that newfound knowledge to her advantage.

She *needed* to use it. Because Martha Smethwick was arriving today.

The woman Weston wanted to marry.

The woman he *would* marry, unless Evie convinced him that she was a better match.

Unless she convinced him that she was a better wife.

A better partner

A better lover.

Dissatisfied with the way she'd curled her hair (this morning, especially, she needed to look her very best as she was formally presented to the other guests, having skipped the receiving dinner the night before) she began to remove the pins in an attempt to loosen her coiffure, and had three of them clamped between her lips when the door unexpectedly slammed inward and Hannah rushed inside.

"Miss Thorncroft!" she cried.

"*Mmmrpph?*" Evie replied, startled by the intrusion. She spat out the pins. "Hannah, what is it?" She took in the streaks of dirt on Hannah's apron, and mob cap sitting askew on the side of the maid's head. "What on earth happened?"

"It was Drufus, Miss Thorncroft." Tears welled in Hannah's eyes as her hands knotted beneath her chin. "I didn't know he was outside."

"Who is Drufus?" Evie asked blankly. "One of the guests?" Her voice rose to a shrill, indignant pitch. "Did one of the *guests* do this to you?"

"No, Miss Thorncroft. Drufus is Lady Brynne's *hound.*"

And Hannah had been walking Posy.

"Oh no," Evie whispered as horrific images filled her head. Tiny and defenseless, the lamb wouldn't have stood a chance against a large dog. "Oh, Hannah, don't tell me–"

"What is going on in here?" Weston demanded as his large, rangy frame filled the doorway. He was dressed in gray trousers and a shirt that was only partially unbuttoned, his black hair damp and curling at the ends. "I thought I heard a shout."

"It's Posy," Evie said, her eyes stinging as she met Weston's gaze. There was a terrible wrenching in her chest, the same kind she'd felt when she had happened to glance out the window and saw four solemn-faced soldiers marching up with the drive...carrying a wooden casket between them. Before they reached the door, she knew. She knew what they were going to say. She knew who the casket contained. Just as she knew that her lamb, like her father, was gone.

And it was foolish to feel this way about a pet when she'd struggled to express her grief over a person. But she had loved Posy. In the same unfettered, careless way that she'd loved father. Careless not because she hadn't cared. But because she'd taken every day with him for granted, as if his presence in her life would never falter. As if his time with her would never end. As if there was always going to be a tomorrow.

Then he'd died. Their tomorrow *had* ended. And with the exception of her sisters and her grandmother, she'd never allowed herself to love like that again. Until she and Weston had stumbled upon an orphaned lamb crying for its mother...and her heart, closed all these years without her even realizing it, had cracked wide open.

"What about Posy?" Weston strode into the bedchamber. Ignoring Hannah, he went straight to Evie and cupped her cheek, his gray gaze intently searching hers. "What is it, Evelyn?"

Later, she would recognize that it was the first time he'd used her Christian name. But in the moment, her misery was too great to notice such small details. "Hannah was taking her for a morning walk. And...and there was a dog. A hound."

"Drufus." The earl closed his eyes. "He's a bloody nuisance, but mostly harmless. Except when he comes across small game. Evelyn...I am so very sorry."

As a single tear trickled across her cheek, she burrowed her face into chest. "She was only a baby."

"Actually–" Hannah began.

"I'll find you another lamb." Weston wrapped his arms around her, cocooning her in a sturdy, protective embrace. "We can go today. Right this minute. We'll get two, if you like. Three even. We'll fill the damned drawing room with lambs. Just...just don't cry."

"I don't want *another* lamb," she said, indignant that he would even dare suggest such a thing. "I want Posy."

"Pardon me," Hannah began, "but–"

"If I could bring her back for you, I would," Weston said huskily, stroking her back. "But find comfort in knowing her last few days were filled with adoration and kindness and warm bottles."

There *was* comfort to be found in that, but not enough to lighten the weight of all the anguish pressing on her shoulders. Distantly, she wondered how Posy's death could cause such sorrow. But then, like water flowing down a mountain, so did grief run through everything.

The pain of loss had no beginning, no end. It could be suppressed, but never forgotten. And as she mourned the loss of a lamb, Evie instinctively sensed it wasn't just Posy that she was grieving. And the Earl of Hawkridge wasn't the only one who had staved off his suffering by surrounding himself in ice.

How hard she'd work to convince herself not to believe in love! She'd even tried to push Joanna into the same mindset, demanding that her sister marry a local suitor not because she *loved* him, but because she did not. And if something perilous had ever happened to Charles Gaines, there would be sadness, but no heartbreak.

It was why...it was why Evie had pursued Weston. To make herself a countess, and get her mother's ring, yes. Those were the reasons she'd maintained on the surface. But the sudden loss of Posy forced her to dive deeper...and in those murky, turbulent waters, she faced the truth.

She had wanted Weston because she never truly thought she'd ever fall in love with him.

And now she wanted him because she had.

Even if it meant risking this terrible agony should he ever leave her.

"I should like a small memorial in Posy's honor," she said hollowly. "I know it probably sounds absurd, but a white stone, or a wooden marker–"

"Anything," Weston said instantly.

Lifting her head, she managed to smile through her tears. He was showing such a sweet side of himself. She'd suspected he was capable of such tenderness. No man who carried a lamb nestled in his arms for an untold number of miles could be all strength and stone. But to have such gentleness directed straight at her...was there any doubt why her frozen heart had melted for this man?

"Miss Thorncroft," said Hannah, hesitantly raising her arm in the air as Weston and Evie gazed into each other's eyes. "If I may...I have something to tell you...that is, I fear there may have been a misunderstanding..."

Evie stifled her irritation.

Couldn't the maid see that she was trying to have a moment here?

"What?" she and Weston exclaimed in unison.

Hannah flushed. "Posy...Posy isn't dead."

Stunned, Evie whirled out of Weston's arms. "She isn't?"

"That is what I've been trying to tell you s-since Lord Hawkridge came in." As the maid darted a quick peek at the earl, her cheeks turned even redder. "Drufus started to chase Posy but, thankfully, a footman managed to grab hold of him before he got to her."

"Then where is she?" asked Weston, splaying his hand across the small of Evie's back.

"I don't know," Hannah said helplessly. "That's why I came to Miss Thorncroft right away. I chased Posy to the stables, but then lost sight of her in the bushes."

The stables.

That was all Evie needed to hear.

She bolted out of the bedchamber, with Weston right behind her.

"But what about the breakfast?" When she nearly fell over her own skirts, Evie yanked them up past her knees. For once, she did not care what she looked like or what others might think of her. Her only concern was getting Posy back safe and sound. Drufus may have been apprehended, but there were any manner of other dangers that awaited a lamb wandering lost around the estate. She might be attacked by a hungry fox, or trampled by a horse, or drowned in the pond.

Evie couldn't allow that to happen.

They couldn't allow that to happen.

Because for once, she and Weston were in complete lock step.

"Hang the bloody breakfast," he said grimly. "This is more important. And this way is faster." Linking his fingers with hers in an ironclad grip, he pulled her to the left and they ran down a narrow servants' corridor that led to a staircase, and the staircase to a door.

Squinting when she stumbled out into the bright morning sunlight, Evie clung to Weston's hand as they raced across a lawn slick with silvery dew. She slipped, her flat slippers affording her no purchase on the wet grass, and she would have fallen had the earl not been there to catch her.

Sliding his arm around her waist, he hooked his fingertips into the curve of her hipbone and tucked her against his body.

"Easy," he murmured in her ear. "I've got you."

Her head turned and, for a split second, she found herself completely and utterly entranced by the stormy depths of his gaze. Beneath the bodice of her dress, her heart slammed violently against her ribcage.

Boom *boom*. Boom *boom*.

Her lips parted.

His eyes darkened.

They leaned in close.

Closer…

"*Baaaaaa.*"

From somewhere up ahead came the unmistakable bleat of a lamb, and the spell broke.

Weston cleared his throat. "We should, ah…"

"Yes," she nodded. "We should."

Keeping a wider distance than before, they hurried to the barn where a stable hand leading a sleek chestnut mare across the front paddock greeted them in surprise.

"My lord," he said, bringing the horse to a halt. "I wasn't told you would be embarking on another ride this morning. Should I have a mount readied for you, or–"

"That won't be necessary," Weston interrupted. "We're here for a sheep."

"A sheep," said the stable hand, appearing confused.

Evie could only assume it wasn't every day the Earl of Hawkridge walked into the stables demanding a farm animal that wasn't a horse.

"About this tall," she said, cupping her hands twelve inches apart. "White. Fluffy. Ears that stick out to the side."

"I am fairly confident he knows what a sheep looks like," Weston said dryly.

"A description cannot hurt anything," she defended.

The stable hand scratched underneath his cap. "Haven't seen any sheep here. Maybe it went to the pond? Something has the swans spooked. They haven't been in the water all morning that I've seen, which is unusual for them. Figured that old snapping turtle was back, but maybe your sheep went over to get a drink and frightened them."

"The pond," Evie repeated.

"This way," Weston said, grabbing her hand.

Off they went, across the lawn and around the side of the house. By the time they reached the pond, Evie was short of breath, but Weston didn't appear the slightest bit winded. On the contrary, their mad dash around the grounds of the estate seemed to have invigorated him.

The wind had swept his hair off his temple in a disheveled wave of obsidian silk. A button at the top of his shirt had come undone, revealing a golden swath of skin that was covered in a sheen of perspiration. There was a light in his eye that she'd never seen before. A glint of happy defiance, as if by temporarily leaving the manor and all of his responsibilities behind, he had stripped himself of the chains that bound him to duty and honor and obligation.

Standing beside the pond, he was just a man looking for a lamb.

And she was just a woman, looking at the man she loved.

While *also* looking for Posy, of course.

Even though Weston's muscular chest was, admittedly, very distracting.

A flash of movement out of the corner of her eye swung her attention to a thicket of reedy marsh plants. Hidden in the middle of them, her tiny tail swishing furiously, was Posy. Chewing on a cattail, of all things.

Warm, welcome relief flooded through Evie.

"Weston," she said, tugging on his sleeve to gain his attention. "There she is."

Kicking off his boots and rolling up his trousers, Weston waded into the water. It appeared Posy, in her eagerness to taste the cattails, had wandered into the pond and gotten trapped on a bank of mud. With a *squelching* sound, Weston pulled her free and extended his arms towards Evie so that she could grab the shivering lamb while he made his way out.

"There you are," she whispered, pressing her face into Posy's soft fleece. "I was terribly worried. You are not to run away like that again, do you understand? I know you're just an animal, and you cannot understand a word that I'm saying, but you're very special to me and I don't want to lose you."

Posy gave a bleat, which Evie took as a yes. Kissing the top of her head, she set the lamb down to dry off on the grass. The mud had gone all the way up to Posy's belly, and she was going to need another bath before she could return to the house.

By the look of things, Weston was going to require a bath as well.

"Are you stuck?" she called out, managing–just barely–not to chortle with laughter at the sight of the earl staggering through the muck. Given that he weighed considerably more than Posy, he'd sunk far deeper into the mud than she had. It was nearly up to his knees, and the harder he tried to get to the shore the higher it went.

"No," he gritted between clenched teeth, "I am not *stuck*."

"What a relief. Then if you're fine, I'll take Posy and–"

"Wait," he called out.

"Yes?" she chirped, batting her lashes.

He glared at her. "You're enjoying this, aren't you?"

"Am I enjoying the fact that the mighty Earl of Hawkridge is stuck in a pond with mud up to his waist and is now dependent on me to help him?" She tapped a finger against her chin. "Let me think...let me think...why, yes. Yes, I do believe I am. Immensely."

"Just find a stick, or a length of rope. Anything that I can use to pull myself out of this Godforsaken quagmire."

"I will," she assured him. "But first, you and I are going to have a chat."

Weston grimaced. "I'd rather not."

"Given your current predicament, I don't know if you have much of a choice. This may take a while. You don't mind if I make myself comfortable, do you?" Splaying out her skirts, she sank to the ground in a graceful flutter of muslin. "There. Now where were we?"

"I was considering letting the mud take me," he said darkly.

She clucked her tongue. "You needn't act as if a having conversation is the equivalent of nursing a sore tooth."

"Isn't it?"

Obstinate rogue, she thought with far greater affection than the first time she'd referred to him as such. Having reached a better understanding of her own feelings, especially those directed at the swamp monster standing in front of her, Evie wanted to clear the air between them. She wasn't nearly ready to confess her love for Weston. Not when there existed the *very* strong possibility that he'd reject her outright.

Last year, while experimenting with adding turmeric to one of her many face creams in an attempt to calm a horribly embarrassing rash of pimples across her cheeks, Evie had slathered the concoction over her entire face. All had seemed well...until she woke up the next morning and her skin was *orange*. That incident (which her sisters still teased her about) had taught her a valuable lesson.

When trying something new, it was best to test a small, inconspicuous spot first.

That's what she was doing with the earl.

Testing.

And keeping her fingers crossed that she did not turn into a fruit.

"I shall make it short and to the point, then," she said, bending her knees and looping her arms around them. "I did not care for the way you last spoke to me, Lord Hawkridge. Our so-called *encounters*, the majority of which *you* instigated, are not lapses in judgment. *I* am not a lapse in judgment."

"Miss Thorncroft—"

"I am not finished." There was, she found, a certain power in knowing that the individual you were speaking to *had* to listen. If this was how men felt when they addressed a room, it was no wonder they talked so much. "There is something between us, Lord Hawkridge. Something tangible. Like a...like a shock of electricity, or a bolt of lightning. And I know you feel it, too. I *know* you do."

A muscle ticked in his jaw. "I won't deny that there is a strong physical attraction between us, Miss Thorncroft. One that I did not anticipate or expect. I will also not deny that my prior use of words to describe our encounters was…poor. Be that as it may, continuing to act upon our baser instincts would be unwise."

"Why?" she asked, canting her head.

"Because…because it just would," he scowled.

"That isn't a reason," she pointed out.

"It's *my* reason."

"Do you want me to get a stick or not?"

"Fine." He threw up his arms. "Our passion must be quelled because there is no future for us, and although I am hardly a paragon of virtue, I am not so evil that I would ruin an innocent."

"Do you see no future between us because you love Lady Martha?"

"What?" His harsh laugh was loud enough to startle Posy, who came bounding over to Evie and hopped onto her lap, cloven hooves digging painlessly into her thighs. "No, I do not love Lady Martha. Why should I ever want to invite such chaos into my life?"

"But you intend to marry her." It was not a question, but a statement. One that Weston did not bother to refute.

"I fail to see where this discussion is headed. There is an apple tree behind you. If you could find a branch–"

"Why her?" Evie persisted. "You could have any woman you wanted. Why Lady Martha? Is there something special about *her* in particular?"

"We've common interests and she will be a satisfactory countess. Miss Thorncroft, the water is not exactly warm. If you'd like to continue this–"

"Have you kissed her like you kiss me?"

Weston's countenance went absolutely blank, like a page that the printing press had accidentally skipped over. "That is none of your concern."

"Then you haven't." That gave her *some* reason to hope. "Have you kissed her at all?"

"I believe this conversation has reached its conclusion. The stick, Miss Thorncroft." His gray eyes glittered with annoyance. "*Now.*"

Evie ignored him. A benefit of being the one on the shoreline.

"When all is said and done, don't you want your marriage to have been more than just satisfactory?" she asked quietly. "I do. I used to think such things were trivial. Love and lust and romance. That tingling sensation you get at the top of your spine when you meet the gaze of someone you desire. The breathless anticipation of that first kiss. The contentment to be found at sitting beside them for supper and sharing the events of your day. But in fact, it is those things, those *moments*, that are the most important of all, I think. Even more so because you cannot place a price upon them." A sad, poignant smile slipped across her lips. "All the titles and all the money in the world cannot purchase love, Lord Hawkridge. It is the one entity that cannot be bought or sold or traded. I wish I had understood that sooner. But I do now, and I know what I want because of it. Do you, my lord? Do *you* know what you want?"

As she met his angry gaze, Evie silently implored him to take that step off the ledge she knew he was capable of, if only because she'd taken it. And if she, the most cynical of all her sisters when it came to love, had permitted herself to fall...then surely Weston could, as well.

For a fraction of a second, there was a flicker in those steely gray eyes of his.

A softening.

A *yearning.*

But before that flicker had the opportunity to grow into a flame, his expression shuttered and all of his emotions were abruptly concealed behind a towering wall of ice that she feared herself incapable of penetrating even with the sharpest of chisels.

"What I *want* is get out of this bloody mud and to not be pestered with such ridiculous questions. This right here," he muttered, more to himself than to her, even though her ears were perfectly capable of hearing him. "This is exactly why I am going to marry Lady Martha Smethwick."

Evie stared at him. She'd poured out her heart. She'd emptied her very *soul*. Which wasn't exactly an easy thing to do for someone who equated being in love with breaking out in hives. And this–*this*–was his response?

Her limbs felt as if they were formed from wood as she stood and gathered Posy in her arms. "If you'd like to free yourself," she said coldly, "might I suggest calling upon your satisfactory fiancée for assistance."

"Where are you going?" he demanded when she began to walk away from the pond. "Miss Thorncroft? You cannot *leave* me here. Miss Thorncroft! God damnit. Don't you dare–"

Closing her ears to Weston's shouts, Evie sailed off towards the manor without looking back.

CHAPTER FIFTEEN

T HE DOOR SQUEAKED on its hinges as Rosemary hesitantly opened the wooden panel a few scant inches and peeked inside. She had waited for her cousin in the solarium for nearly twenty minutes, but it appeared they'd gotten the timing wrong, or else she was terribly early, for she'd been the only person there with the exception of the servants.

Ordinarily, she would have been content to remain in the company of the staff. She'd even brought a book with her, just in case. But all of the silver platters on the long banquet table were covered, and she was starving, and with no sign of the breakfast beginning anytime soon, she had marched off in search of food.

The manor was so vast that she hadn't the foggiest idea of which hallway led where, and not wanting to stray far from the solarium, she'd gone straight across the foyer to what she assumed to be a parlor. There was a low buzz of voices emanating from somewhere else but, as a general rule, Rosemary preferred not to socialize on an empty stomach. Truth be told, she preferred not to socialize at *all*, but the idea of trying to maintain a conversation while dreaming about blueberry cobbler was particularly abhorrent.

"Hello?" she said hesitantly. When there was no reply, she opened the door a bit wider and her empty belly rumbled with delight when she saw the array of pastries, coffee, and tea beckoning to her from across the room.

She'd nearly reached the table of sweets and was eyeing a plate of golden crumpets drizzled with raspberry jam when an unexpected masculine voice nearly had her leaping out of her borrowed dress.

"Oh my Sir Reginald!" she gasped, swirling around just in time to see a head pop up from the other side of a sofa. And not just *any* head. Oh, no. This head, with its tousled black hair sticking in every direction and pale, bloodshot eyes, belonged to none other than the Duke of Hanover.

Rosemary had never actually *met* the duke. Their social circles were such a distance apart they might as well have been on different planets. But she knew who he was. Everyone did. Because…well, because he was a duke. A *handsome* duke. A handsome duke who was not married, which had made him the target of every eligible miss in all of England and its surrounding countries. With Rosemary being the notable exception.

Not that she hadn't admired His Grace from afar. Just because she was a wallflower didn't mean she was blind. But while her nose was often in a book and her mind in the clouds, she had enough common sense to know that she had a better chance of tossing a knotted line of bedsheets into the night sky and catching a falling star than she did of catching the attention of the infamous Duke of Hanover.

"Could you be a love," he croaked, his voice rough as gravel, "and bring me a cup of coffee?"

Rosemary looked to her left, then to her right. "Are you…are you talking to *me?*"

Squinting, he sat up a little straighter and cast his arm across the back of the sofa. "Is there someone else here?"

Her eyes as wide as the crumpets she'd been on the brink of devouring, she slowly shook her head.

"Aye, then I'm talking to you. Coffee. Please." He blinked soulfully at her. "I'm begging you."

Rosemary's arm shook ever-so-slightly as she poured rich brown coffee, still steaming, out of a silver pot and into a cup. Carrying the cup around the front of the sofa she delivered it to the duke, and as she passed it from her hand to his, their fingers brushed. When a jolt passed through her at the small, accidental contact, she gasped and nearly spilled the hot liquid down the front of his shirt.

"You're a sweetheart," he groaned as he guzzled the coffee.

Rosemary experienced another jolt.

The Duke of Hanover had just called her a sweetheart.

Her, Rosemary Amelia Ursula Stanhope.

Clearly, he did not know to whom he was speaking.

Or maybe he did, and he was just being extraordinarily kind.

Like a baker who threw spare breadcrumbs for the pigeons.

Or a philanthropist who donated his old clothing to orphans.

"I…thank you, Your Grace."

"Have we met?" As he finished his coffee, his eyes–gray with thin streaks of red through the white–traveled across her with unnerving intensity. You look familiar. Wait–let me guess," he said when her lips parted. "You're Lord Henley's eldest daughter. Lady Victoria."

As shyness overtook her, Rosemary could only bite her lip and shake her head.

"No?" The duke's brow creased. He sat up even taller. "Lady Emma Crowley."

Lady Emma Crowley was blonde with green eyes.

She shook her head again.

"Hmm. I was sure I had it that time. Ah! Now I remember." With a roguish grin, he snapped his fingers. "Miss Penny Snow. How could I forget? Especially after that night we drank the champagne beside the fountain and you asked for me to search for your missing hairpin." He lifted a brow. "Such an odd place to find it, beneath your skirts. But there it was."

Heat exploded across Rosemary's face. "I-I-I am not Penny Snow," she stammered.

The duke's brow lowered. "Well then, who the devil are you?"

"N-no one of consequence, Your Grace."

"You have to be *someone*. Surely I would have noticed you before, unless…will this Season be your first? That's it," he said confidently. "You've not yet made your debut."

"I've attended every ball that you have been at for the past three years, Your Grace." Rosemary was not offended that he could not remember her name or even recall her face. Given how well she and the back corner were acquainted, she'd be more shocked if he *did* know who she was. A horse didn't notice a patch of weeds in the middle of its field. And the Duke of Hanover had no reason to notice a wallflower whose head was buried in a book more often than not.

"My name is Miss Rosemary Stanhope. I am under the guardian-ship of my grandmother, Lady Ellinwood."

The duke's gaze showed no signs of recognition.

"My cousins are Miss Evelyn and Miss Joanna Thorncroft," she tried as a last resort.

"*That's* why you appear so familiar to me. You look like them."

"I do?" she asked, inordinately pleased by the comparison. Evie and Joanna were two of the most beautiful women she'd ever seen. If the duke thought she and her cousins shared similar characteristics, then that could only mean he considered *her* to be beautiful as well. Evie's refashioning had worked! Before all that awful bandoline had been yanked out of her hair, no one had ever told her that she was beautiful. Mostly because they'd never taken the time to notice her, but also because she wasn't. Beautiful, that is. But who was she to argue with the Duke of Hanover? Even though he hadn't said as much in so many words, the implication was almost certainly there!

"Eh…" Lurching to his feet, he scraped a hand across the bristle covering his jaw and peered at her more closely. "Maybe not."

"Oh." Disappointment caused her shoulders to hunch, a bad habit that her grandmother had been trying unsuccessfully to break her of since adolescence. "That's–that's quite all right."

"'Tis your eyes. They're not blue enough."

"I'm...sorry?" she offered.

Without warning, the duke reached out and cupped her chin. His countenance a study in concentration, he turned her head from side to side, then brought their faces intimately together. Another half-inch, and their noses would be touching.

"Remarkable," he breathed.

Her chest rose and fell in quick succession. "What–what is?"

"Your eyes. The color of them. I've never seen the like before. Like the hazy light of dawn after a night filled with storms when everything is wet and ruined except for the sky. It's neither blue, nor gray, nor violet. But a combination of all three that tells the sailors the danger has passed and they can set their compasses for home." His thumb traced the edge of her jaw in a feathery-soft touch that caused her breath to quicken, and then stop altogether. "That's what color your eyes are, Rebecca. The color of home."

He gazed at her a moment more. And for an instant, Rosemary actually thought she might be kissed by the Duke of Hanover. Then he shook his head, as if waking from a trance. He grinned, gave a wink, and then he was gone, whistling a merry tune under his breath as he sauntered out of the parlor, leaving an open door and a shocked wallflower in his wake.

"Rosemary," she whispered, running her fingertips across her cheek where his hand had burned into her flesh. "My name is Rosemary."

WESTON WAS GOING to murder Evie.

After falling face first into the mud and crawling his way to shore, he had collapsed, exhausted, onto the bank...whereupon, he'd been chased away from the pond by a pair of hissing swans. Vowing to place swan stew on the dinner menu, he had retreated to the manor. But no sooner had he placed one muddy foot inside than Brynne had ordered him to go clean up in the stables.

"You *stink*," she'd told him, her nose wrinkling as she waved a hand in front of her face. "What happened? Never mind. I don't even want to know. I'll have your valet send out a change of clothes. Just make yourself presentable. And be sharp about it, as the breakfast is about to start and you are performing the opening toast."

And that was how the esteemed Earl of Hawkridge found himself to be bathing in a *horse trough* while dreaming up all sorts of ways to make Evie suffer for having the audacity to walk away from him. When he saw her again...when he saw her again, he had half a mind to draw her over his knee, flip up her skirts, and spank her bottom red.

Although that was likely to be more of an enticement than a punishment.

Bloody hell.

Even when he was furious with her, he still desired her.

Closing his eyes, Weston dunked his entire head into the cold water and ran his fingers through his hair. When he was finally cleaned, he emerged from the trough and met the amused gaze of his valet, Albert Jenkins, who'd been in his employ for the better part of a decade.

"Don't say a word," he warned.

"Wouldn't dream of it, my lord," Jenkins replied even as his brown eyes twinkled with merriment.

Cursing under his breath, Weston toweled himself dry and dressed quickly in the attire his valet had provided. Jenkins, always mindful of small details, had even brought out a jar of pomade and Weston used it to slick his hair straight back in a stern, formidable style that perfectly matched his current mood.

"Has everyone assembled in the solarium?" he asked.

Jenkins nodded. "Everyone but you, my lord. Lady Smethwick and her daughter, in particular, are looking forward to seeing you."

Weston didn't know why that information should cause his mouth to sour, as if he'd bitten into a lemon. He liked Martha. She was an excellent conversationalist, mostly because she never argued or tried to provoke him. Unlike a certain American that he knew. Time spent with her was akin to a pleasant ride through Hyde Park during the height of the promenade hour. Alternately, being in the company of Evie was like a wild, reckless ride through the Scottish moors with perilous cliffs looming at every turn.

"When did Lady Martha and her mother arrive?" he questioned absently. Proper decorum dictated that he should have been there to welcome them personally to Hawkridge Manor. And Martha's mother, a thin woman with prominent eyebrows that he suspected (but had not yet confirmed) were drawn on, was nothing if not properly decorous.

"Half an hour ago, my lord," Jenkins replied.

No so long, then. Surely his future mother-in-law wouldn't harbor a grudge over thirty minutes. Not that he particularly cared either way; he wasn't marrying Lady Smethwick, after all. But neither did he care to be the recipient of passive aggressive glares across the table while he was trying to enjoy his bacon and poached eggs.

It went without saying that he *would* have greeted them...if he hadn't been trapped waist-deep in mud. For that, he blamed Evie. As well as that troublesome lamb of hers.

He never should have gotten involved to begin with. But when he'd heard Evie cry out, his first instinct had been to run to her as fast as humanly possible. And when he saw those luminous blue eyes wet with tears...how could he *not* have held her? In that moment of heartbreak and hopelessness, he would have gladly traveled to heaven itself if that's what it took to get Posy back. He'd have traded his wealth. His title. His properties. Everything–*anything*–to heal Evie's hurt.

Then it turned out that Posy wasn't dead, just missing. But instead of calling up a footman to go searching for the lamb, as any reasonable earl would have done, as he *should* have done, he'd gone to find her himself. In the midst of a house party. With his esteemed peers waiting for him below stairs and his soon-to-be fiancée arriving any second, he had raced off with Evie. As if she were the only person that mattered. And the worst part…even worse than the filthy muck and the attack swans (however, they came in a close second)…was how terrifyingly *right* it had felt to do so. To abandon all of his commitments and responsibilities to focus solely on Evie. To make her, for however brief a time, the center of his universe. To put her needs above all else. And, most importantly, to make her smile again.

That was all he'd wanted to do when he had set off to find Posy.

To take away Evie's tears…and replace them with a smile.

The kind that lit up her entire face and made the corners of her eyes crinkle and her nose scrunch.

Like when she'd gotten foxed and doubled over with laughter at absolutely nothing. Or the wondrous grin that had captured her mouth when he'd caught her peering over the stall at the newborn foal.

If he could bring *that* smile back to her face, all would be well.

And it had been.

For approximately four seconds.

Until she got some idea in her head that they "were going to have a chat".

Six little words that had been striking fear in the hearts of men since the beginning of time.

She'd ended that tortuous discussion by asking him what he wanted.

As if he knew anymore.

As if he had any *goddamned* idea.

Weston knew that he wanted poached eggs for breakfast instead of boiled.

He knew that he wanted to buy another railroad line to expand his empire.

He knew that he never wanted to bathe in a horse trough ever again.

But as to what he ultimately wanted in love and in life?

He'd thought it was a biddable wife to let him carry out his duties sans interruption.

Now...now he wasn't so certain.

And that uncertainty throbbed like a splinter burrowed under his nail bed.

"Jenkins," he said abruptly as they entered the house. The foyer was empty, the quiet clink of glassware and the muted hum of voices revealing that everyone had gathered in the solarium where they were waiting for him to deliver his opening toast. The official start of a house party that had already proven to be more trouble than it was worth...and it was only the first day. "I've a task for you. One that I'd like carried out with the utmost discretion."

"Anything, my lord."

"I need a complete list of all the eligible bachelors in attendance. Their names and titles along with how much they are worth. If they've any debts outstanding, or improprieties attached to their names. I should also like to know any pertinent hobbies." He paused. "Also, if they are fond of animals. Specifically of the woolly variety."

"Woolly variety, my lord?" asked Jenkins, appearing mystified.

"Sheep," he said impatiently. "I need to know if they like sheep."

"If you don't mind my saying, that is oddly specific."

Weston's jaw tensed. "Can you get the list or not?"

"I should have it for you by the end of the day."

"Good. Good," he repeated, and he started to run his hand through his hair before he remembered that he'd set it with wax. Muttering another curse, he excused his valet and took care to compose himself before he set out for the solarium to give his welcome address.

CHAPTER SIXTEEN

"**Y**OU ARE STARING," Rosemary whispered in Evie's ear for the third time.

Nearly bobbling her fork, Evie managed to catch the utensil before it dropped into her lap. On a sigh, she set it down beside her plate. She hadn't been using it anyway; her appetite having vanished as soon as she joined her cousin and the rest of the guests for breakfast and her gaze landed upon Lady Martha Smethwick.

She'd known it was Lady Martha without needing to be told, as Weston's intended bride was exactly as Evie had pictured her. Slim as a willow, with golden hair and large brown eyes (such an easy color to remember that Evie suspected the earl had been playing her for a fool in the carriage when he'd pretended not to recall their shade), Martha was the epitome of an English Rose. Everything about her, from the graceful way in which she sipped her glass of water to the sound of her voice to the way she cut into her bacon, was perfect.

She was perfect.

Of course, Weston would want to marry her.

If Evie was an earl in search of a wife, she'd want to marry Martha as well.

Even her laugh sounded like wind chimes.

It was quite irritating, actually. But for all that Martha's presence set Evie's teeth on edge, she couldn't seem to make herself look away.

Thus the staring.

"What can you tell me about her?" she asked Rosemary in a low tone so as not to be overheard by the other guests. The table–the longest she'd ever sat at–was filled to overflowing with all facets of the British aristocracy. There were lords and ladies. Dukes and viscounts. Businessmen and scholars. It would take Evie a day, if not more, to learn everyone's name. This even after they'd all gone around at Brynne's invitation and introduced themselves.

When it was Evie's turn, there'd been an excited buzz of chatter. Much to her surprise, it had rapidly dwindled. Given the stir that she and Joanna had made when they attended the Countess of Beresford's ball, she'd been expecting all sorts of questions and gossip. But it appeared the *ton* had a short attention span, and while the return of Lord Dorchester's illegitimate daughter and her sister had made headlines last week, they were already sniffing after a more exciting scandal. Especially given that Evie's mere presence at the house party indicated that the Westons had accepted their American blood into the family fold with no more drama to be had.

"Who?" Rosemary asked as she slathered butter onto a piece of toasted bread. She peered at Evie's untouched plate of food. "Are you going to eat your eggs?"

"Take whatever you'd like. And I want to know about Lady Martha Smethwick."

"Oh." Biting off a piece of bread, Rosemary chewed thoughtfully. "There's not much to tell, really."

"Is she positively awful?" Evie asked hopefully. "Does she kick small puppies and terrorize children?"

Rosemary blinked. "Not that I've ever seen. She is always kind to me. One of the few diamonds that is."

"Diamonds?"

"A term used in the *ton* to describe a debutante of the highest quality," her cousin explained. "It's not as common nowadays, but were

Lady Martha born at the beginning of the century, that's what everyone would have called her. I'm more of a quartz, myself. But Lady Martha...definitely a diamond of the first water." Rosemary stabbed a chunk of roasted potato with her fork. "Did you know she is rumored to soon be engaged to the Earl of Hawkridge? Grandmother heard whispers that it might even happen *here*, during the house party."

"I've heard." As Evie slumped in her chair, she wished she could slide right under the table. Having seen her competition firsthand, she recognized that her plan to woo Weston away from Martha had been a fool's errand all along. She may have been a diamond in Somerville, but in England, without a title or a dowry or any social influence of which to speak of, she found herself in the same category as Rosemary.

Quartz was by no means an ugly or undesirable gem.

But it certainly did not compare to a diamond.

Weston was going to marry someone else.

And there was nothing she could do about it.

"I...I need some fresh air." Several heads turned when Evie shoved her chair back and stood up, including Brynne's, who was seated several chairs over to her left.

"*Are you all right?*" Weston's sister mouthed.

Evie summoned a tight grin and gave a curt nod. Squeezing behind the row of chairs, she managed to keep her pace at a slow, measured walk until she'd quit the solarium.

And then she ran.

"WHAT ARE YOU waiting for?" Brynne hissed, giving Weston a sharp nudge with her elbow. "Go after her!"

His gaze pinned to the door that Evie had just exited through, he brushed off his twin's demand with an irritated hitch of his shoulder. "You've only just finished chastising me for being late to the breakfast, and now you want me to leave in the middle of it?"

"There are some things more important than proper etiquette."

"You go after her, then."

Brynne sipped her champagne, then flicked him a smug glance over the top of the crystal flute. "I would, but I am not the one she is trying to escape. I don't know what you did, West, but you need to make it right."

"I didn't *do* anything," he snapped, even as his fists clenched into knotted balls of tension beneath the tablecloth. "Unless you count the fact that I rescued her damned lamb. Again."

"Is that why you came in dressed like a pig in slop?"

"I do not wish to discuss it."

"Maybe not, but there is clearly something you and Miss Thorncroft *do* need to discuss."

"Why do women always insist on talking about their problems?" he wondered out loud. "Why not do it the manly way, with pistols at dawn? Either one party or both is killed, and whatever issue they may have had is instantly resolved without a single sentence needing to be exchanged."

"Because dueling is illegal, and the world would be a safer, calmer place if battles were won with words instead of weapons." She nudged him again. "*Go to her*, you lummox. Before it is too late."

"What do you mean, too late?" he frowned. "The house party has only just started."

His twin gazed at him pityingly. "If you truly don't know the answer, then I'm not sure you can be helped. I *do* hope that I am wrong. For your sake, as well as Miss Thorncroft's."

"You're speaking in riddles," he grumbled. But he couldn't help but look at the door again. "Someone should check on her. Just to ensure she isn't choking or in need of some other assistance. Since you cannot be bothered, I suppose it falls upon me as the host to ensure that Miss Thorncroft is all right."

The corners of Brynne's lips twitched. "I suppose it does," she said gravely.

"You're a brat," he informed her before he pushed his chair back. "You know that, don't you?"

"So you've told me a thousand times over. Oh, and West?" she said as he stood up and placed his linen napkin on the table.

He could feel curious eyes upon him, but no one in attendance would dare have the audacity to question his decision to leave the breakfast preemptively. Without meaning to, he glanced at Lady Martha. She was staring demurely at her plate, but must have sensed his shift in attention for her head rose and she met his stare with a pleasant smile which he made a passing attempt at returning.

She was the one he should have been chasing after, if he was to chase after anyone. That being said, Lady Martha would never quit a room before the meal was over. Nor would she leave him stranded in a pond, or allow him to ravish her in the stables, or hide with him in the bushes while a farmer shot at them for stealing a sheep.

And yet it was *Evie* he was going to find.

The bloody bane of his existence...and the woman his blood still hummed for, even now.

"What is it?" he bit out, glaring at Brynne. He knew his twin was plotting something. She had that glint in her eyes. The kind that she got whenever she was starting a painting and was throwing all manner of colors at the canvas to see what stuck.

"Try, for once, to follow your heart instead of your head. I believe you'll be pleasantly surprised with where it leads you."

Not bothering to justify such drivel with a response, he traced Evie's steps out of the solarium whereupon he promptly lost her trail. There was no sign of his quarry in the hallway or the foyer, but after a maid informed him that she'd seen a guest fleeing in the direction of the library, that was where he found her.

Surrounded by books, she sat perched on the windowsill, a breath-taking vision in violet satin with sunlight in her hair and a wistful smile curving her mouth.

"You changed your dress," Weston observed gruffly as he stepped into the room and closed the door behind him to afford them the privacy he instinctively sensed that they were going to require. Because there was no reality, no world in this one or next, in which he could see her sitting there, like a stunning goddess of old torn straight from the pages of Greek mythology, and *not* kiss her.

"You changed your shirt," she said without looking at him.

"I changed more than that." An oak floorboard, polished to a dull shine with beeswax and sealed with varnish, creaked beneath his foot as he walked to the middle of the library and stopped beside a round table piled high with books. "Thanks to you, all of the clothes I had on will likely need to be burned." He stared at the slender line of her neck where a single curl lay nestled, glossy mahogany against sheer ivory touched with the slightest hint of pink. "Why did you run from me at the pond, Miss Thorncroft?"

"You called me Evelyn, before. In my bedchamber."

"Did I?" he said, startled. He did not recall that particular detail.

"Indeed," she said, keeping her gaze on the glass. Beyond the window, the sky had turned an ominous gray, signaling bad weather...both outside the library and within it. "And I did not run. I walked at a fast clip."

Picking up a book from the table, he tossed it aimlessly from his left hand to his right. "I could have drowned."

"One does not drown in twelve inches of water."

"Twelve inches of mud, you mean, with water on top of it."

"Yet here you are, alive to pester me."

There was an edge in her voice he'd never heard before. Even from across the room, with her facing away from him, he felt its sharp bite.

"Are you angry with me, Miss Thorncroft? Is that why you left the breakfast? To sit and sulk by your lonesome over some imagined transgression of mine that I am unaware of?"

"I am not *sulking*." Finally, she turned her head to look at him. Her expression was fierce, but her eyes, those big, beautiful blue eyes that a man very well *could* drown in if he wasn't careful, were filled with sadness. "I've fallen in love with you."

The book fell to the floor.

His heart plummeted along with it.

"Miss Thorncroft, I…"

"It's not your fault," she said with a dismissive wave of her hand. "It's mine. I put myself in this situation. I thought…I had *planned*…to marry you. For your money, and your title, and my mother's ring."

An icy chill passed between Weston's shoulder blades.

"You planned *what?*" he said in a very soft, very dangerous sort of tone. The kind that sent anyone who did not want to die a painful death scampering for the hills. But Evelyn stayed where she was and regarded him calmly.

"Don't look so shocked." She rolled her eyes. "Did you honestly believe I put myself through a hundred mile trek in the desert for my good health?"

"It was eight miles in the countryside," he growled. "And you were free to return to London at any time. Instead you–you *inserted* yourself here under false pretenses and–"

"Please," she scoffed, raising her palm. "I am not some Yankee spy come to pilfer all of your precious gold. I was after a good match, the same as every other debutante sitting in that solarium. Besides, if I'd told you what I wanted on the first day of our journey, you'd have tossed me out of the carriage without waiting for it stop. No use denying it."

As loath as Weston was to admit it, she had a point. The entire *ton* was built on the basis of matching young, eligible women with young (and sometimes not so young), eligible men. They did not refer to it as the Marriage Mart for nothing. Still, he'd have preferred that Evie had revealed her motivations outright...even though he most likely *would* have thrown her out of the carriage.

"Why tell me now?" he asked.

"Because I am no Lady Martha Smethwick."

His temple creased. "Of course not. You're...you're Miss Thorncroft."

He'd almost–almost–called her "my Miss Thorncroft".

Which was how he thought of her, deep down.

As his.

Only his.

To hold, to kiss, to argue with.

Except she *wasn't* his. And he wasn't hers. And it was for the best that they were getting this all out in the open now so that he could proceed with finding her a suitable husband.

"I am," she said quietly, and although her mouth smiled, her eyes remained sad. "I am Miss Thorncroft. A penniless American who made the grave error of falling in love with a man far, far above her station. It should make a lovely book, if only I could change the ending."

She looked at him then. At him and *into* him. Where he kept all of his innermost shame and secrets. Where he never let anyone look, not even Brynne. Not even himself. And he knew what she was asking. He knew what she wanted. But he couldn't give it to her. Not today. Not tomorrow. Because what she truly desired...what she deserved...he was incapable of giving to anyone.

"I am not a writer, Miss Thorncroft. And even if I were..." A lump formed in his throat. Hard and knotty, like a burl in a slab of pine. "Even if I were, I believe all endings have a way of serving their intended purpose. This one is no different, and I would not change it."

"You're certain," she whispered.

The lump expanded. "I am."

For a long while, Evie was silent. He watched her closely, waiting for a tear to form or a cry of anguish to tumble from her lips. If she'd made but a sound, he would have gone to her. He would have been helpless not to. But her eyes remained dry, and when she spoke, her voice was remarkably even.

"Then I shall see myself out, Lord Hawkridge. If you could arrange a carriage to take me back to London—"

"Wait." As something akin to panic clawed at him, he moved in front of the door. As if that small motion in and of itself could somehow keep her trapped in the library forever. Because as much as he did not want to marry her, he also did not want to let her go. "You...you cannot leave yet. The house party has barely begun, and...and Brynne would be devastated if you disappeared without an explanation."

"Your concern for you sister is admirable, Lord Hawkridge, but I am confident that she will be fine." Evie slid off the windowsill and approached the door, but he refused to move away from it. "I fail to see why you are making this immeasurably more difficult than it needs to be," she said as twin blotches of color appeared high on her cheeks. "Have I not embarrassed myself enough already?"

"You want a husband," he said desperately. "I can find one."

She placed her hands on her hips. "A husband is not a lost sock. You cannot simply look underneath the bed and *find* one."

"I am an earl and the heir to a dukedom. I can do whatever I damned well please. Give me...give me three weeks." What the devil was he doing? Weston hadn't the bloodiest idea. He only knew that he'd do anything, say anything, to keep Evie from leaving Hawkridge Manor. From leaving *him*. "Three weeks," he repeated. "There's more than half a dozen eligible suitors here. You can have your pick, after I've had them weighed up. Any would consider themselves fortunate to marry you."

She stared at him incredulously. "I told you that I love you. I've never said that to a man before. And your response, your *solution*, is to find someone else for me to marry?"

"Isn't that what you wanted? A wealthy, titled husband." He felt like he was hanging off the edge of a cliff and grabbing for anything that would prevent him from falling. "I can give you that."

"You can *give* me a husband," she sneered. "How charitable of you."

"It wouldn't be charity."

"Then what, precisely, would it be? I have no dowry to offer."

"Then I'll provide one."

Her eyes slowly cooled, like a sheet of ice spreading across a lake. "Why?" she asked. "Why would you do such a thing?"

Because it will keep you here, for just a while longer.

Because when another man marries you, I'll no longer want you.

Because you've driven me absolutely mad, and this is pure insanity.

"Because when I retrieved my family ring, I robbed you and your sisters of the financial means with which to support yourselves. Consider this repayment in kind."

"Repayment in kind," she repeated. "You are going to procure me a husband because you stole my mother's ring."

When she put it *that* way…

"Yes," he said unabashedly. "Yes, I am."

"And it won't bother you?" she asked, studying him closely. "To see me marry someone else?"

Bother him?

It was going to bloody well *kill* him.

But it was better than the alternative.

It had to be.

It had to be, or else everything he'd convinced himself of was a lie.

"No." Through sheer force of will, he managed to keep his tone detached. Emotionless. Aloof, when he was anything but. "It won't bother me in the slightest."

Hurt flashed in her eyes, but she blinked it away, like a speck of unwanted dirt.

"Fine. A rich husband in exchange for a stolen ring. It could be worse, I suppose." She lifted her chin and even though she was at least six inches shorter than he was, she somehow managed to look down her nose at him. "But you have two weeks, not three. It has come to my attention that my sister is still in London, and I should like to see her sooner rather than later."

Two weeks.

Fourteen days.

It was both too long…and not nearly long enough.

For an instant, his gaze betrayed him as it slipped to her mouth. If things were different, if *he* were different, he'd snatch her into his arms and kiss her until the embers in the fireplace faded to black and rain poured from the heavens. But the very second she'd admitted that she was in love…with *him*…everything had come into sharp, unrelenting focus.

Their attraction towards each other was no longer a harmless dalliance. There were real emotions involved. And if he wasn't careful, if he wasn't mindful of his words and his actions, there would be real hurt as well. Something that he was intrinsically cognizant of. For as cold and aloof as he could be, it was never Weston's intention to cause deliberate harm.

He knew what it felt like, to give love and never experience the sweet warmth of its return. The agony of emptying himself out, again and again, in the hopes that if he just gave more, or earned better marks at school, that his father might finally, finally love him enough to show even the smallest hint of interest in his only son's wellbeing.

But the Marquess of Dorchester never had.

Years ago, Weston had resigned himself to the fact that he never would.

And he'd made peace with that. Even better, he'd made himself into someone who did not require love to survive. But the price for encasing a heart in ice was a steep one, and he was paying it now.

Maybe…*maybe* he'd be able to love Evie as she loved him.

But he wasn't going to base a marriage on such a tenuous assumption.

"If there is nothing else?" she said, arching a brow.

"No." Tamping down the tendrils of desire that threatened with a stern hand, Weston gave a curt shake of his head. "There is nothing."

"Splendid. I shall see you at the picnic, then." She glanced at the window where the clouds had grown even darker. "If we are not rained out, that is."

Trailing frost in her wake, she brushed past him and sauntered out of the library.

CHAPTER SEVENTEEN

I T RAINED FOR the next four days straight.

Trapped inside lest she wished to succumb to a good drenching, Evie spent a large portion of her time with Rosemary. The cousins explored the manor's vast art collection, worked on their embroidery, listened to an impromptu recital put on by Lady Martha (who, it went without saying, was a consummate pianist with a lovely soprano), and spent a memorable night skidding down a marble hallway in their stockings after imbibing too much wine at dinner.

For the most part, Evie managed not to think about Weston at all...until came the night, and he was *all* she could think about.

Staring up at the canopy above her bed while rain pummeled the windows and wind howled through the trees, she went over every conversation they'd ever had, beginning with when they'd met.

He'd asked her to dance and without knowing anything about him except that he had the most arresting stare she had ever seen, she'd accepted.

When she had bumped into his chest (his fault, as he'd pulled her into a turn a tad too forcefully), she'd been surprised at the spark she felt. The first sign that they were always destined to catch fire.

"I am sorry, my lord," she'd said, even though she hadn't been. Not really.

"The error was mine," he had replied, although the gleam in his gray eyes revealed that he wasn't sorry for it.

"I suspected as much, but am always loath to point out other's errors unless they are deserving of it."

"And I am not deserving of critique?" he'd asked.

"That remains to be seen," she had replied coyly.

Moving in flawless unison, they'd waltzed around a slower couple and Weston's hand had slid just a little further down her back than propriety allowed.

"What is your name?" he'd wanted to know. "You are not from around here."

"Was it the accent that gave it away?"

"That, and I never forget a face."

"Do you find it memorable?" she'd asked. "My face, that is."

"You're beautiful. Only a blind man could forget you."

"And you're not blind."

"I am not," he'd confirmed.

"Just rude, then, for asking me to introduce myself to you when it is a gentleman's duty to introduce himself to the lady."

He had grinned at her. A scoundrel's smile, she remembered thinking. If only she had savored it more, as she'd yet to see it again.

In the present, Weston was...guarded. In both his actions *and* his reactions. But that night at the ball, before she'd told him her name, he'd been remarkably more relaxed. Charming, even. And perhaps...perhaps a tiny part of her had started falling even then.

"I never said I was a gentleman," he had said.

Her eyes had sparkled with coquettish amusement. "That's fine, as I never claimed to be a lady."

Unfortunately, things had gone downhill from there, and had culminated in Weston telling her to sod off before he'd stormed away.

Such a charmer, that earl.

And now she couldn't sleep but for thinking of him.

Evie rolled onto her stomach, then her side. She placed a pillow over her head. Under her head. Kicked the blankets off, then dragged them back on. At last, with a loud, annoyed huff of breath, she gave in to her Weston-induced insomnia and padded downstairs and into the kitchen in search of a warm glass of milk.

The house was still and silent, almost eerily so, causing her to cast an apprehensive glance over her shoulder as she retrieved some milk powder from the pantry and mixed it with water before pouring it in a kettle to heat in the stone hearth where a handful of logs glowed red and orange.

There was a stove, a massive, iron beast fueled by coal, but it had been shut down for the night and she dared not attempt to revive it. Thankfully, while a tad old fashioned, cooking in the fireplace was all but foolproof and as she poured her steaming milk into a mug, she silently thanked whatever servant had thought to bank the fire.

While Evie hadn't enjoyed the mindless chatter and socialization over the past few days as much as she'd anticipated that she would, she *did* love having a bevy of maids and footmen at her beck and call. Why, she barely could set an empty teacup down before it was filled again! There was no cleaning for her to do. No laundry that needed washing, or food that had to be prepared. Courtesy of Hannah, she didn't even have to style her own hair if she didn't want to.

Being waited on hand and foot was a welcome respite from arguing with Joanna and Claire over whose turn it was to scrub the water closet.

It was a life she could easily become accustomed to...just not with Weston.

Sliding onto a stool, she stared pensively into her cup as she waited for the milk to cool. She should have been pleased that Weston was taking the effort to find her a husband. A wealthy, titled husband who would give her everything she'd ever wanted. While Weston married Lady Martha and received everything *he'd* ever wanted.

It was the perfect happily-ever-after.

But then why didn't she feel particularly happy?

A rustle of movement had her squinting at the doorway. While she'd brought an oil lamp from her room and the fireplace emanated a soft glow of light that staved off some of the shadows, it remained quite dark.

"Who is there?" she demanded. "If you're a rat, I must warn you, I've a very shrill scream and...oh, it's just you."

"You sounded more excited about the rat," Weston said dryly as he entered the kitchen. Unlike Evie, who wore a green silk wrapper over her high-necked cotton nightdress, he was in his clothes from dinner, although he'd since discarded both his jacket and cravat. "Do you mind if I...?" He gestured at the stool opposite hers.

"Go ahead. I couldn't sleep, and hoped some warm milk might help." Resting her elbows on the table, she picked up her cup with both hands and eyed him over the rim as he sat down. "What are *you* doing awake at such an hour?"

"Catching up on ledgers, mostly."

"You don't have an accountant for such things?"

"When I'm able to, I like to go through the books myself. The harvest will be coming in soon, and it's important to have an accurate tally of last year's crop yield to compare."

She sipped her milk. "Is there nothing you don't try to control?"

"No," he replied simply. The edge of his mouth curled upward. "But I'll be the first to admit that I've been less than successful with you in that regard."

"Thorncroft women have always been difficult to manage."

"That much is clear." He folded his arms and leaned forward until they were only a few inches apart, their nearness made all the more intimate by the dim lighting. "Should I expect the same streak of stubbornness in Joanna?"

As Evie's pulse fluttered in response to Weston's close proximity, she deliberately cast her gaze to the side. "My sister is even worse."

Weston snorted. "I find that hard to believe."

"Claire is the best of us. The kindest, and the gentlest. I miss her very much." Evie didn't know why she was talking to him about her family. Only that it seemed natural to do so. As if this wasn't the first time they'd met in the kitchen late at night to share anecdotes about themselves over warm milk, but the fiftieth.

"It must be difficult, to be so far from home," he said, his gray eyes gently probing.

"It is," she acknowledged. "But at the same time, it isn't. I…I've come to enjoy England." Her lips twisted in a rueful smile. "Despite all of the rain."

"We do receive more than our fair share."

"But your gardens are all the prettier because of it. And how are you to appreciate the sun if it is always shining?"

"How indeed?" he murmured, his gaze skimming across her wrapper before it returned with almost comical abruptness to her face. "Would your sister consider coming here to visit you? Or does she have a husband who would keep her close to home?"

"Claire is not married, but she is sweet on the butcher's son." Evie paused to take another sip of milk. "He gives her extra bacon slices in our meat order every week."

"If that isn't true love, I don't know what is."

"And yet, you don't believe in it."

"Believe in what?" he said guardedly, as if he already knew the answer to his own question, but wanted to give her the opportunity to ask a different one.

"True love. Or any love, for that matter."

He was silent for a moment, his shuttered stare impossible to decipher. When he did speak, it was with all the wariness of a solider trying to avoid underground explosives on the field of battle. "It isn't that I don't believe in love. I understand that it exists. I've seen it, in all its varied forms. I love my sister. I love my horses. I love this estate."

He'd omitted his father, Evie noted.

And her, but then he had already said as much when she had given him her heart and he'd offered to find her a husband.

Rather like handing a baker money for a decadent chocolate cake and receiving a plain loaf of bread instead.

Bread wasn't bad, per se.

But it was a far cry from chocolate cake.

"Do you love Lady Martha?" she dared to ask, and found herself holding her breath as she awaited his reply.

"I do not," he said without hesitation. "Neither does she love me. And our marriage shall be the better for it. Love, especially love between a husband and wife, is an...unnecessary complication." He lifted his shoulder in a negligent shrug. "I've no love for my valet or my butler, yet they are an intricate part of my household."

Evie blinked. "Then you intend for your wife to be a servant."

"I *intend* for my wife to serve a role," he corrected. "As I will serve a role for her. Love need not muddy the waters."

She wanted to argue with him. But how could she, when she'd recently been of the same exact opinion? For her entire adult life, with the exception of these past two weeks, she'd thought precisely as Weston did. That a marriage was not something to be romanticized, but a contract between two willing parties.

A husband would provide his wife with protection, a generous allowance, and a good name. In turn, a wife would give her husband a male heir, manage his household affairs, and be a consummate hostess. Love was an afterthought.

Oh, it was nice if it occurred.

But it certainly was not a *necessity*.

Or so she had believed...until she'd fallen in love herself.

And splatted face first onto the ground.

"I have been meaning to ask, why are the walls barren?" she asked in an obvious and deliberate attempt to steer the subject towards safer ground. "The manor's architecture is stunning. The crystal chandeliers are divine. The furniture is of the highest quality. But why is everything so...white?"

"Brynne says it reminds her of a mausoleum," he said wryly.

"I do not disagree with her."

"When my parents lived here, my mother took it upon herself to redecorate every room down to the wall hangings. Apparently, it had not been updated for nearly half a century and the style was somewhat...garish. Or so I've been told. She finished right before my sister and I were born, and..." He cleared his throat, then glanced at Evie's half-filled cup. "Do you mind if I...?"

"Please," she said earnestly. "Help yourself. If you'd like me to make another–"

"This is fine," he said, lifting the cup to his mouth, and her thighs unconsciously pressed together as he touched the same spot where her own lips had been. "After my mother died, it's said that my father went a tad mad in his grief. He stripped the entire household of anything that reminded her of him, and had it painted white. I've simply yet to get around to changing it. An adequate project for the future Countess of Hawkridge, I should think."

As Evie searched Weston's gaze, she felt a tug in the middle of her chest. There was such restrained pain in his eyes. Buried beneath all of the stoicism, of course. But it was there, all the same. Especially now that she knew to look for it.

What a terrible message it must have sent to a vulnerable young boy, yearning for approval, that the marquess had loved his wife so much that her passing had caused him to tear an entire house apart. But he hadn't cared enough about his son to bother to show up at Weston's convocation. The most important milestone in a gentleman's life, with the exceptions of marriage and the births of his children.

And the Marquess of Dorchester hadn't been there.

How could Evie's mother have had an affair with such a heartless man?

At least she finally understood why Anne Thorncroft would have chosen to give up everything England had to offer her and return to the arms of a kind doctor who had valued his wife and daughters and service to country above all else.

"I am sorry," she murmured, reaching across the worktable to splay her fingers on Weston's forearm and feel the quiver and clench of his muscles through the thin fabric of his shirt.

"You've nothing to be sorry for," he said curtly. "All of this happened a long time ago. Before you were even born. It has nothing to do with you."

Couldn't he see that it had *everything* to do with her?

With them?

As much as she was a product of her upbringing, so was Weston a product of his. No doubt he thought that if his father had loved his mother a little less, then the marquess wouldn't have fallen apart after she'd died and rebuilt himself with stone.

It was clear, both from what he'd said and the actions he'd taken, that Weston was trying to avoid a similar destiny by eradicating love from his marriage altogether. But in doing so, he'd already condemned himself to the same fate as his father.

He'd just used ice instead of rock.

But if Evie could change her views on life and love and the pursuit of happiness...then maybe...just maybe...Weston could as well.

With a little coaxing, that is.

"You've not spoken of passion, or desire, or lust," she said, dropping her voice to a throaty whisper as her hand skimmed up his arm to his bicep. She traced the muscle with the tip of her finger, marveling at its firmness. There was no question that the Earl of Hawkridge kept himself physically fit. Or that he was failing–miserably–to resist the pull of his baser instincts.

"What of them?" he rasped, his eyelids sliding to half-mast as she continued her exploration of his body. Having made her way to his shoulder, she flattened her palm and slid it ever so slowly along the hard ridge of his collarbone before dipping to his chest. If she touched his nipple as he'd touched hers, would it have the same effect? All that pulsing heat centered in a circle of nerve endings, his considerably smaller than hers.

But no less sensitive, she discovered, a catlike smile stealing across her lips as she rubbed her thumb across his nipple and he all but toppled off his stool.

"Aren't those qualities you should like to have in a marriage? You're right. Love is a complication." She flitted him a glance from beneath the thick fringe of her lashes. "But surely you don't intend to deny yourself of all the pleasures that come from taking a wife. Or shall you delegate the making of an heir to the butler?"

"You're playing with fire, Evelyn," he said thickly.

"Oh," she purred, her ribcage pressing into the edge of the table as she extended her arm as far as it would go and began to walk her fingertips down the middle of his torso, "but I so enjoy the burn."

CHAPTER EIGHTEEN

E VIE MAY HAVE been the one playing with fire.

But Weston was the one being consumed by it.

Flames lapped at his self-restraint as her inquisitive hand trailed across his chest. He steeled himself against the heat. The temptation. The savage desire to take and be taken. But even as he resisted, he knew it was a battle he was losing. A battle he no longer wanted to fight.

And thus he threw up his white flag...and surrendered.

He surrendered to the attraction between them. An attraction that had begun as a spark on the ballroom floor, and had since grown into a raging inferno.

He surrendered to his primal urges, long stifled beneath layers of propriety.

But most importantly...he surrendered to Evie.

Exquisite, alluring Evie. An ebony-haired siren wrapped in silk and sin, just as he'd envisioned her. Except the reality of having her in his arms was far better than any dream.

His stool clattered to the floor as he shoved to his feet. A single step, and she was his, her hands clutching his hips as he spun her forcefully around on her seat.

She tilted her head back and gazed up at him in wordless anticipation, her throat giving a delicate jerk as she swallowed and then wet her lips, affording him a tantalizing peek at her pink tongue. Her dusky nipples were swollen and erect, their pointed shape clearly visible through the thin fabric of her wrapper and nightdress. Bathed in the glow of firelight, her slender body was all but quivering for his touch.

She reached for him, but he gently deflected her arm. With midnight at their backs and sunrise hours away, they'd all the time in the world. And he intended to use every second to bring her pleasure.

He began by removing the pins from her hair. One by one, he set them beside her on the table. When the last had been freed, her curls tumbled down around her shoulders in a tumultuous curtain of black satin. Weston sucked in a sharp breath. Pinned against the table with her hair undone and her eyes heavy with lust, Evie had never looked more arousing.

A log shifted in the hearth. As sparks danced in the air, he sank his fingers into her lush mane and lowered his mouth to hers in a kiss that was as deliberately slow as it was consuming.

Their lips parted. Their tongues entwined. Their bodies throbbed.

Cradling the back of her skull with his left hand, he used the right to untie the sash holding her wrapper closed. A few deft tugs and the garment slithered down her arms to pool at her waist before it slipped, already forgotten, onto the floor. Uncovered, her cotton nightdress clung to her curves. It was simple and plain, the only decoration a blue ribbon trimmed in white lace stitched across the bodice. But then, Evie's natural beauty needed no frills or adornments.

He kissed her again, lingering over her lips with lazy abandon as he explored every inch of the warm, damp cavern inside of her mouth. She whimpered with impatience, a tiny, mewling cry of suppressed desire that went straight to his loins. Grabbing the hem of her nightdress, he yanked it past her thighs and then up over her hips, before whisking it off the top of her head.

Completely exposed to his gaze, she didn't shy or blush. Not his Evie. She was a woman empowered, a woman *in* power. Over him, his body, his mind...his heart and soul. A beckoning tilt of her chin, a lascivious smile, her fingers sweeping in tantalizingly slow motion across her ribcage before she cupped her own breasts...and she controlled him. All of him. Every bit. Even the parts he'd sworn that he would never give to anyone.

His mouth went to her neck, her shoulder, her collarbone...and then her nipples. Drawing one bud between his teeth to lick and nip and suckle, he permitted his hands to continue further down, across her slightly rounded belly to the curls between her thighs where she was wet and wanting.

Her legs fell shamelessly apart as he petted her there; stroking along the pearl of her womanhood before delving deeper. To the first knuckle, the second, the third, he gradually sheathed his finger all the way within her velvet heat.

He groaned when he felt her clench around him. Reaching for her hand, he guided it to his trousers where he was as hard and as hot as a railroad pike in the midafternoon sun. Lightly wrapping her fingers around him through his pants, she gave a small, experimental stroke along his shaft from base to tip. He jerked in her embrace, as inexperienced as it was, and would have spilled his seed then and there had he not grinded his teeth together with such force that a ligament popped in his jaw, loud but painless.

"Bloody hell," he gasped. With a flinch, Evie withdrew her hand.

"Did I do something wrong?" she whispered, blue eyes luminous in the lamplight.

His only answer was to take her wrist and direct her back to his cock as he sought her mouth.

Time blurred after that. Or maybe it ceased it exist altogether. Weston didn't know. Quite frankly, he didn't care. There were a hundred different things he had to do come morning. Obligations. Duties. Ledgers. God, were the ledgers never ending. But in this kitchen, in this moment, in this sweet paradise of carnal pleasure, his only concern was Evie.

Their breaths grew more frantic, their motions more uninhibited, their passion more desperate as they recklessly plunged towards oblivion. And when the mountain crumbled beneath their feet and they spread their wings, they took flight together.

"WE DID NOT spill the milk," Evie noted, somewhat impressed.

"So we didn't," Weston said gruffly as he shook out her wrapper, then held it out.

After adjusting the arms of her nightdress, she accepted it gladly. Without the warmth of the earl's body pressed against hers, and with the fire in the hearth all but extinguished, a slight chill had overtaken the air.

Needing to give her heart a chance to resume its normal rhythm and her scattered thoughts to organize, she took her time with the sash. When it was finally tied and she was properly dressed, she flitted a glance at Weston. He'd moved across the room to the fireplace, exposing half of his countenance to the muted light from the dying flames as he stood with an arm braced against the wooden mantel that stretched the length of the hearth.

As if he could feel the weight of her gaze upon him, he looked at her over his shoulder, and she braced herself, both inwardly and out, for the rejection that she knew was to come. But even though she understood that their interlude had probably changed nothing, she did not regret it.

Not a word, not a kiss, not a touch.

Especially not a touch.

The feelings he'd elicited from her body…it had been like a burst of sunlight.

No, not a burst.

Burst was far too mild a word.

An explosion, she decided. An *explosion* of sunlight.

And now came the shadows. Slithering, sneaking their way in to douse the light and dampen her spirits.

"I suppose this is the part where you tell me what we just did was a mistake," she told Weston quietly. "That it won't happen again, and you're *terribly* sorry–"

"But I'm not," he cut in. "I'm not sorry. And whatever that was,"– he gestured at the chair behind her–"it wasn't a mistake."

Her lips parted. "Then...what...you...I..."

"I don't have all the answers." He ran a hand across his face. "Hell, I don't have *any* answers. This is a position I've never found myself in before."

"You mean you've never ravished a woman in the kitchen?" asked Evie. At his resulting flicker of guilt, she gave a peal of delighted laughter. "You rake, you have! Who was she? A maid? A lady? Your mistress? Do tell. I should like to know what company I keep."

His eyes narrowed with annoyance. "It occurred once several years ago, and she is now happily married with several children. The hour is getting late, Miss Thorncroft. We should seek our beds."

"Yes, we should," she agreed.

But neither of them moved, and as the air grew noticeably heavier, Evie wound her arms around her chest to brace herself against the brewing tempest.

"Do you still plan to ask for Lady Martha's hand in marriage?"

"No. Yes." He raked his fingers through his hair, and muttered a curse. "I don't know."

"You don't know," she repeated slowly. "Tell me, Lord Hawkridge, what is it you *do* know?"

His eyes, as dark and volatile as a storm cloud, shot to hers. "I know that I should not desire you as I do. I know that it was easier when I hated you. And I know...I know that no matter what I do, I cannot stop thinking about you. Those are the things that I know."

It was better than the cold slap of rejection that she had anticipated.

But it was far from the declaration of love that she needed.

"Then let me tell you the things *I* know," she said, proudly lifting her chin. "I know that I will not be a second choice. Not for you. Not for anyone. And I know that I will not leave my heart in your hands indefinitely. So take care to treat it kindly while you have it, Lord Hawkridge. For you may miss it far more than you realize when it's gone."

With that dire warning, she left the kitchen to seek her bed…and pray for a dreamless sleep.

CHAPTER NINETEEN

THE NEXT MORNING, Evie slept past breakfast and awoke to discover that the majority of the houseguests had made their way to the village for an afternoon of shopping and a tour of the local sights. She considered joining them, but decided to remain at Hawkridge Manor instead in the hopes that some peace and quiet might settle her thoughts.

When she went downstairs, with Posy bouncing energetically behind her, she discovered she wasn't the only one who had forgone a trip to the village.

"Your Grace," she greeted the Duke of Hanover upon finding him sitting by himself in the solarium. "I did not expect to see you here. Are the local sights of no interest to you?"

"As the pub doesn't open until after two, no, not really." He tipped his cup of coffee towards the sideboard. "The eggs have gone cold, but the salmon isn't half-bad. Won't you join me for a belated breakfast, Miss Thorncroft?"

"I would be happy to, although I shall pass on the salmon. I must confess I've never had much of an appetite for fish." Filling a plate with fresh cantaloupe sliced into neat squares and a few thin slices of beef, she also made sure to spoon blueberries into a bowl for Posy (the lamb had already devoured two bottles of warm milk) before sitting across from the duke who was studying Posy with a raised brow.

"Does it bite?" he asked warily.

"Posy?" Evie said with a laugh. "No, she is completely harmless, I can assure you."

"I knew a French count who kept a pet tiger in his bedchamber." Sterling scratched his freshly shaven jaw. Unlike the last time they'd met, he looked–at least by all outward appearances–to be sober and was handsomely dressed in a navy blue jacket with a high collar, satin waistcoat, gray breeches, and leather boots splattered lightly with mud, indicating he'd recently come from a ride.

"Oh?" she said, stabbing a piece of fruit with her fork.

"It went well, for a time. Until the tiger ate him."

Evie paused with the cantaloupe halfway to her lips. "The tiger...ate the count?"

"Indeed. Very messy affair. His heir was pleased, though." The edge of Sterling's mouth curled. "He was the one who gave the count the tiger."

"Surely you jest."

"Most times, yes. But never about anything as serious as premediated murder by jungle cat."

"How horrific for the poor count."

"I feel worse for the tiger, to be honest. Lord Dubois was a small little weasel of a man. He couldn't have tasted very good. Probably quite chewy."

"An unfortunate event all the way around then," Evie said solemnly.

"Indeed. Well, now that we've gotten the gruesome death and maiming portion of our discussion out of the way...how are things proceeding? With our Lord Hawkridge, that is. Still madly in love with him?"

She frowned. "I was hoping you might have forgotten I said that due to your...ah..."

"Drunken stupor?" He grinned at her. "No need to dance around the truth on my account. And while I only vaguely recall you begging to be my mistress and me doing the honorable thing and declining to preserve your womanly–"

Evie gave an unladylike snort. "Is *that* how you remember it?"

"Yes. I'm sure that is precisely how it happened."

"What an interesting memory you possess, Your Grace."

"Sterling," he corrected. "As I was saying, while I do not recollect our conversation by the stairs, I do remember, in great, embarrassing detail, everything that was spoken on the terrace. Give or take a few sentences here and there. By the by, did you happen to see what happened to the hat I was wearing? It happened to be my–"

"Second favorite," she interrupted. "Yes, so you told me. After you threw it over the balcony."

The duke's brows knitted. "Did I?"

Evie nodded. "I'm afraid so."

"That explains why my valet hasn't been able to find it among any of my belongings. Maybe I'll wait before telling him," he said thoughtfully. "It's kept Higgins busy, at any rate. Now, where were we, Miss Thorncroft? Ah, that's right. You were about to tell me how you could be in love with a scoundrel like Hawkridge and not with a perfectly honorable, well-behaving gentleman like me."

"Well-behaving?" she said, the edges of her mouth twitching. "You propositioned me on a landing, Your Grace."

"Although, as I said, my recollection of that particular part of the evening is blurry at best...that *does* sound like something I would do," he admitted.

"As far as how I came to be in love with Weston..." On a sigh, Evie laid down her fork and glanced woefully at Posy, who had finished off the blueberries and was licking the bowl with some enthusiasm. "If I knew that, I would immediately make myself fall *out* of love with him."

"Going that well, is it?" Sterling said dryly.

"It is not *going* anywhere," she said in frustration. "Aside from a few passionate encounters–"

"Do tell," the duke breathed.

"–it seems as if we're right where we started. Weston still plans to ask Lady Martha Smethwick to marry him, and to make matters even worse, he wants to find *me* a husband. A repayment in kind, he said, for taking my mother's ring and robbing my sisters and me of financial independence."

"Odd, I never fancied Lord Hawkridge as a matchmaker."

"He's not." Reaching beneath the table, she gave Posy an absent pat between her ears. "If he cannot even match *himself* with the right person, I've no idea how he plans to match me. I think it's just a means to keep me distracted."

"Or a way to keep you at Hawkridge Manor."

"Maybe," she said doubtfully. "If he *really* wanted to keep me here, he could simply propose."

"Ah, but what kind of story would that make?" Sterling asked. "The cold-hearted earl and the gorgeous American meet, fall in love, and get married? The readers would perish of boredom before the fifth chapter. There needs to be *angst*, my dear. Emotional turmoil. Will-they-or-won't-they. High drama at its finest. *That's* what makes a good romance."

"Why, Your Grace," she said with some amusement. "Have you been reading Austen?"

Sterling crossed his arms. "Even if I had, I'd never admit it."

"Then you've no opinion on Mr. Darcy?"

"That tosser?" The duke's lip curled. "Elizabeth could have done a far sight better."

"He came around in the end." And so, she hoped, would Weston. "Have you ever been in love, Your Grace?"

"Yes," he said darkly. "I wouldn't recommend it."

"Neither would I. I hadn't planned to, you know. Fall in love with

Weston, that is." She placed her elbow on the table and plopped her chin into the palm of her hand. She shouldn't have been admitting such intimate thoughts and feelings to a man who was, for all intents and purposes, a complete stranger. Not to mention a duke, besides. But she felt comfortable around Sterling in the same way that she felt comfortable around Joanna. And without her elder sister to confide in, a renowned rake and libertine would have to make do. "I just wanted to marry him for his money and title."

Sterling patted his chest. "A woman after my own heart."

"Then somewhere between there and here, that all changed." Her shoulders slumped. "This is why I never wanted to fall in love. Especially with someone who did not reciprocate my feelings."

"Weston is madly in love with you," Sterling said confidently, as if he were declaring that the sky was blue or water was wet. "He's just too much of a stubborn arse to admit it. Give him a bit more time yet to get his head on straight. Once he does, you'll have your Mr. Darcy."

There *were* striking similarities between Weston and Jane Austen's fictional protagonist. They were both aloof, unapproachable, emotionally detached men. Why, Mr. Darcy even had a sister! But that was fiction, she reminded herself. And this was real life. And even though Miss Austen had been immeasurably talented, even she could not have dreamed up a character as impossibly stubborn and infuriatingly obtuse as Weston Weston, Earl of Hawkridge. Even if she had, what heroine would have possibly been foolish enough to fall in love with such a man?

"How can you be so certain?" she asked Sterling glumly.

"Because he's as miserable as you are. And if that isn't a sign of being in love, I don't know what is. Chin up, my dear," he said encouragingly. "If Hawkridge ends up being too blind to see what's right in front of his face, then you could always marry me and become a duchess. Depending on if I'm summoned before the House of Lords and convicted of murder, you might never have to see me. Just spend my wealth as you see fit."

"It wouldn't be the most *terrible* thing in the world," she allowed.

Sterling grinned. "That's the spirit!"

When Posy bounded over to the door, her little tail wagging, Evie stood up. While the lamb possessed remarkable intelligence for such a small creature and was very nearly housebroken, she wasn't completely immune to accidents.

"Have a good rest of your day, Your Grace. I'm sure we'll see each other again soon."

"For the last time, it's Sterling," he admonished lightly. "And I'm sure we will. Best of luck, Miss Thorncroft. You're damned well going to need it."

AFTER A LONG, tediously dull dinner, Weston accompanied his houseguests out to the gardens where torches lit the night sky and cool, crisp air hinted of autumn nights soon to come.

Brynne had organized a popular parlor game for them all to play, but given the number of people involved, had decided to host it outside. After directing all of the men to the left side of the garden and all of the women to the right, she gave each lady an unwound spool while to the gentlemen she handed the end of a piece of thread that had been twisted around bushes, across fountains, and under statues, creating a veritable maze of colorful string.

Often played with the lights dimmed or, in this case, outside in a dark labyrinth of narrow stone pathways and towering hedges, the game was little more than an excuse to kiss or fondle a comely lady–or lord–without repercussion or judgment.

"Every person had been randomly assigned a partner," Brynne announced to a flurry of excited titters and giggles. "The first couple to unite their spool with the end of their thread shall be declared the winner! Are you ready?"

"Last time I did one of these, Lady Dunlop groped my bollocks,"

Sterling grumbled from beside Weston where they stood shoulder to shoulder at the end of the line.

"The dowager countess is nearly eighty years of age and half-blind," Weston said mildly. "I'm sure it was an accident."

"She knew exactly what she was doing."

"How was it?"

The duke shrugged. "Wasn't the worst grab and tickle I've ever had. Who are you hoping you're paired with? Lady Martha, I suppose."

"I haven't given it much thought," Weston lied.

Normally, such frivolous games were beneath his level of interest. Something to endure rather than enjoy. But as he glanced at the string he had tied around his wrist so as not to lose it in the dark, he couldn't escape the knowledge that there was only one woman he wanted to find on the other end.

And it wasn't Martha Smethwick.

For the entire dinner, and the hours preceding it, he had tried to gain Evie's attention. But whether by accident or design, her focus had always been on another. And when he'd seen her speaking exclusively with Mr. Greer during dessert, it had taken all of the self-control he had in him not to launch across the table and demand that his fellow board member immediately remove his hand from the back of Evie's chair lest Weston cut it off with a bread knife.

Jealousy was such an ugly emotion. Red, angry, and pulsing. Like a pustule that needed to be lanced.

But it was also revealing.

Even more so for Weston, as he'd never experienced jealousy like that before. He'd never felt strongly enough about someone *to* experience it before.

Until Evie waltzed into his arms...and turned his entire bloody world upside down.

He could go on, ignoring the obvious. Put his head to the ground and plow ahead with the life he'd planned. The life he'd told himself that he wanted. The life he'd convinced himself that he *needed*. But while Weston recognized his own obstinacy, he refused to submit to stupidity. And that's what ignoring Evie and his feelings for her would be.

Sheer, unforgivable, stupidity.

Because what they had between them…it was more than a physical attraction. It was deeper than a passing fascination. And it wasn't going away. Not if he found her a husband. Not if he married Lady Martha. Not even if he put a thousand miles and a thousand years between them.

Yesterday, today, tomorrow…it would always be Evie.

No matter what obstructions he threw in their path.

No matter what lies he told himself.

No matter what lies he told *her*.

For there was one more thing that he knew. One thing he'd kept from her in the kitchen. One thing he could not–he dared not–tell her. And what was a lie, if not telling someone the truth? Even if that truth meant stepping off the edge of a cliff and falling into the unknown.

"What are you two still doing here?" Brynne asked, frowning at both Weston and Sterling as she approached, carrying a small lantern. "If you hadn't noticed, the game has started."

Blinking, Weston realized belatedly that all of the guests had begun following their strings while he'd been trapped inside his own head. There was much shouting, high-pitched giggling, and even a few curses as men and women alike were forced to crawl under benches, through flowerbeds, and even over each other.

"Why don't you have to play?" Sterling demanded.

"Because someone has to declare the winner." Brynne's hazel eyes glittered with amusement. "And because I don't want to."

"Well that's not fair."

"When *you* organize a house party, you may set whatever rules you wish. In the meantime, go." She pointed her finger at Sterling, then gave her brother a not-so-gentle push. "Your participation is mandatory, not suggested."

Sterling turned beseechingly to Weston. "Hawkridge, my dearest friend–"

"I am not going to argue with my sister on your behalf."

"Pox on both of you." Drawing his string taut, the duke headed off in the direction of a mulberry tree, grumbling under his breath all the while.

"Who have you paired him up with this year?" Weston asked, lifting a brow.

Brynne's smile was secretive, and a tad mischievous. "Someone I think he'll be pleasantly surprised by."

"And my partner?"

"You know I cannot tell you that."

"As long as it's not Lady Dunlop." The corners of his eyes crinkled. "I hear she's quite the minx."

Brynne stared at him in astonishment. "*Weston.*"

"What?" he said defensively. "Do I've something on my face?"

"No, you told a jest. *And* you're grinning."

"People tell jests all of the time."

"Maybe, but *you* don't."

He rolled his eyes at that. "It was a quip, Bry. And not a particularly clever one at that. You needn't act as if you've just uncovered the Eighth Wonder of the World."

"Maybe not the eighth. But seeing my brother happy *is* a wonder." Her gaze softening, she reached out and tugged the thread around his wrist. "Best start following this, West. I've a feeling you are going to like what it leads you to."

CHAPTER TWENTY

AFTER TEARING HER gown on a rosebush, sinking up to her ankles in a puddle, and having her bottom "accidentally" grabbed by Lord Ellis, Evie decided to sit on a bench and wait for her Prince Charming to come to her.

Let *him* fend off the thorns and the mud and the lecherous old men. She'd just sit here, thank you very much, and count the stars.

She was nearing number eighty-seven when she heard the crack of a branch. The bench her string had led her to was isolated from the rest of the garden by a circle of shrubbery. There was a fountain in the middle, its marble basin reflecting the silvery light of a full moon, and a single stone pathway leading in and out.

While she'd been waiting for her (very late) prince to arrive, Evie had heard any number of couples successfully finding each other, their union generally marked with clapping...or, in a few notable instances, the rustle of fabric and telltale silence. She didn't have a way to account for exactly how many guests still remained in the game, but she had a feeling it wasn't many. For all she knew, she and her partner were the last ones left.

"Over here," she called out when she heard another branch crack underfoot.

Rustling leaves, a muttered curse, and then...

"There you are." Shooting her a disgruntled glare as he forcibly squeezed his large frame between a pair of boxwoods trimmed into narrow columns, Weston stumbled into the clearing and brushed himself off. "I've been looking everywhere."

"Well I have been right here. *Waiting*," she said with pointed emphasis.

Scowling, he plucked a shiny green leaf out of his hair. "The point of the game is that you follow your string. Not sit on a bench and have me do all the work. Do you have any idea how many damned bushes I've crawled through?"

Lifting her gloved hand, she made a show of studying her fingers in an attempt to disguise her surge of tingling excitement upon seeing him.

She had spent most of the day in the company of Rosemary. The cousins had made bows for Posy, and then ventured out to the stables to see the newborn foal who was already growing by leaps and bounds. During dinner, she'd found herself in a pleasant conversation with Mr. Greer, a charming businessman, whose knowledge of the rapidly developing railway industry had been both interesting and informative.

But from sunrise to sunset, even though she'd not spoken to him directly, she found her mind preoccupied with Weston. What he was doing. What he was thinking. If he'd proposed to Martha yet. There was no ring upon the lady's finger, but with less than a fortnight remaining before the end of the house party, time was of the essence.

For everyone.

After her chat with Sterling at breakfast, Evie's waning hopes that Weston might still come to his senses had been somewhat renewed. But she'd told him the truth when she'd said that she was not going to leave her heart in his care forever.

Perhaps not even for a fortnight.

Love required a certain amount of vulnerability...and faith. She had demonstrated both when she'd shared her feelings with Weston by the pond, and again in the kitchen. But she could not continue to remain defenseless indefinitely.

She *did* love the earl. Of that, she was certain. But if he continued to deny that love, to turn it away, or worse, to ignore it, then she'd rather have her heart in her own care and be alone than leave it with someone who did not appreciate its value.

"I am sure I don't know how many bushes you crawled through," she replied coolly. "Nor do I particularly care. Can we return to the manor now? Is the game over?"

"The game *is* over." Weston's shadow, long and lean, rippled across her as he stepped around the fountain and placed his hands on his hips, muscular thighs spread apart and head cocked ever-so-slightly to the left. "But we're not returning to the manor."

At the sheer intensity of his stare, her breath hitched. "We're–we're not?"

"No," he said. "Not until we've gotten some things straight."

"What things?" she whispered.

"It's become obvious that we cannot continue in this vein. That there are…there are feelings involved. Strong feelings. Feelings that I cannot continue to ignore."

This was it, she thought with a quiver of anticipation.

He is going to tell me that he loves me.

That he cannot wait to marry me.

That he wants to spend the rest of his life with me.

"Yes?" she prompted when he fell silent. "What else?"

His brow furrowing, his gaze went to the ground, then slowly rose to her face. "I…I have come to care for you, Miss Thorncroft."

"Care for me," she echoed when it became clear that was all he was going to say. "You *care* for me."

"Very much," he said, frowning, as if her reaction–or notable lack thereof–was not what he'd been anticipating.

"Oh," she said, her voice rising an octave. "You care for me *very* much. I see."

"Isn't that...isn't that what you wanted to hear?"

"Is that the only reason you said it, then? Because you thought I *wanted* to hear it?"

With the slowly dawning trepidation of someone who realized they'd just stepped into quicksand and were sinking rapidly, Weston both literally and figuratively began to retreat. "I...I am afraid I don't understand, Miss Thorncroft. I was under the impression that you would be pleased if I admitted how I felt."

"I am pleased," she said shrilly. "Do I not *look* pleased?"

"Not particularly, no."

"Maybe that's because I've served you my heart on a sterling silver platter, and you've just given it back to me on a tin plate." Anger and disappointment filled Evie in equal measure as she surged to her feet. "I am happy that you care for me, my lord. Truly. I also care for things. Like this–like this fountain." She gestured blindly at the marble statue in the middle of the glade. "Or this dress. Or these shoes, which are splattered in mud and most likely ruined."

Weston's frown transformed into a scowl. "You're acting irrationally."

"Maybe I am!" she exclaimed, flinging her arms wide. "But that's what love does to people. Or so the poets would have us believe. It makes them act irrationally. Fearlessly. Courageously. It took great courage for me to admit that I love you. I've never said that to a man before. I'd never planned to say it. Or maybe I did, but I wouldn't have meant it. Not really. Because I've never felt this...this *deeply* for anyone as I do for you. And to hear that you *care* for me...caring is all well and good. It certainly has its place. But it isn't love. So I'll ask, because you haven't offered to say it." She took a deep breath. A bracing breath. A potentially life-changing breath, depending on what awaited her on its release. "Do you love me, Weston?"

In a carefully neutral tone devoid of emotion that made her want to curl her hands into fists and pummel his chest, he began, "I care for you, Miss Thorncroft. Very much, as I said. One day, perhaps, that may turn into something that closely resembles–"

"Oh!" she cried, stomping her foot. "You're *impossible.*"

Unable to trust herself not to say something she'd come to regret in the morning once cooler heads had prevailed, she shoved past him and stormed towards the manor in a fit of indignation...and bitter, heartbroken dismay.

He could, Weston acknowledged in hindsight, have handled that better. Which was why he took it upon himself to seek out Evie before she sought her bed.

The hour was rapidly approaching midnight, but the game in the garden had filled everyone with renewed energy, and with the exception of Lady Danbury and a few other elderly guests, the main receiving parlor was a hive of activity as wine and gossip flowed freely.

Taking a glass of port from the tray of a passing servant, Weston indulged in a leisurely sip while he perused the room, staying to the back so as not to invite conversation. Unfortunately, despite his efforts at remaining inconspicuous, he was almost immediately singled out by none other than Lady Martha Smethwick.

"My lord," she said by way of greeting as she sidled up beside him and dipped into a graceful curtsy. "How did you find the gardens?"

Reluctantly placing his search for Evie on hold, Weston forced a tight-lipped smile. "Green, Lady Martha. Quite green."

"Oh, Lord Hawkridge," she giggled, her gloved fingers glancing off the side of his arm. "You are *such* the comedian. Who were you partnered with?"

"Miss Thorncroft," he said absently. "Lady Martha, if you will excuse me–"

"The American? I've not yet had the opportunity to speak with her, but she seems lovely. How do you find the weather, my lord, now that the rain has ceased?" Martha smiled, revealing even white teeth and the fluttering hint of a dimple. Her blonde hair was swept back from her delicate features in an intricate twist of curls, and her curves, slight as they may have been, were on full display in a yellow gown with a low bust and cinched waist. She was a beautiful woman; her reputation as one of the *ton's* premiere jewels well deserved. And she would make a perfect countess.

For someone else.

Because he no longer wanted perfection and all of the varied shades of blandness that accompanied it. He wanted...he wanted tension, and discord, and someone who would disagree with him. Zealously. And then make love to him with just as much passion.

He didn't want to stand in a parlor drinking port and discussing the bloody *weather*.

He wanted to be knee-deep in a pond with his boots stuck in the muck while the woman he loved challenged him from the shoreline. He wanted to ravish her in the stables, and the kitchen, and every other inappropriate place that would cause a woman of Martha's gentle breeding to faint at the mere thought of intimate relations being performed outside of the marital bed. He wanted to rescue orphaned animals, and go for long walks, and trade sarcastic quips over dinner.

And while he hadn't been able to give Evie the words he'd known that she wanted, that she *needed*, he felt them. Deep down inside, where it mattered most, he *did* love her. With everything he had. With everything he was. With everything he wanted to be.

"Excuse me, my lady," he said abruptly. "But there is someone I must speak with."

"Can it not wait?" Martha asked. "We've hardly had a moment to exchange more than a few words, my lord. When I received your invitation to attend the house party, I assumed..." She trailed delicately away. "But perhaps I was mistaken."

Damnit.

While he'd done little to encourage Martha's attention this past

Season, he hadn't actively *discouraged* it. Which meant that he couldn't merely push her aside without giving her the chance to find a proper replacement, or else the *ton* in all of its sharp-tongued cruelty would run wild with stories of how the Earl of Hawkridge had thrown over one of their own for an American.

The gossip would be meaningless to him. But he wouldn't want it to affect Martha, or her future prospects. She'd done nothing wrong, and he'd not let her shoulder the blame for his own indecisiveness.

"Would you like to take tea with me tomorrow in the music room before breakfast?" he asked. "There is something that we should probably discuss."

Martha's eyes lit. "Yes, of course. I would like that very much."

"In the meantime...have you met Mr. Greer?" Snagging Henry's arm as the poor unsuspecting fellow walked past on his way to the sideboard, Weston all but flung him into Martha's path. "Lady Martha Smethwick, might I introduce you to Mr. Henry Greer. Mr. Greer is the eldest son of Lord Crawford and a member on the board of Midland Railway Company. His assets are quite numerous and he is one of the smartest people I know. Isn't that right, Mr. Greer?"

"Ah..." Visibly caught off guard by the unexpected praise, Henry tugged at his collar where a dull flush had begun creeping up his neck. A personable gentleman with a slight bookish quality about him, he'd make as fine a husband as any for a lady of Martha's standing. Whereas it once would have been unthinkable for the daughter of a viscount to marry down in rank, such a match was now quite common courtesy of a surge in wealth amidst the working class.

The nobility was a dying breed. And those who insisted on clinging to the old ways of tenant farming and inheritance to fund their lavish spending habits were falling ill the quickest.

In three or four decades, mayhap even fewer, Weston doubted that there'd be much of an aristocracy left in England. Or the world over, for that matter. A good thing, in his opinion, as he'd never defined himself by his title...only the obligations that tied him to it.

"I don't know if I would describe my holdings as *numerous*–" Henry began.

"Nonsense," Weston said firmly. "What don't you take Lady Martha to get some refreshments, and you can tell her all about them."

Watching with some amusement as they walked away, their heads bowed together and Martha's hand lightly resting in the crook of Henry's elbow, he drained his port and set the empty glass aside on a table. But he'd no sooner caught a glimpse of Evie's dark hair beside the piano than Brynne approached him wearing a slightly quizzical smile.

"What have you done?" she asked, nodding towards the sideboard.

He followed her gaze to where Martha and Henry were leaning over a platter of coconut macaroons drizzled in chocolate and shrugged. "Matchmaking isn't as hard as people would lead you to believe."

"No," his twin agreed, "it isn't. All you really need is a common interest and a flicker of attraction. Sometimes not even that much. But why are *you* matchmaking? More importantly, why are you matchmaking for Lady Martha? Did she decline your proposal?"

He needed something stronger than port, Weston decided, if they were going to have this discussion here and now. "Come to my study," he said. "I'll explain everything there."

"You mean abandon my duties as hostess and leave our guests to socialize by themselves?" Brynne asked with a feigned gasp of horror. Her eyes twinkled. "Give me five minutes and I shall be right behind you."

As he left the parlor, Weston felt...free. As if a great burden had been lifted off him. One that he had carried for such a long time that it had become a part of him, like an arm or a leg. Had he done nothing to escape its weight, it would have continued to sit there. To grow heavier, and heavier, until one day the boy he used to be, the boy who had yearned for love above all else, would have been utterly eclipsed by the man who refused to believe in it.

Pouring himself a glass of his second-best scotch, he stood by the window as he waited for Brynne to join him. He knew that she'd long been hoping that he would listen to his heart instead of his head. Hoping that he would choose Evie instead of Martha. Hoping that he would be the first male in his family to marry for happily-ever-after instead of calculated convenience.

And his sister was right, bugger it.

She'd been right all along.

Not that he was stupid enough to tell her that.

"No need to knock, Brynne. Come right in," he said brusquely when a quiet fist tapped on the door. Except it wasn't his twin who entered the study, but rather his butler.

"My lord," Mr. Stevens said formally.

Weston lowered his scotch. "Is something amiss?"

"It is your father, my lord."

He stared at the butler in stunned silence for the span of three seconds, and then recovered enough to ask several question in rapid succession. "Has there been an accident? Is my father ill? Does he require the services of a doctor? Has he sent for me?"

"No, my lord. As far as I am aware, the marquess is in excellent health."

"Then by God, what is it?" Weston demanded.

"Your father...your father is *here*."

"Here?" he said blankly.

"At Hawkridge Manor, my lord. Your father is here at Hawkridge Manor."

CHAPTER TWENTY-ONE

H IS FATHER WAS here.
Of anywhere Weston would have preferred the Marquess of Dorchester to be–the ground being one of them–this was the worst place, and the worst *time*, his father possibly could have chosen to finally make an appearance.

Like a shark smelling blood in the water, had he known, somehow, that his only son and heir was on the brink of happiness? Or was he here for some other purpose?

There was only one way to find out.

"Send him in, Mr. Stevens," Weston said grimly, and then he sat behind his desk to wait.

When Jason Weston, Marquess of Dorchester, entered the study, the first thing Weston noted about his father was how *old* he appeared.

Maybe it was due to the fact that they hadn't seen each other in person for over a year. Or maybe it was simply because children always tended to view their parents through a lens that was unchanged by days, or months, or even years. Whatever the reason, it was clear that the marquess had aged considerably since they'd last occupied the same room.

Jason's hair, once as black and thick as his son's, was thinning and gray. His face had more creases. The back of his hands, when he removed his leather gloves, had more veins running through them.

His mouth was thinner. Flatter. His forehead more pronounced. But his eyes...cold, piercing, and gray...his eyes were exactly the same.

"Son," he said bluntly as he crossed the study and helped himself to a generous pour of scotch. "You appear healthy enough. A bit pale, perhaps. You should get outside more."

Five seconds in, and Weston's teeth were already on edge, his hackles raised, his hands knotted underneath his desk.

"Father," he replied just as curtly. "What are you doing here?"

"This *is* the annual house party, is it not?" Jason settled himself in an oversized chair and crossed his legs at the knee. "I presumed my attendance was expected."

"Expected, yes. Counted on, no." Weston forced himself to take a deep, even breath. Their last discussion had ended in an argument. Which wasn't a surprise, in and of itself. But it was the topic of that argument, namely, his father's American mistress, Anne Thorncroft, which had him proceeding with extreme caution. "You must have heard by now that your daughter and her sister have come to England."

"Joanna and Evelyn Thorncroft." The marquess glanced into his scotch before he raised the glass to his mouth and took a liberal swallow. "Yes, I am aware. It has also come to my attention that Jacob Thorncroft was killed during the War Between the States, leaving his three daughters and mother on the brink of destitution. I've already made arrangements for my solicitor to reach out to Joanna and settle a modest sum of ten thousand pounds in her name, to be used at her discretion."

A fortune, by anyone's standards.

And no less than what Joanna deserved.

Just a few weeks ago, Weston wouldn't have thought so. He'd have been angry–furious, even–that his father was bestowing a sizable inheritance upon an illegitimate daughter he'd never recognized, nor even met. But time (and Evie) had changed his perspective. And in his newly unfrozen heart, he wanted Joanna to get every penny. Even though...

"She may not accept it," he remarked.

"Of course she'll accept." Jason snorted into his scotch. "It's free money."

"Money cannot make up for a lifetime of anonymity."

The marquess' eyes chilled. "You know as well as I that Anne chose to raise her daughter in America, with another man as her father. It was not my decision. I merely honored it."

"Jacob Thorncroft died over six years ago. Had you loved Anne as much as you claim, then you'd have kept aware of–"

"How *dare* you question my devotion," Jason snarled, slapping his hand on the armrest of the chair. "I did love Anne. I loved her so much that I let her go, and I ensured our daughter's future financial security by giving Anne that blasted ring. Had you not taken it back, the Thorncrofts would have had wealth in perpetuity. *You* caused this. Not I."

As Weston met his father's steely, scornful gaze, he resisted the urge to shift in his chair. At five and twenty, how was it that he could still feel as if he were a lad of twelve, desperate for the marquess' approval...and withering beneath his contempt?

"I did nothing but return something to our family that never should have been bestowed outside of marriage," he said evenly. "Regardless of how strong your feelings were for Joanna's mother, the ring was not yours to give away. There were other means you could have used to provide for her and your daughter. Had you married Anne–"

"Do you think I didn't *try*?" Without warning, the marquess hurtled his empty glass of scotch across the room. It struck the wall and shattered, bits of glass exploding in a shower of crystal. "I asked her to marry me a dozen times. But she couldn't live in this life, and I couldn't leave it. So she left. With our child in her belly. And then…even then, I held out hope…" His countenance ravaged by desolation, Jason tilted his head back to look at the ceiling. "But she died of scarlet fever, and my hope died with her."

Weston stared at his father, stunned into speechlessness. Never, in his entire life, had he seen the marquess display this much emotion. He hadn't even known Jason was *capable* of feeling this strongly. But apparently, he was. Apparently, for his deceased mistress, he'd felt everything…until Anne's death robbed him of all compassion.

"You still had me," Weston said quietly. "You had me and Brynne. Your *children*."

"You were given the best tutors and nannies and governesses that money could buy."

"A tutor is not a father. A nanny is not a father. A *governess* is not a father."

The marquess slowly lowered his chin, and regarded his son with a heavy gaze. "I'd lost my wife, and the woman I loved. I was not in any shape to be a father when you and your sister were young. And as you grew older…as you grew older, it was easier to stay away. To distance myself from anything and anyone that reminded me of what it felt like…"

"What it felt like to what?" Weston asked when his father fell silent.

Jason closed his eyes. When he opened them, they were filled with an anguish so bleak that Weston felt the strike of it in his own heart. "What it felt like to love."

EVIE HAD TRIED to smile and nod her way through the rest of the evening as if nothing was amiss, but when she continued to catch herself searching for Weston's familiar face amidst the sea of guests, she knew it was time to retire to her room for the night.

Bidding farewell to Rosemary, she made her way upstairs where she was greeted by Posy, bouncing on the middle of the bed.

"Poor thing," she murmured when the lamb gave an excited bleat and launched herself off the mattress. Scooping Posy up into her arms, Evie pressed her face into the lamb's soft white fur and sighed. "You haven't gotten much attention today, have you? Not with all that's gone on. It's not fair for you to be stuck in this room all day while I'm doing other things. As soon as you're a bit bigger, we'll have to see about putting you out to live with the other sheep. Would you like that?"

Posy butted her head into the middle of Evie's chest, causing Evie to laugh. As soon as she did, the tension she'd been unconsciously carrying with her ever since leaving Weston in the gardens began to unravel, and after fetching a cloak to cover her gown, she carried Posy outside for a final romp before bed.

Using the servants' stairs so as not to disturb the ongoing revelry in the drawing room, she set the lamb on the grass, already damp with dew, and smiled with warm, cozy delight as Posy gamboled across the lawn, kicking and bucking.

"She's getting bigger," Weston remarked from the shadows, and Evie nearly fell as she spun around to face him and the flat soles of her shoes slipped on the wet grass.

"What–what are you doing lurking about?" she gasped, pressing a hand to her pounding heart.

"You mean what am I doing enjoying some fresh air while standing outside on the grounds of my estate?" he asked, a dark brow rising as he stepped away from the wall of climbing ivy that he'd blended so effortlessly into that she'd walked right past him without noticing his presence.

She gave a clipped nod. "You're right. It is your estate. I'll just fetch Posy, and we'll–"

"Don't go," Weston said hoarsely, and the raw, haunted glimpse of vulnerability she saw in the depths of his gaze made her heart ache. "Please."

"What happened?" she whispered, fingertips gliding across his temple as she pushed a lock of inky black hair out of his eyes.

He leaned into the palm of her hand. "My father has paid me an unexpected visit."

"Oh. I...I understand." She didn't. Not really. How could she, when he'd hardly spoken of his father at all? Everything she knew about Weston's relationship with the marquess had come from a third party. But she didn't need to be privy to every intimate detail to see that he was hurting.

And that he needed her to comfort him.

"It's all right," she murmured soothingly. "It's going to be all right."

"I need..." He trembled; a hard jolt that traveled the length of his entire body. Lifting his head, he spanned her waist with his hands. "I need *you*, Evelyn."

She was still frustrated with him. Irritated. Mayhap even a little angry. But how could she deny him such a request when it seemed as if his very life depended on it? Especially when she needed him just as much.

If not more.

The dark scruff on his jaw scraped against her skin as she grasped the sides of his face and rose up onto her toes. A brief, searching look into his eyes and then she pressed her lips to his.

At first, the kiss was soft. Gentle. Almost delicate, like the underside of a rose petal. But it wasn't long before the spark between them caught fire, and they were both basking in the glow of the flames.

Madness in the moonlight, she thought dimly as his tongue slid between her lips and her nails dug into the nape of his neck.

Their kiss was feverish.

Desperate.

Daring.

Anyone could have glanced out the window or walked out the

door and seen them, but Evie didn't care. Neither, it seemed, did Weston. Their only concern was each other...their only care was how fast they could sate the restless yearning building inside of them.

He backed her up against the side of the manor where ivy climbed a wooden trellis. Glossy green leaves tangled in her hair as Weston captured both of her wrists and raised her arms above her head, leaving her helplessly exposed to his ravenous, carnal appetite.

"Evelyn. Evelyn. Sweet Evelyn." He repeated her name as if it were a prayer as his mouth skimmed down her throat. She writhed against him, instinctively arching her hips so that all the pulsing heat centered between her thighs rubbed against his hard, throbbing arousal.

He kissed his way to her breasts, impatiently shoving the folds of her cloak aside so that he could suckle her nipples through the sheer layers of fabric that comprised her bodice. When he dropped to his knees and released her arms, she helped him yank up her skirts and quivered like a bowstring drawn taut at that first electric touch of his tongue against the most intimate, sensitive part of her entire body.

Her head thrashed against the ivy as he pleasured her, first with his mouth, and then with his fingers, and then both at the same time in an undulating rhythm that sent her spiraling into oblivion with such savage speed she hardly had time to catch her breath before he drove her off the edge again...and *again*.

When he rose to his feet and sought his own release with his hand, she clung to him, burrowing her face into the valley beneath the slant of his collarbone. And when it was over, when their desires were finally sated, they clung to each other as their harsh breathing stained the air and their heartbeats gradually slowed.

Without a word, Weston helped her straighten her dress and fix the lay of her cloak so that it concealed her breasts and the wet circles his wicked tongue had left behind before he shoved his shirttails back into his trousers and adjusted his jacket.

"Thank you," he said, tenderly brushing a curl off her cheek.

"For what?" she asked, tilting her head back.

"For being there when I needed you most. Evelyn, I–"

But much to Evie's annoyance, whatever he was about to say would have to wait, for with a spill of light and a shout of laughter a trio of drunken guests spilled out of the servants' entrance.

"I say," said the man in the middle, peering out into the darkness. "Is that a wolf?"

"Don't be silly," said the woman beside him. "It's clearly a cat."

"A cat wolf?" the third, another woman, slurred. "Never 'eard of it."

"Actually," Evie chimed in as she left Weston standing in the shadows, "it is a lamb. Her name is Posy."

"Posy," the man repeated.

"Told you it wasn't a wolf," said his companion, nudging him in the ribs.

"I knew that," he said defensively.

"Come along now, Posy. It's time for bed." Evie patted her thigh, and the lamb obediently bounced over. Casting a discreet glance over her shoulder, she met Weston's gray, possessive gaze...and with the curving hint of a smile, she scooped Posy into her arms and went inside.

EVIE WOKE AT dawn the next day. She knew that Weston took an early ride each morning, and she wanted to try to meet him upon his return before everyone gathered for breakfast in the solarium.

She dressed with great care, mulling over her wardrobe for the better part of an hour before she settled on a frothy pink gown with satin stripes on the skirt and silk flower trim along the bodice.

The dress was far more suitable for a ball than a breakfast, but it wasn't every day a woman became engaged to the man she loved! And after their encounter by the trellis, she knew, she just knew, that

Weston was going to ask her to marry him. Or, if not an outright proposal, surely he would confess his feelings. His *real* feelings. Because surely he never could have displayed such wrenching vulnerability to someone he only cared about.

He loved her.

She was convinced that he did.

And after this morning, she'd have the words she needed to validate giving him her heart to have and to hold.

"You're up early, Miss Thorncroft," Mrs. Grimsby, the housekeeper, noted as Evie all but floated down the main staircase. "And don't you look nice! Pretty as a painting, dear."

"Thank you," Evie beamed. "It's a beautiful morning, isn't it?"

"It is nice to see the sun after all that rain," Mrs. Grimsby agreed. "The birds are happy as well. I've rarely heard them chirping this loud. Is there anything I can help you with, Miss Thorncroft?"

"Yes, as a matter of fact. Has Lord Hawkridge returned from his ride yet?"

"Oh, he didn't go on his ride this morning."

That gave Evie pause. "He didn't?"

"No. If you are looking for a word, I believe he is in the music room. At least, that's where he was the last time I walked by."

It was all Evie could do not to jump with excitement. "Thank you, Mrs. Grimsby!"

"Wait!" the housekeeper said with some alarm. "He's not–"

But whatever Mrs. Grimsby said was drowned out by the excited elated buzzing in Evie's ears as she picked up her skirts and dashed off down the hall.

She found the door to the music room slightly ajar. Out of habit born from eavesdropping on her sisters, she peered through the tiny gap in the wood before she announced her presence...and all of the blood drained from her face at what she saw.

At first, she didn't believe it.

She blinked.

Rubbed her eyes.

Even pinched herself again, just to make sure she wasn't dreaming.

But this was no dream.

It was a waking nightmare.

For there, in the middle of the room on a blue velvet sofa, sat Lady Martha Smethwick. And beside her, down on bended knee, was Weston.

Biting her lip to stifle her cry of dismay, Evie stumbled back from the door.

And then she ran.

All the way to London.

CHAPTER TWENTY-TWO

THIS TIME, THE carriage's axle did *not* break (a small miracle but, at this point, Evie would take whatever she could get) and she arrived in England's busiest city by late afternoon. She had the driver bring her straight to Mrs. Privet's Boarding House; the last place she knew Joanna to have been with any certainty.

It was strange to walk through the front door and into the velvet walled lobby with its sagging floors and moth chewed furniture. In some aspects, it felt as if only yesterday she and her sister had come here to request lodging. Fresh off the ship that had ferried them across the Atlantic, they'd been energetic and hopeful. Joanna more so than Evie, as she'd still been queasy from spending the better part of a month spitting up into a bucket. But they had both been looking forward to what London might bring them.

For Joanna, the secrets of her past.

For Evie, a handsome duke to marry, as if they were low-hanging fruit that she had only to pluck off the tree. A notion that she'd found herself quickly disabused of. While dukes were plentiful in all of the romantic novels that she'd occasionally stolen from Joanna's bedside table, it immediately became clear that their abundance in real life had been greatly exaggerated.

The one thing Evie *hadn't* been searching for?

Love.

Which made it an even crueler twist of fate that it was the one thing she'd found.

As she rang the bell on Mrs. Privet's desk and waited for someone to come down the stairs to assist her, she could not help but reflect on how different she was now than she'd been then. If she were to stand in front of a mirror that somehow revealed all of her innermost thoughts and desires, she doubted if her past self would even recognize the woman that she'd become.

How vain she had been! Vain, and foolish, and appallingly arrogant to ever believe that she wanted a life without love. That money and social clout were the most important things a person could have, and everything was secondary. Including her own happiness. For while she might have had the respect and admiration of her peers had she married for wealth and status alone, she would have eventually lost the respect and admiration she had for herself.

And she never would have found true happiness.

The poets were right, it appeared.

Pompous literary lyrists that they were.

In the words of Alfred Tennyson, it really *was* better to have loved and lost then to have never loved at all. A difficult lesson that she was glad to have learned. For even though her heart was broken, the pain was a sign that she'd had a heart to break.

And wasn't that a beautiful thing?

"Miss Thorncroft!" a familiar voice rang out from the top of the staircase. "What are you doing here? I did not expect you back for another week at least."

"Mrs. Benedict." Smiling warmly at the widow as she hurried down the stairs, Evie embraced her at the bottom. A longtime resident of the boarding house, Mrs. Benedict had befriended Evie within the first few days of her arrival. While Joanna was doing heaven knew what with her private detective, Evie and Mrs. Benedict had played many a game of whist, strolled through Hyde Park, and even dined at the Claridge Hotel.

"I've come to see Joanna," she explained as the two women broke apart. "My cousin, Miss Rosemary Stanhope, joined me at Hawkridge Manor and shared that my sister did not depart London as planned. Have you seen her? Is she still staying here?"

An odd flicker of emotion passed over the widow's countenance. "I...I *have* seen her. Recently, as a matter of fact. But she is not here at the boarding house."

"Then where has she gone?"

"To live with Mr. Kincaid."

Evie's eyes widened. "To *live* with him? Are you certain?"

She'd known that Joanna choosing to remain in England could only mean that she and Kincaid had worked out whatever ills were plaguing them. But surely her sister would have known better than to completely tear asunder her reputation by deciding to live with a man she was not related to.

Or maybe not.

Joanna was nothing if not stubbornly impulsive, and when she fixed her heart on something, she often lost her head.

But to have become a private detective's *mistress*...

That surely went beyond the pale, even for Joanna.

"It appears I've arrived not a moment too soon," she said grimly. "Can you direct me to Mr. Kincaid's residence? I've never been there before."

Mrs. Benedict nodded. "It is not difficult to find, nor is it far. Just follow this street out to its end, turn left, and..."

"Someone–someone is at the door," Joanna gasped as the unmistakable sound of a fist knocking on wood carried up the stairs and into the bedchamber where she laid sprawled on her back across the mattress.

"They can come back later," Kincaid murmured against her flesh. "After *you've* come. For the second time."

"It would be the third, actually, and they sound quite insistent." Tightening her grip on the wooden spindles that comprised the headboard of their very large bed, Joanna pulled her naked, slender body upright. Her hair spilled across her shoulders in a riotous curtain of flame. "We should see who it is. Maybe it's a new case."

On a sigh of exasperation, Kincaid lifted his head from between her thighs and sat back on his haunches. "You're serious, aren't you? You really want to stop in the middle of our lovemaking to go answer the door."

"It *is* the afternoon," she pointed out. "Besides, what if it's another client? Another *wealthy* client." She arched her eyebrows suggestively. "It would be our third one this week."

"Only because you let it slip that I am representing the Duke of Hanover." Reaching around her, Kincaid grabbed his spectacles off the bedside table and slipped them onto his face. As his eyes came into focus, he used them to glare at her. "You never should have that let slip. Sterling requested my discretion."

"But Sterling isn't even in London, is he?" she said lightly. "And it's not as if I put out an advertisement in the paper. I merely told a few people, who told a few other people. You should be *thanking* me. In less than a month, you've seen more business than all of last year. Which reminds me. I think we should put a sign out front. It would lend an air of professionalism and impress our more esteemed clientele." She spread her hands apart as if the sign was directly in front of her. "Thorncroft and Kincaid, Private Investigators."

"If you were a private investigator, which you're not, your name wouldn't be first on the sign. Furthermore, that isn't even your—get back here," he demanded, grabbing her ankle when she tried to slip off the bed. "I'm not nearly finished with you yet."

Squealing, Joanna let herself fall back onto Kincaid's hard chest. But when he began to kiss his way down her neck, she resisted.

Barely.

"They're still knocking. It must be important."

"It better be," he growled.

They helped each other dress, Joanna's layers of garments taking considerably longer to put on, and went to answer the door together.

"Please pardon the delay," Kincaid began. "We were–"

"EVIE!" Joanna screeched, launching herself at her sister with such force that they were both propelled off the front steps and onto the stone pathway. "What are you doing here?"

Prying Joanna's arms off her neck, Evie coughed and said, "I could ask you the same thing. I *will* ask you the same thing." Her blue eyes flicked to Kincaid, who was standing in the doorway, then narrowed on Joanna. "What are *you* doing here? Mrs. Benedict said that you've moved in. But that cannot be true. Even you wouldn't do anything so reckless." She hesitated. "Would you?"

"Come in, and I'll explain everything." She pushed her sister past Kincaid, then glanced back him over her shoulder. "You don't mind if we borrow your office, do you?"

"I–"

"Splendid." Ushering Evie inside the room (which was now, courtesy of Joanna's organizational skills, meticulously clean), she shut the door in Kincaid's face and leaned against it. "I'm so glad to see you. I've *missed* you," she said with feeling, and it was true. Despite the happiness she had found with Kincaid, she'd been unable to escape the vague notion that something was missing. And it wasn't until the door had opened and she'd seen Evie's face that she realized she wasn't missing something, but rather *someone.*

"I've so much to tell you," she said, clapping her hands together. "I had planned to surprise you when you returned from the house party, but this is even better. Is it done?" Her head tilted. "I could have sworn it was for the entire month."

"It was," Evie said shortly. "I left early. Jo...are you...and Kincaid...er..."

"Intimate?" Joanna grinned. "Yes, exceedingly so. But I already know what you're thinking, and it's all right."

"How can sleeping with a man out of wedlock be all right?" Evie cried. "Never mind what it will do to your good name. When Grandmother hears of this–"

"Kincaid and I were married two days after you left for Hawkridge Manor. I should have sent word," she said in a rush when Evie paled. "But it happened so fast, and it was a small ceremony. There were no guests. Just our two witnesses, Mrs. Benedict and James. We'd like to return to Somerville and have a reception in the summer with you, and Claire, and Grandmother. Maybe even Rosemary could attend, if she wouldn't mind the travel."

Evie was silent for such a long while that Joanna began to fret.

"I am sorry," she began, raising her arms beseechingly. "Please forgive me. You should have been there. I know that. But you'd only arrived at Hawkridge Manor, and I did not want to pull you away so soon, and–"

"James is a cat," Evie interrupted.

"What?"

"James." Her sister's dark brows drew together in bemusement. "You told me that James was a witness for your wedding, but he is a cat."

"Oh. Yes, well, we couldn't find anyone else at the last minute and the vicar's eyesight wasn't very good, and..." Joanna relaxed when Evie began to laugh. "You're not angry."

"No, I'm happy for you. I am. Of course I wish I could have been there, but I understand why I wasn't, and you're right, we'll have a grand celebration this summer. I'm happy for you. So very, very h-happy." Evie's voice cracked and, all of a sudden, she wasn't laughing, but crying.

Stunned, Joanna ran across the room and wrapped her arms around her sister as Evie's entire body shook with sobs. There were only two times she recalled that Evie had ever cried. Or at least, that she'd seen her cry. The first, when Evie was of school age and a bully by the name of Violeta Arbor had mocked her dress. And the second, when she'd tried out some sort of new cream and her entire face and neck had turned as orange as a carrot.

"Evelyn, what's *happened?*" Joanna said, aghast.

Lifting her tear-stained countenance from where she'd buried it the crook of her sister's shoulder, Evie drew a deep, trembling breath. "I fell in love."

Had her sister revealed that she'd joined a traveling circus and would be performing with elephants, Joanna might have been more prepared.

"You...you fell in love," she repeated, slowly and carefully, to ensure that was what Evie had really meant to say.

"Is that so impossible to believe?" Evie asked, lifting her head.

"No, no," she said hurriedly. "It's just that...well...I was under the impression you didn't believe in it. Love, that is."

"I've always believed in it," her sister sniffled. "I simply didn't think it was advantageous for me, personally."

"And now?"

"And now it turns out I was right. Love isn't advantageous." More tears brimmed in Evie's eyes. "It's *awful.*"

Taking Evie by the arm, Joanna gently guided her out of the office and across the hall to the parlor. Once plain, barren, and all but screaming "a bachelor lives here", she had since turned it into a cheerful receiving room for clients, complete with serene paintings of the countryside, calming blue draperies, and a matching set of second-hand furniture upholstered in striped satin and trimmed in rosewood. Sitting her sister on a sofa, she sat directly beside her and clasped their hands together.

"Speaking from experience," she began, "love *is* awful. It was for me, at first. But love is also grand. And...and magnificent. And glowing."

Evie wiped her damp nose with her sleeve. "Do I look like I'm glowing?" she said miserably.

"Well, no," Joanna admitted.

"That's because the man I fell in love with just proposed to someone else."

"Oh." Desperately, she searched for the right words to bring a glimmer of light to a situation that seemed as dark as it could possibly get. "That's..."

"Not good."

"No." Sometimes, Joanna supposed, there weren't any right words. There was just pain. To be felt, and absorbed, and reckoned with. "That's not good at all. I'm sorry, Evie."

"The worst part is that I didn't *plan* to fall in love with him." She gave a bewildered shake of her head. "It just...*happened*. And I thought it had happened to him, too, but it must not have, or else he wouldn't have asked Lady Martha Smethwick to marry him. Do you know that she is a diamond? I was a diamond, in Somerville. But here...here I'm just stupid quartz."

Joanna had absolutely no idea what Evie was talking about.

"Quartz is pretty," she said tentatively. "I love quartz."

"No one *loves* quartz."

"Well I do. And if this man you've fallen in love with had an ounce of sense in his head, he would love it, too." Joanna paused. "Who *is* he, by the way? A guest at the house party, I presume."

Evie pursed her lips. "Weston. I've fallen in love with Weston. Whom I hate. And don't look surprised. I told you I wanted to marry him."

"Wanting to marry someone for their fortune and falling in love with them are two very different things. If I recall, the last time we spoke about Weston, you referred to him as a 'selfish, domineering, arrogant lout'."

"He's all that and more."

"And yet you love him?"

"I didn't say I was *happy* about it."

Joanna sighed. "Thorncroft women *really* don't do anything the easy way, do they?"

JOANNA HAD JUST gotten Evie settled in the guest bedroom with a cup of hot tea and a slab of chocolate when someone knocked on the door again.

"Who is it *this* time," she muttered under her breath as she hurried back down the stairs and through the narrow foyer, James trailing after her like a silent black shadow. Kincaid had stepped out shortly after Evie arrived; as much to give the sisters privacy as to follow a new lead on the Duke of Hanover's case.

It appeared there'd been a sighting of Hannah, the lady's maid who had worked for the duke's mistress...and had disappeared, somewhat suspiciously, a few days before Eloise's untimely death.

If Kincaid could find Hannah, and question her, it might prove to be the break in the case they desperately needed. For thus far, despite their best efforts, Kincaid and Joanna had been unable to unearth any evidence that pointed at anyone *other* than Sterling as the murderer. Which was particularly vexing, given that he was innocent.

Someone very clever had gone out of their way to frame the duke...and they'd done an excellent job at covering their tracks.

"I'm almost there!" she called out irritably when the knocking grew louder and more insistent. Despite her earlier insistence that Kincaid answer the door, she was of half a mind to let whoever this was come back at a later time so that she could focus all of her attention on Evie.

She'd never seen her sister in such a state.

Then again, she'd never seen her sister in love. And having just gone through the process herself, Joanna could attest to how painful it could be when things did not turn out how you expected them. Thankfully, she and Kincaid had worked through their differences and she had never been happier. She only hoped that, soon, the same might be said of Evie.

When whoever was on the other side of the door struck it hard enough to rattle the brass knob, Joanna flicked a glance at James. "If it's someone come to rob us, I'll grab Kincaid's pistol from the office and you scratch his eyes out. Deal?"

James gave a loud meow, which she took as a resounding yes.

"Do you know," she said as she opened the door, "it's appallingly rude to–*you*."

The man on the other side of the threshold frowned at her. "Do I...*Joanna*. I mean to say, Miss Thorncroft." Visibly taken aback, he removed his hat and raked a hand through his hair, shoving a wave of inky black off his temple. "I...I..."

"Actually, it's Mrs. Kincaid now." Joanna's smile could have been carved from the edge of a razor blade. "Won't you come in...brother?"

CHAPTER TWENTY-THREE

L OOKING AT IT now, Weston supposed that he should have expected to see his half-sister at the residence of the man she was romantically involved with. *Make that the man she was married to,* he corrected himself silently. But from the moment he'd reached London, his only concern had been finding Evie.

He had discovered she was missing when she did not come down for breakfast. Eager to see her, to speak with her, to share his heart with her, he'd gone straight to her bedchamber. But when he knocked on the door, she wasn't there. Instead, he'd found Hannah, her lady's maid, in the midst of packing all of Evie's beloved dresses into a traveling trunk. And he'd known, even before Hannah told him, that she was gone.

"When?" he'd asked tersely.

"Half an hour ago, my lord," Hannah had replied.

"Did she say anything?"

"She asked me to have her things sent to a boarding house in London, and for me to look after Posy. She...she didn't appear herself, my lord." At that revelation, the maid had ducked her head and spoken to the ground as she mumbled, "I would have gone straight to you or Lady Brynne, but Miss Thorncroft asked for my discretion. I...I wasn't sure what to do." Anxiously, she'd lifted her head. "I hope I did not do anything wrong, my lord."

"The only person who did something wrong was me," he'd said darkly before he spun from the room and ordered the first footman he saw to ready his fastest horse.

After that, everything was a blur until he had arrived in London and gone straight to the boarding house. Evie wasn't there, but a kind widow named Mrs. Benedict was, and she had directed him on where to go next.

"Mr. Kincaid's residence isn't too far," she'd said. "Just a few blocks. You won't even need a hackney if you don't mind going by foot."

He'd run the entire way. Not stopping to catch his breath...or to consider that Evie wasn't the only Thorncroft who might be waiting behind the private detective's door.

"Coffee or tea?" Joanna said pleasantly. She had taken him into her husband's office and invited him to sit in a chair while she stood behind the desk, as clear a message as any he'd ever received of who was in charge.

"Neither, thank you," he declined.

"Good. Then you can tell me why you broke my sister's heart and how you intend to fix it."

Right to the matter at hand, then.

"I–" He paused when he felt something brush against his pant leg. A glance down revealed it was a black cat with green eyes and bared fangs. As he met the feline's gaze, it gave a hiss and swatted at his calf. "Bloody hell."

"James is not overly fond of liars or thieves." Joanna braced her arms on the desk and leaned towards him. "Given that you've already proven yourself a thief, I would strongly advise you against lying."

"I hadn't planned on it."

"Excellent."

"Where is Evelyn? I need to–"

"My sister is currently resting. I have never seen her this upset. If you've done her irreparable harm, Lord Hawkridge, I am afraid I'm going to have to kill you." While Joanna tempered her threat with a smile, there was no doubt in Weston's mind that she meant every word.

"I never wanted to hurt Evelyn. I came here to tell her that I..." When his throat tightened, he broke off and stared intently at a blank space on the wall. "The words I want to say are for her to hear. Your sister...your sister has changed me for the better. And I will not lose her." Distraught, he met Joanna's steady gaze. "I *cannot* lose her. Which is why I must speak to her."

Joanna was quiet for nearly a minute.

Just as Weston was considering if he'd be able to make it to the door before James used his claws and teeth to carve into him like a roasted ham, she finally spoke.

"Evie is upstairs. The second door on the right."

Relief washed over him. "Thank you."

"Lord Hawkridge," she said as he turned to leave the office. "When you are done groveling for whatever it is you've done, I should like us to make the time to get to know each other. Aside from you stealing my mother's ring and breaking my sister's heart, I've a feeling we might get on splendidly."

"I...I should like that as well," he said gruffly and, to his surprise, he really meant it. Where once he could not have cared less if he ever saw or heard from Joanna Thorncroft again, now he wanted to build a relationship with her.

Not because of Evie.

Well, not *just* because of Evie.

But because family was what you made of it. His father had taught him that, if nothing else. And if Evie would have him...if Evie would have him, he wanted to make something wonderful.

EVIE LIFTED HER head off the pillow when a quiet knock sounded at the door. "Come in if you've more chocolate," she told Joanna. "Otherwise I am going to try to take a nap."

"I'm afraid I haven't any chocolate," a deep voice replied as the door swung inward. "But hopefully, I've brought you something better."

On a gasp, Evie scrambled into a sitting position and yanked a pillow against her chest as if it were a shield of iron instead of a soft pile of feathers sewn in cotton. "What are you *doing* here?" she asked, gaping at Weston. "When–when did you leave Hawkridge Manor?"

"As soon as I realized that you had," he said simply. His hands sliding into the pockets of his trousers, he regarded her with a vaguely bemused expression, as if he'd been presented with a puzzle that he couldn't quite solve. "You *left* me, Evelyn."

"You gave me no choice, Weston." Dashing her fingers beneath her eyes to remove any stray tears, she straightened her spine and regarded him with as much composure as she could muster, given the circumstances.

Evie hadn't abandoned the manor in an attempt to lure Weston away. It was not some grand plan to get him to come after her. Rather, she'd left because she couldn't physically stand to remain in the same house as the earl...and his future countess. Listening to people congratulate them, raising a champagne glass in their honor...it would have been too much to bear. Seeing another woman wearing her mother's ring wouldn't have just broken Evie's heart. It would have *shattered* it. And she knew, as clearly as she knew her own name, that she'd never be able to find all the pieces.

Thus she had run, as far and fast as she could. And in all that running, she had never–not once–allowed herself to think that Weston might actually follow. Yet here he was all the same. Dressed in the very same clothes he'd worn yesterday. His hair tousled and his face red from the wind, as if he had galloped the entire way.

To her.

"What are you doing here?" she repeated quietly. "Why have you come?"

"It was not only me you left behind." Stepping into the room, he closed the door behind him. Sunlight trickled in through the window beside the bed, softening the stern brackets around the edges of his mouth. "Posy will wonder where you've gone."

Evie hugged her pillow closer. "I left her in the care of my lady's maid. She'll feed her with a bottle until she's grown enough to be with the other sheep. I couldn't bring a lamb to London."

"And an earl?" he asked. "I suppose you couldn't bring one of those either."

"I would have, but I–" She stopped herself short. "It doesn't matter."

"It matters to me." He moved closer. "*You* matter to me, Evelyn."

Her brow creased with annoyance. "You've an odd way of showing that."

"I know I haven't made any of this easy. For you, for me. I was...I was in a constant battle, between my head"–sliding his hand free of his pocket, he grimaced as he tapped a finger against the side of his skull–"and my heart. A long time ago, I made the decision that I never wanted to be hurt or disappointed by anyone ever again. But in order to do that, I had to close myself off. From the bad *and* the good. From what had been, but also from what *could* be. And I grew so accustomed to being in that isolated room that I never even noticed when the walls closed in and the light turned to shadow."

"Why...why are you telling me all this?" she asked, wetting her lips.

"Because I would have stayed in that dark, windowless room for the rest of my life if not for you." His mouth curved in a wry grin, the first she'd ever seen. It made him appear more youthful. More carefree. As if an enormous weight had been lifted off his shoulders. "You didn't just open the door, Evelyn. You kicked the damned thing down."

"I *have* been told I am very strong for my size," she said modestly.

His grin deepened. "I should have just walked right through the door the minute you kicked it down. It was open, and you were standing on the other side of it. Bold, and brazen, and beautiful. I didn't know what to make of you. Hell, part of me still doesn't. But I *do* know that I never want to lock myself in that room again, I want the light, Evelyn. I want you."

It didn't feel real.

He didn't feel real.

But wasn't that the very definition of a dream? All of your wildest fantasies come true. Except it was happening while she awake. Unless she *was* asleep. Slightly panicked, Evie pinched the inside of her elbow.

"Ouch," she exclaimed, and Weston chuckled.

"Come here," he beckoned, extending his arms.

"Why?" she asked, even as she set her pillow aside and slid off the edge of the bed. The floorboards were cold against her bare feet, but Weston's hands were warm when he gently grasped her face, his thumbs resting on the edge of her jaw as his fingers splayed across her cheeks.

"Because," he said huskily, "when I tell you that I've fallen in love with you, I want to be able to look straight into your eyes. Do you know that since the day I met you, I have started noticing blue everywhere? The sky in all its varied shades, the water, even the damned curtains. But there is no blue more clear, nor more stunning, than the blue in your eyes."

As the floor tilted beneath her, Evie grabbed on to the lapels of Weston's jacket to steady herself. "You've fallen in love with me," she echoed, unable to keep the astonishment out of her voice...or her heart from doing a joyous leap within her chest. "Is this...is this a jest?"

"No, I am not jesting. Nor would I about something this important. I may have resisted falling at first "

"*May* have?" she said, arching a brow.

Another grin, this one even bigger than the last, as if his facial muscles had been frozen along with his heart, and when his chest had finally thawed so had every other part of him. "All right, I chained myself to a boulder. But you held the key. All this time, *you* held the key. I could have no more not fallen in love with you than the sun could stop shining in the middle of a summer day, or the rain could stop falling in the midst of a storm." His knuckles brushed across her cheekbone as he tucked a loose curl behind her ear. "Loving you was always inevitable, Evelyn. *Always.*"

It was everything she had wanted to hear. Everything she had dreamed of. Everything she had waited for.

And she was at a complete and utter loss of words for how to respond.

Her mouth opened. Closed. Stunned, she could only blink slowly at him, like a fish staring out of a glass bowl.

The man she loved beyond reason, the man she wanted to spend the rest of her life with, had just confessed his love for her…and she'd turned into a goldfish.

"Why, Miss Thorncroft," Weston drawled, as if he sensed her dilemma and was thoroughly amused by it. "Have I done the impossible and rendered you speechless?"

"I-I am not *speechless*," she said defensively. "I just…don't know what to say."

"Unless I am mistaken, that is the very definition of–"

"Oh, just be quiet and kiss me." Rising onto her toes, she pressed her mouth to Weston's and with a low chuckle, he obeyed her request.

There were no need for words after that.

At least, not for a very long while.

But when they eventually surfaced from their haze of passion, there was something Evie needed to say. Lifting herself up on her elbow (somehow, they'd ended up sprawled on the floor in a tangle of limbs), she absently drew a circle in the middle of his abdomen with her finger.

"But what about Lady Martha?" she asked, stealing a glance at him from beneath her lashes. "I *saw* you proposing to her in the parlor. That was why I left. I could not bear the thought of you marrying another."

Capturing her wrist, he raised her hand to his lips and kissed the back of it as he gazed steadily into her eyes. "I was not proposing, I was searching for an earring that she dropped. And explaining that while she will undoubtedly make a man very happy one day, I am not that man. I took it upon myself to steer her in the direction of a good friend of mine. If I had to guess, she'll soon have the proposal that she wanted. Which reminds me..."

Rolling nimbly to his feet, he briefly scoured the room before he found his jacket draped over a bedpost. From an interior satin pocket, he pulled a square wooden box, and from the box he removed a gold ring with a ruby heart in its center and a diamonds on the side.

A ring that had belonged in his family for generations...until it was given away to an American with Evie's blue eyes, Joanna's willful spirit, and Claire's tender heart.

"When my father gave this ring to your mother, he broke a long-standing tradition," Weston said quietly as he knelt in front of Evie and reclaimed her hand while she sat absolutely still, intent on his every word. "You see, the men in my family are not meant to love their wives. Or if they do, it is a happy convenience that occurs over time. But for all of his many faults, the Marquess of Dorchester loved Anne Thorncroft. More than he loved my mother. More than he will ever be capable of loving Brynne or me. And I am glad that he did. I am *glad* that he loved her, for if he hadn't...if he hadn't, this ring never would have led me to you."

"Weston." When tears threatened, Evie blinked them away. She wasn't about to ruin this moment by letting her eyes get anymore puffy than they already were. "I never wanted this. I mean, I *did*." She gave a watery laugh. "But only because I desired your title and your wealth. I wanted to be the Countess of Hawkridge. I wanted to incite envy wherever I went. I wanted those who had turned me away to feel poorly for their decision, and beg me to be their friend once again."

Weston frowned. "Is this a declaration of love, or a list of reasons why I *shouldn't* marry you?"

"You made *me* wait long enough," she said, flicking his thigh. "You can wait a little longer. I'm just getting to the best part."

"By all means, then, continue."

"*As* I was saying...I wanted frivolous things. Prideful things. Things that would never make me happy in the end. And it took falling in love with a stubborn, arrogant, mule-headed–"

"Maybe we can skip this part," Weston interjected.

Another flick. "*–handsome*, intelligent, protective earl to fully understand that love is what's important. Love is what will see you through the years. Love is what will keep you warm at night, and greet you each morning. Money, prestige, social influence–they are no substitute for what matters most." Her lips curved. "Not to say it *hurts* anything that you're an incredibly rich nobleman who will one day inherit a dukedom, but–"

"Be quiet and kiss me," he ordered, dragging her onto his lap.

"And now?" she asked, looping her arms around his neck after she'd pressed her mouth to his in a quick, impertinent kiss.

"Marry me. Marry me, Evelyn, and be my wife." Reaching between them, Weston gently placed her mother's ring upon her finger.

It fit perfectly, and even though Evie had never tried it on, she knew, somehow, that it would.

"Yes," she said, and now she did let herself cry, but they were happy tears and her smile blossomed through them, like a flower unfurling its petals to soak in the first gentle mist of spring. "Yes, I will marry you. I will love you. I will be yours, always."

In the end, there was nothing else to say but that.

EPILOGUE

"A CORRESPONDENCE FOR you, my lady. From Lord Hawkridge."

Brynne paused in her painting and carefully set down her brush. A light breeze moved through the gazebo, tickling her hair against her cheek as she rose from her chair to accept the letter. "Thank you, Mae. Please tell Cook that I shall take dinner out here this evening. The sunset promises to be a beautiful one, and I wouldn't want to waste such colors by sitting inside."

The maid nodded, curtsied, and then returned to the house where a massive cleaning was underway. The last of the guests had left early in the morning, and the estate was almost eerily quiet. Taking full advantage of her newfound solitude, Brynne had retreated to the gazebo where she'd been painting for hours, stopping only to rest her wrist and take a stroll around the pond to toss breadcrumbs to the swans.

Leaning against the railing, she opened her brother's letter. As she read it, a smile slowly dawned, and by the time she'd reached the end, she was all but beaming.

"You lummox," she murmured with great affection. "You did it."

Dearest Sister,

I am writing to let you know that I have chosen to remain in London until Christmas. I invite you to join me at your earliest convenience.

You shall be pleased to know that I have asked Miss Thorncroft to marry me, and she has accepted. If you would do me one small kindness, do refrain from saying "I told you so".

I have also met and spoken with Joanna. Our initial meeting began with her threatening to murder me. I should think you will like her very much.

If you are amendable, which I have a feeling you will be, I should like to have all of us spend the holiday together at Hawkridge Manor.

We are, after all, a family.

With my love,
Weston

After reading the letter twice, and then once more for good measure, Brynne tucked it into the pocket of her burgundy frock coat and resumed painting.

As it often did, the rhythmic strokes of the bristles across canvas soon carried her away to another place, dimming the sights and the sounds all around her. When she was in the midst of transferring her art from her mind onto the paper, she might as well have been in a castle high in the clouds, or a ship in the middle of the sea, or a cottage deep in the woods.

Such was her level of absorption that she did not hear the sound of approaching footsteps until they were on the steps of the gazebo and a shadow, long and dark, fell across her line of vision.

"Could you step to the side, please, Mae?" she asked without glancing up from the easel. "I fear you're in my light."

"Is this better?" a deep, achingly familiar voice drawled.

The shadow shifted to the side and Brynne, her face draining of all color, let the brush slip through her bloodless fingers and fall to the ground in a splatter of blue paint. As her stomach pitched and her pulse raced, she rose to her feet and met the amused amber gaze of the last person on earth she had ever wanted to see again.

"Get out of here," she whispered, raising her arm to point at the drive. "Before I pick up that brush and stab you through the heart with it."

Lord Lachlan Campbell clucked his tongue. "Now, Bry, me love…," he said, flashing his teeth in a wolfish grin. "Is that any way tae greet yer husband?"

THE END

About the Author

Jillian Eaton grew up in Maine and now lives in Pennsylvania on a farmette with her husband and their three boys. They share the farm with a cattle dog, an old draft mule, a thoroughbred, and a mini-donkey—all rescues. When she isn't writing, Jillian enjoys spending time with her animals, gardening, reading, and going on long walks with her family.

Made in the USA
Monee, IL
23 April 2021